# Hemlock Row

Also by this author

*The Lancefield Mysteries*

*Salvation Hall*

*The Redemption*


*The Rose Bennett Mysteries*

*Dead on Account*

*Dead Ringer*

*Death Duties*

*Death Benefit*

*Dead & Buried*

# Hemlock Row

*A Lancefield Mystery*

MARIAH KINGDOM

~ Perceda Press ~

This novel is entirely a work of fiction. Any resemblance to actual persons, living or dead, or to events, locations or premises is purely coincidental. Salvation Hall, the Lancefield family, the Woodlands Plantation, Hemlock Row and the village of Penwithen do not and have not ever existed, except in the author's imagination.

First published in digital form 2023 by WL Fowler

Copyright © Mariah Kingdom 2023

This paperback edition Perceda Press 2023

Mariah Kingdom asserts the moral right to be identified as the author of this work.

A catalogue record for this publication is available from the British Library

All rights reserved. No part of this publication may be reproduced, stored in a retrieval system or transmitted in any form or by any means, electronic, mechanical, photocopying, recording or otherwise, without the written permission of the author and/or publisher.

ISBN 978-1-8380834-7-2

Cover design by www.ebooklaunch.com

*'It is very important not to mistake hemlock for parsley...'*

*Denis Diderot, philosopher, 1713-1784*

# 1

Hemlock Row.

She could see the familiar lamp post on the corner of the lane, its faintly-yellowing glow casting a tentative halo of light above the cars parked far too close to the corner. In a few short steps, she would be turning right, down towards the trio of perfectly-proportioned Georgian townhouses nestled deep in Edinburgh's New Town. Soon she would be letting herself into number three and walking down the hallway, shoes kicked off, her socks slithering on the highly-polished mahogany floorboards that led to the warmth and comfort of the kitchen.

She would have to account for her unexpected return, of course, although she knew that it wouldn't be an issue. She would be met with understanding, her appearance welcomed by her host, and no doubt there would be hot chocolate, conversation, and perhaps even commiseration before she made her way up to the familiar confines of the guest room to sleep off what might have passed for disappointment.

She turned her head to check the road behind her, just as the familiar outline of a black cab turned into Northumberland Street with a squeal of unoiled brakes, and she lifted a hand to shield her eyes from the glare of its approaching headlights. In a moment it was past and she swiftly crossed the road, slipping between the parked cars that lined the kerb, and pausing to draw in a breath as she landed on the other side just a few feet from the corner.

The cold was nipping at her fingers now, the bone-aching February chill biting through the fabric of her gloves, and she shoved her hands into the pockets of her coat as she turned on her heel to head off down Hemlock Row. She could see number three ahead of her, three storeys high above the ground, its pink-tinged sandstone profile standing proudly behind the entrance to the mews lane.

Safely home.

Her pace quickened as she approached the mews, the narrow lane that led from Hemlock Row to curve around behind the houses. Lit by a quartet of old-fashioned street lights – tall, cast-iron Victorian standards out of keeping with the terrace's Georgian heritage – the night-time atmosphere that emanated from the lane could be nothing short of unnerving. The flickering of a faulty lightbulb in the second lamp from the end gave rise to an eerie, intermittent darkness, and as she stepped quickly off the pavement she turned her eyes down towards the cobbled surface of the roadway, closing her ears to the sounds of scurrying and scratting that echoed from the darkest depths of the mews.

In a moment her foot was on the lowest of the stone steps that led up to number three's impressive, black-painted door and she took her right hand from her pocket to wrap her fingers around the railings that lined the stairway. She was breathing heavily now, her renewed anxiety heightened by an irrational fear of whatever lay in the mews: rats scurrying with unease from one overflowing dustbin to another, resourceful feral cats secreted in the gaps between the now-deserted stable blocks, perhaps even a hungry urban fox looking for a morsel to stave off its hunger, and then she laughed softly under her breath. There was nothing in that lane that could cause her any harm; no four-legged predator big enough or brave enough to present any sort of threat to a fit, healthy, grown woman just about to enter the safety of her temporary home.

Nothing *in* the mews.

But then, head down, she hadn't seen the nameless, faceless predator that had emerged silently *from* the mews just seconds after she had crossed the cobbled lane. She hadn't heard the two-legged creature, far more dangerous than any rat or cat or fox, as it stepped softly across the pavement to stand behind her at the foot of the worn, stone steps.

And only too late did she feel the heat of its breath on her neck as she bent her head to examine the keys that her left hand had pulled from her pocket; feel the force of its fingers as they clamped around her face, crushing her lips into the unyielding bone beneath her skin; feel the void beneath her feet as it lifted her, voice stifled, into the air to carry her swiftly off down the mews lane and into the intermittent darkness.

There was nothing in the lane to see what horrors came next; rats and cats and foxes, all had scattered. Only the moon bore witness as the hand that clasped her face loosened its grip and her body slumped to its knees beneath the second lamp from the end. Only the sky was watching as that hand took hold of the soft, woollen scarf around her neck to pull it tightly, ferociously against the soft, white, delicate skin of her throat. And only in the fleeting seconds that the faulty lightbulb threw out its transient, watery glow could her dying breaths be witnessed as they reluctantly left her body, floating noiselessly and frostily up into the crisp and cloudless sky.

## 2

'So, how does it feel to be back in Edinburgh?' The voice at the end of the phone line carried a forlorn note behind the soft, Cornish burr. 'It must bring back memories?'

Kathryn Clifton leaned back against the pile of crisp, clean pillows at the head of the bed, and considered the question. 'It feels weird.' She tucked the phone into the crook of her neck. 'I know the place so well; I read for my degree here, began my career, married, set up home...' She continued the list in her head.

*Discovered that my husband had been unfaithful here, lost the home that I had begun to cherish, waved goodbye to my future...*

But she wasn't going to spoil a conversation with Ennor Price by dredging all of that up again. 'It's water under the bridge now. I think I'm ready to move on.' And she had Price himself, at least in part, to thank for that. 'Anyway, David and Stella live in Palmerston Place. It's miles away from where I lived.' She glanced around the bedroom as she spoke, taking in the stylish, understated soft furnishings and the tasteful, muted colour of the walls. 'It's very kind of them to put me up, you know. I didn't expect it. I would have been happy to stay in a hotel.'

'You're still trying to keep up the illusion of a professional boundary then?' He was teasing her now. 'You're not fooling anyone, Kathryn. You're not the Lancefield family's consultant genealogist anymore. You're part of the Lancefield firm now: part of the bricks and mortar. There was never any question of you staying in a hotel.'

Unseen, Kathryn pouted. 'I still stay at The Zoological Hotel when I'm in Penzance. Why would I do that if I wasn't still trying to maintain a professional boundary?'

'So that you and I could meet up regularly for supper without the Lancefields interfering?' He laughed softly down the phone line. 'Given the number of crimes I've had to investigate that involve the family, it wouldn't really be appropriate for me to visit their home socially, would it? Lucy's and Philip's murders, Becca and Zak Smith's hate campaign, not to mention…'

'I know.' Kathryn shivered. 'Not to mention Dennis Speed and Emma Needham.' She sucked in her cheeks. 'So please don't. Don't mention them. I know that Lucy's and Philip's deaths were nothing to do with me, and I know that it wasn't my fault that Becca decided to make the family suffer for what happened to Philip. But Dennis and Emma?'

'You weren't responsible for either of those deaths, Kathryn.'

'It was my work which led to their deaths. It was only because the family were left without an heir that Richard asked me to track down members of the extended Lancefield family. It sounded like such a simple request. It never occurred to me that someone might lose their life as a result.'

'They didn't.' Ennor's voice was gentle now. 'I'll say it as many times as I have to. You were not responsible for those deaths. Dennis and Emma died because Jason Speed refused to accept that he wasn't a fully paid-up member of the Lancefield family. You might have been responsible for identifying Dennis and Jason as distant members of the family, but you weren't to know that Jason was illegitimate, any more than you could have known that his father had chosen to keep that from him. And you weren't to know that he was cold-blooded enough to murder his girlfriend and his adoptive father in a bid to keep that a secret from the Lancefields. Jason committed those murders because he saw a material opportunity and he refused to let it go. He wanted to take advantage of Richard and David

Lancefield and pass himself off as a legitimate member of the family in order to benefit financially. You said it yourself at the time, Kathryn; he wasn't interested in the family, just in what the family could do for him. He was even deluded enough to think that he might position himself as Richard and David's heir and inherit the family fortune.' Ennor fell silent for a moment. And then he said, 'I hope you're not regretting this latest escapade after you've put so much effort into it already?'

Was that how he thought of Eva McWhinney? As an escapade? 'Are you suggesting that my hard-won success in turning up another Lancefield cousin is some sort of game?' She clicked her tongue against the roof of her mouth. 'David doesn't think it's an escapade. He met with Eva yesterday. They had lunch at the Caledonian Hotel and I hear they got on famously. He was singing her praises all through supper this evening. He's quite taken with her.'

'Well, I'm glad if it's working out well. Especially if she takes the invitation to connect with the family in the spirit in which it was intended.' Ennor paused, and then asked, 'She's a doctor, isn't she?'

'Yes, a specialist at the Edinburgh Royal Infirmary. And affluent enough not to need any of the Lancefield fortune, thanks to inheriting a significant amount of property from her own line of the family.'

'So why do I detect a hint of reservation?'

'Do you?' He knew her too well. 'It was something that Stella said to me earlier this evening. That, and you reminding me how many members of the Lancefield family have already died.' Kathryn raised her eyes to study the bedroom ceiling, tracing the contours of the ornate plaster cornice that ran around its edges as she spoke. 'All of that, coupled with the knowledge that some of those victims died because of my work.' She puffed out a sigh. 'Stella said, David is quite besotted with Eva McWhinney, and I can't help wondering if it's because of her appearance. And I didn't fully understand what she meant by that until David showed me a photograph.'

'A photograph of Eva?'

'Yes. He took the picture on his phone, with her permission. So that he could send it to Richard.' Kathryn drew in a breath. 'There's no question that Eva is a member of the Lancefield family, Ennor. She's the spitting image of Lucy.'

\*

Richard Lancefield settled back into his favourite, well-worn armchair and patted his knee with a gnarled hand. The wire-haired terrier beside the chair needed no other invitation. Samson launched himself clumsily into the air and landed on the old man's lap, more by good luck than good judgement.

It took a few moments for the animal to settle. 'You will see, Marcus, that Samson and I have grown a little older while you have been away. Neither of us is quite as agile as we used to be. It's been a most uncomfortable winter.' One that he could feel in his bones. 'But we are both delighted to be reunited with you, my boy. I can only say that you have done the Lancefield family proud.'

At the other side of the Dower House sitting room, Marcus Drake perched uncomfortably on the edge of a shabby, damask-covered sofa. He was leaning forward, his broad shoulders hunched, his forearms resting wearily on his knees. 'I did my best.' He sighed out the words and then straightened his back, stretching out a hand to retrieve a small glass of brandy from a nearby wine table. 'I can't say it's been the best winter for me either, but it's over now. Now I just want to rebuild my life.'

'And we will do everything we can to help you.' Richard observed the young man with a pang of remorse. 'We will always be grateful to you for speaking up and taking responsibility for Philip's death. I'm sorry that I couldn't be at the trial myself, but I understand from David that our legal team were outstanding.' Which was all to the good, given the leap of faith required from Marcus to put his trust in them. 'I take it that everything was made quite clear to you at the time. That you understood why it was necessary for you to plead guilty?'

'I was told that it would help my case if I pleaded guilty to involuntary manslaughter. That admitting to unlawfully killing Philip, without the intention to kill, would make all the difference.' Marcus sipped on his brandy and then shot a glance at Richard. 'But it wasn't true, was it? The legal team positioned it to suggest that I thought Lucy was still alive, and that I was trying to stop Philip from killing her. But I didn't know whether she was alive or dead. I just wanted to kill the bastard.'

'Tush.' Richard put up a hand. 'Don't say any more, my boy, not even in the privacy of these four walls. I don't want to know what you thought. What matters is that you are home with us now.'

'But I still don't understand how. They've tried to explain it to me, but it doesn't make any sense. How could I plead guilty to manslaughter and walk away without a custodial sentence?'

'Because the sentencing was at the discretion of the judge. The fact that Philip's death was caused by your attempts to defend Lucy reduced your culpability for the crime.' The old man spoke slowly, as if speaking to a child. 'Everything was reasoned out most carefully. We knew that the starting point for sentencing would be two years. With a reduction for your early guilty plea, your remorse, your previous good character, the lack of premeditation and the assistance you gave to the prosecution by being open about the facts of the case, the sentence was set at twelve months.'

'Then I should have been imprisoned for twelve months.'

Richard shook his head. 'You had already spent six

months on bail in Edinburgh, with a curfew condition and electronic tagging. And the remaining six months of your sentence was suspended in recognition of the financial compensation that I have paid to Philip's partner and child on your behalf.'

'You mean, you paid them off?'

'I sought to make amends in recognition of their loss.' It also didn't hurt that the judge responsible for sentencing was the son of one of Richard's oldest friends, but he wasn't going to add that to his explanation.

'But the way I disposed of the bodies…'

'Enough.' Richard held up his hand. 'There is nothing to be gained by raking over what's done. You have been given a gift. Only an ungrateful man questions the giver and looks at the price tag.' He softened his voice. 'What's done is done. Now, I want you to try to put it all behind you.'

'Behind me? And how the hell am I supposed to do that?' Marcus stared into his almost-empty brandy glass. 'By running away to St Felix?'

'Spending time on the Woodlands Plantation isn't "running away". I see it as a possible solution to a problem. It will be four years and six months until your conviction is spent. You needn't spend all of that time in the Caribbean, but I think the more time you spend out there, the more your wounds will heal. You will forget, in time, what's happened. For now, we are just delighted that you are home with us at Salvation Hall.' The old man narrowed his rheumy eyes. 'Of course, there are others who need to come to terms with these events. Becca and little Frankie, to name but two.' He licked his lips. 'You know that Becca no longer works for us?'

'David told me that you had let her go and that she's moved out of her estate cottage. Is it true that her family made threats against you both because of what I did to Philip?'

'Perhaps.' Although there might be many other reasons.

'Whatever the case, she still lives and works in the area and she will not take kindly to seeing you free to live your life. We kept the full extent of her malice from you while you were in Edinburgh awaiting trial because we didn't want to add to your woes.'

'Is that why you arranged for me to have a holiday immediately after the trial?'

'It's one reason. Although I didn't think that you would mind a change of scene. I've stayed on Burgh Island many times myself, and always found the experience to be a healing one.' Richard tilted his head. 'I hope you know, Marcus, that I would rather have you here with me at Salvation Hall so that I can thank you every day for the sacrifices you have made for the family. But I know that wouldn't be practical, at least not until the dust from the trial has settled. I've already spoken to Nancy and she is willing to travel out to St Felix with you, to introduce you to the Woodlands Estate and its residents. With your agreement, I would like to book flights for you both to travel out on Monday. In the meantime, you would be wise to keep your head down and avoid Becca Smith. There is plenty to keep us occupied. We can discuss the duties you might undertake for us on the plantation, the frequency of your visits home to England, and what we see as your role to support David on your eventual return to live full time at Salvation Hall.'

'You seem to have it all mapped out for me.'

'I put all of this forward to you as a suggestion, Marcus. I am not so foolish as to think you will just cave in to an old man's will.' A knowing smile lit Richard Lancefield's face. 'And you haven't yet seen the island of St Felix for yourself. There is always the possibility that, once you do, you might prefer never to set foot on English soil again.'

# 3

Detective Chief Inspector Alyson Grant rested a shoulder against the sandstone wall to the rear of 3 Hemlock Row and folded her arms across her chest. It was cold in the mews lane, and barely light, and there was no question that she had grabbed the wrong coat in a hasty exit from her flat. But it was too late now to do anything about that. She gave an involuntary shiver and nodded towards the body on the ground. 'What do we know so far then?'

Detective Sergeant Ross Pearson pulled a notebook from the pocket of his overcoat and flipped it open. 'The victim's name is Geraldine Morton. She's a cardiology specialist at the Edinburgh Royal Infirmary. She's been staying as the guest of a friend at number three.' He pointed vaguely in the direction of the house. 'She was discovered by a neighbour this morning, the lady who lives at number one.' He squinted down at the notebook. 'Her name is Eileen McDonald. She was walking her dogs along the front of the row and they set off barking as they reached the turning for the mews. They were pretty wound up, so she let out the lead and followed them down here to see what the problem was.'

'Did she know the victim?'

'Only by sight. She'd seen her once or twice, going in and out of number three. She raised the alarm there first and it was Geraldine Morton's friend, Eva McWhinney, who called the police.'

'And what time was that?'

'Around six thirty.'

DCI Grant's brow furrowed beneath a thick, dark fringe. 'How long do we think the body has been here?'

'We're still waiting for the pathologist, but her clothing is wet and there were some heavy rain showers in the early hours of the morning. So I'm guessing she's probably been here all night.'

'And nobody missed her? Not even the friend?' Grant pushed herself away from the wall and bent her knees, effortlessly crouching down beside the corpse. 'Why did nobody miss you, then, hen?' She cast experienced eyes across the young woman's face, taking in the cold, bloodless pallor of the skin and the tiny flecks of frost that glittered along the long, motionless eyelashes. 'How old would you say she is, Ross? In her late thirties? Early forties?' Old enough to be a cardiology specialist anyway. 'She's a nice-looking girl.' Grant swept her eyes across the victim's body, still safely cocooned in a long, padded coat. 'But it doesn't look as though she's been interfered with. So we'll be needing a motive.' The detective pushed herself back to her feet. 'It looks like she's been strangled with that scarf, it's cut into the flesh of her neck.'

'Yes, I noticed that.' Pearson flipped the notebook shut and slipped it back into his pocket. 'And I wondered why nobody had missed her. I've had a brief chat with Eva McWhinney, and she reckons that Geraldine had worked a shift at the hospital yesterday, and then spent the evening with a boyfriend down in Leith. She'd told Eva that she might stay over if they opened a bottle of wine, and not to worry if she didn't hear from her.'

'So why is she staying here at all? Doesn't she have a home of her own to go to?'

'She has a flat in Marchmont, ma'am. But she's having the kitchen and bathroom refitted, and Miss McWhinney offered to let her stay here while the work was being carried out. They've been working together for some time and are quite good friends.'

'And the boyfriend?'

'His name is Alec Henderson, but that's all I have at the moment. Miss McWhinney said they only met a few weeks ago. It wasn't a long-standing relationship.'

DCI Grant dug a cold hand into the pocket of her coat and pulled out a packet of cigarettes. 'Usual drill then, Ross.' She glanced up at the rear of Hemlock Row as she pulled a cigarette from the packet. 'I want you to wait for the pathologist and get a provisional time and cause of death. Then I want a door-to-door, covering all properties that might have seen or heard something sixty minutes either side of the estimated time of death.' She pushed the cigarette packet back where it came from and fished in the other pocket of her coat for a cigarette lighter. 'I want somebody down to the infirmary to check on her movements yesterday, and somebody down to Leith to interview the boyfriend. If he hasn't been told yet, he needs to know.' She slipped the cigarette loosely between her lips and cupped a hand around the end as she lit it. 'Where was Eva McWhinney yesterday evening?'

The cigarette bobbed up and down as Grant spoke and Pearson took a precautionary step backwards. 'She said she was here all evening, alone. She was in the drawing room at the front, watching the television and catching up on some reading. She did go down to the kitchen several times, to make coffee and some supper, but she didn't hear anything as she moved around the house.'

Grant turned her head and squinted up at the building. 'Where's her bedroom?'

'On the first floor, at the front.'

'And how did she take the news of her friend's death?'

'Calmly.' He turned his own eyes to follow Grant's gaze. 'I couldn't say that she wasn't affected by the news of her friend's death, she did look saddened. But there was no hysteria, no crying. I thought she was rather brave about it all.'

'So, she's a good-looking young woman too, then?'

Pearson's boyish face flushed pink. 'She's a doctor, ma'am. I put her reaction down to the fact that she deals with illness and death on a daily basis.'

'She's not a doctor, Ross, she's a consultant. And I'm the Queen of Sheba.' Grant pulled the cigarette from her lips and pointed down the mews lane with it, scattering a shower of tiny sparks into the air. 'That looks like the pathologist now.' She dropped the cigarette to the floor and stepped on it, twisting the sole of her boot to stub it out. 'Let me know how you get on with him. If you want me, I'll be in there.' She jerked her head back towards the house. 'Having a wee chat with your calm, not-necessarily-good-looking medic.'

\*

'More coffee, Kathryn?' David Lancefield lifted the cafetiere from the kitchen table and began to refill her cup without waiting for an answer. 'I always need an extra cup myself in the morning.'

Kathryn watched as he carried out the task. 'I certainly need a kickstart this morning. I think the journey up from Cornwall yesterday tired me out more than I'd realised. That, and the excellent supper that Stella prepared for us.' It had never occurred to Kathryn that David's wife might be up to cooking a meal of almost cordon bleu standard. Life was certainly full of surprises. 'It was kind of Stella to go to so much trouble. And kind of you both to accommodate me while I'm in Edinburgh.'

'Nonsense. Apart from anything else, your presence here gives us more opportunity to talk about Eva and the McWhinney family's connection to us.' David smiled a mischievous smirk. 'And as Stella has absented herself for her yoga class, I hoped we might make a start on it this morning. It's been delightful to meet up with Eva, and she is so well-disposed towards the idea of making a connection with the family that I can't wait to hear more about how we are related.'

'Then I hope I'm not going to disappoint you.' Kathryn added sugar to her coffee and stirred it. 'Have you shared any family information with Eva yet?'

'I've told her everything I know about our own direct line of the family. She knows that my father and I are the end of the main line of descent, and that's how we inherited the estates. I've explained that you are researching the family's heritage and that you've identified a sibling group of four ancestors as being key to the way the family divided from the beginning of the nineteenth century. And I've told her a little about the Liverpool line of the family.' David's gentle, grey eyes momentarily clouded. 'But I confined myself to the basic facts, just enough to explain how that line of the family relates to the rest of us, and how lucky we are to have welcomed cousin Barbara into the fold.'

'And how much of Eva's ancestry did you discuss with her?'

'Again, just the basic facts. I explained that her branch of the family is descended from Charlotte Hestor Lancefield and her husband, James McWhinney.' David's brow furrowed as he contemplated the question. 'Of course, Eva already knew most of that. She has a family Bible, Kathryn, which I'm very keen that we should see. She tells me that it outlines the McWhinney family from the birth of James and Charlotte's first child, all the way down to Eva herself.'

'Indeed?' Kathryn's cheeks dimpled. Not six months ago she would have struggled to raise a spark of interest in David, he was so indifferent to his family's history and heritage. And here he was now, waxing lyrical about family trees and family Bibles. 'Did Eva know that James McWhinney was the consulting doctor on the Woodlands Plantation before his return to Edinburgh?'

'There is a mention of it in the family Bible, I believe. But she didn't know anything much about Woodlands, nor that Charlotte was a member of the family which owned it. Charlotte is listed in the Bible as "the daughter of Thomas Moses Lancefield and Lysbeth Quintard of Penwithen,

Cornwall, and St Felix".' His frown deepened. 'I hope you're not going to tell me that we are looking at another serious rift within the family here, Kathryn. I'm not sure that my nerves would be up to it.'

She would have to break the news to him gently then. 'There would be little point in my lying about it, would there? But something did happen which led to a cooling of relations between various branches of the family. The Lancefields didn't approve of certain practices that McWhinney carried out while he was responsible for medical care on their plantation. I'm afraid there was a falling out and James returned to Edinburgh, bringing Charlotte with him. They didn't completely lose touch with the family; I have found letters between Charlotte and her brothers Benedict and Richard, and her sister Maria.' Now wasn't the time to reveal the content of those letters. 'What I can tell you is that, on this occasion, the Lancefields were not at fault. They appear to have been acting in the best interests of the slaves who worked on their plantation.'

'So the problem was with McWhinney himself?' David scowled his disapproval. 'Is this going to be another distressing tale? Was he incompetent or neglectful?'

'He certainly wasn't incompetent. Far from it. In fact, all of the evidence I've seen so far points to him being highly scientific in his approach. As to whether the story will cause distress, I would say that very much depends on one's own value system and outlook. As a medical practitioner, for example, Eva may look at things with a pragmatic and scientific eye. After James returned to Edinburgh he built a successful medical career, and generation after generation of McWhinneys followed him into the medical profession, including Eva herself.'

'Then what on earth was wrong with the man?'

A difficult question to answer. Kathryn picked up her cup and slipped a finger through the delicate handle. 'I'm afraid it was a question of ethics, David.' She sipped on the coffee without looking at him. 'And what an individual feels about the idea of medical experimentation.'

\*

It was warm in the kitchen at Salvation Hall.

Richard hitched up the sleeves of his thick, cotton shirt and folded his thin arms on the kitchen table, tilting his eyes to look up at his secretary. She was standing at the kitchen counter, her back to him, her attention fixed firmly on brewing a pot of tea.

It never failed to amaze him what a delightful creature Nancy Woodlands was. A secretary in name, a personal assistant, a beauty, a wit, a practical and capable young woman… he would miss her when she travelled again to St Felix, even though Kathryn would be back from Edinburgh by then to take her place. The exchange would be a relatively seamless one, and Kathryn was the wisest of friends and the kindest of helpers.

But she wasn't Nancy. And however deeply she immersed herself in the Lancefield family's heritage, she would never remind him of St Felix in quite the way that Nancy did.

'Would you like a biscuit, Richard, or is it too soon after breakfast?' His secretary glanced across her shoulder, regarding him with warm, solicitous eyes. 'I don't want to be accused of leading you astray.'

'No one could ever accuse you of that, my dear. But I had better decline.' He puffed out his disappointment as she carried the teapot and milk jug over to the table. 'Shall we begin our morning session in here? There seems little point in retiring to the library.'

'As you wish.' She dropped onto a chair at the other side of the table. 'Shall we start with the arrangements for the dinner party? I've set the time for drinks at seven thirty and dinner at eight. The caterers have promised me that they will be here at six o'clock sharp. And the menu is as you requested: liver paté to begin with, consommé, roast rib of beef and a sticky toffee pudding with crème anglaise for dessert.' Her dark eyes narrowed with a hint of rebuke. 'I thought you might have chosen something with a Caribbean twist, given the occasion.'

'Nonsense. We need to wave the boy off with some good British fare. Marcus will have plenty of time to enjoy the local food when he gets to St Felix. And so will you.' Richard studied her face as he spoke. 'You are still comfortable about taking him over to St Felix?'

'Of course. Why wouldn't I be?' She put out a manicured hand to nudge the old man's arm. 'And even if I wasn't, do you think I would pass up the chance of another trip home?' Her cheeks dimpled with a smile. 'I'm not so sure that Marcus is comfortable with it, though. I haven't had a chance to speak to him at length since he returned to Salvation Hall, but he doesn't look to me like a man ready to reinvent his life.'

That was hardly a surprise. 'Marcus has been through a dreadful ordeal; he lost Lucy, he lashed out at Philip with the most painful of consequences, and he's been constrained to a narrow life with his mother in Edinburgh while awaiting his trial.' Dear God, being confined with Stella Drake Lancefield for five or six months would be enough to drain the life from anyone. 'He's had the worry of the trial, not knowing what the outcome might be. And now, unless I'm mistaken, he is showing definite signs of survivor guilt. The boy needs a new life in the sun. And that's what he's going to get.' The old man nodded to himself. 'I spoke to him yesterday evening on his return, and he understands the need to move on quickly. I've told him about the dinner party – that David and Stella and Kathryn are flying back from Edinburgh on Saturday to celebrate his release and to wish him well – and he's going to spend Sunday tying up a few loose ends here. So I'd like you to book the flights to St Felix for Monday.'

'Monday?' Nancy arched a perfectly groomed eyebrow.

'You want me to just drop everything and go to St Felix on Monday?'

'Tush, girl. Anyone would think I was sending you to purgatory.' Richard pushed out his thin lips. 'You needn't stay out there longer than a few days if you don't want to. Just long enough to introduce him to everyone at Woodlands and get him settled. Your mother is going to take charge of him, and if he feels homesick we can send Stella and David out for a visit.'

'And what is he going to do while he's out there?'

'He's going to familiarise himself with Woodlands. I want him to learn how the plantation works and how we make it profitable. And I want him to meet everyone who works there. I want him to get to know them. Now that I can't travel there myself, I want him to be my envoy, my eyes and ears. To tell me what is working and what isn't, and to suggest improvements where necessary.' Richard turned his head away to look out of the window. 'And when I'm gone, I want him to do the same for David.'

'I see.' Nancy ran her tongue around her teeth. 'And what if Marcus doesn't want the job? What if he just wants to come back to England and start a new life here?'

The old man turned his gaze back across the table, and a smile tugged at the corners of his lips. 'My dear girl, what on earth would possess a young man of Marcus Drake's talents to turn away from the prospect of a comfortable and rewarding life on a beautiful island like St Felix?'

# 4

The drawing room of number three, Hemlock Row, was the epitome of understated elegance. Dark green walls contrasted sharply with crisp, white-painted woodwork and a pair of oversized gilt-edged mirrors hung in recesses to either side of the fireplace. A large oil painting in an ornate frame rested proudly on the black, marble mantelpiece, and if DCI Grant didn't know better she would have sworn it was an early study of Hemlock Row itself.

She was seated at one end of a blood-red velvet sofa, her notebook balanced precariously on her knee, her pale lips pressed tightly together in momentary contemplation of the woman seated opposite. It occurred to the policewoman that Eva McWhinney, seated between the cushions that adorned an uncomfortable-looking chaise longue, was also the epitome of understated elegance. For a woman who had been raised in alarm at some ungodly hour, and asked to identify the body of a murdered houseguest, she was conveying a remarkable impression of quiet, unruffled refinement. Dressed in a pair of neat woollen trousers and a pale pink cashmere sweater, her blonde hair coiled effortlessly into a chignon, she reminded Grant of someone famous and familiar. Grace Kelly, perhaps, or maybe Tippi Hedren. Little wonder that the impressionable DS Pearson had been so easily smitten.

Grant loosened her lips and forced a smile. 'I know you've already answered DS Pearson's initial questions. But I'd be grateful if you could run through a couple of things again with me, in more detail.' She tapped her pen gently on the notebook. 'I understand that Geraldine was staying with you because work was being carried out on her flat in Marchmont?'

'Yes. She was having the kitchen and bathroom refitted and the work was going to take just under a month.' Eva's voice was as sleek as her appearance. 'I gave the address to your colleague. Someone will need to let the workmen know what's happened.'

'I'm sure he has that in hand.' As if the police didn't have anything better to do with their time. 'Do you know when the work was due to be completed?'

'At the end of next week. Geraldine had already been here for two and a half weeks. She kept in touch with the foreman by phone and popped back home every few days to see how the work was progressing. As far as I know, it was going to plan.'

'So she was planning to stay on here for at least another nine to ten days.' Grant looked down as she added a note to her notebook. 'I believe that the neighbour who found the body came here to tell you before the police were called in.' She glanced up. 'Is that correct?'

'Yes. I'm afraid Eileen was distraught. I brought her into the house and calmed her down. And then I went outside to see for myself.'

'You weren't afraid to go out there then?'

'Afraid?'

'It would still have been dark at that time of the morning. It didn't occur to you that killer might still have been out there?'

A flicker of surprise crossed Eva's face. 'I didn't think of that. Only about Geraldine, lying out there in the cold. I wanted to see for myself, to see if there was anything I could do to help her.'

'But you were too late.'

'Much too late. I would estimate that she'd been dead around six or seven hours.' Eva blinked, as if trying to banish the memory. 'It's not easy to think of her lying out there all night, so close to home.' She leaned forward towards DCI Grant. 'I'm assuming that she was strangled? I saw the scarf around her neck, it had cut into the flesh.'

'I'm afraid I can't comment on that at this stage. We haven't had a report from the pathologist.' Grant glanced down at her notebook again and scribbled in it as she spoke. 'While you were out in the lane, did you notice anything suspicious? Anything to pique your curiosity? An unfamiliar vehicle, a gate open that might be usually kept locked, anything of that sort?'

'I'm afraid not. But I'll admit that I didn't really pay much attention. I was so shocked by what I'd seen that I came straight back into the house and called for the police.'

'Of course.' Grant placed her pen gently down on her notebook. 'You believed that Geraldine had gone straight to Leith after she worked her shift, didn't you? And that she was planning to stay there if she and her boyfriend opened a bottle of wine. But presumably, she changed her mind and didn't bother to let you know.' Only now was the plethora of possibilities beginning to dawn on the detective. 'Assuming that she did travel to Leith, and that she spent the evening there, how would she have travelled back to the New Town?'

'I'm sorry, I don't understand what you're asking.'

'Well, she's been seeing this boyfriend – Alec Henderson, is it? – for a few weeks now. I'm just wondering how she usually travelled back from Leith. Taxi? Bus? It's too far to walk.'

Eva leaned back against the chaise longue. 'I don't recall her travelling back from Alec's at any other time. I think yesterday evening might have been the first time that she'd been to his flat. I know she'd been to the theatre with him, and the cinema. And they'd been out for dinner a few times.'

'Have you met him, Eva?'

'No, I haven't.'

'So Geraldine didn't bring him here at any time?'

'If she did, she didn't tell me.' Eva looked away for a moment and then turned back to DCI Grant. 'She wouldn't have brought him here without telling me. She was too well-mannered for that.'

'Geraldine was a good-looking girl, wasn't she? Did she have a lot of boyfriends?'

'No. She was quite a shy person, really. She was married, some years back, but the marriage failed. She threw herself into her work afterwards. I would say that Alec was the first person she had dated for quite some time.'

'Did she confide in you about the relationship?'

'No, she didn't. As I said, she was quite shy.' The idea seemed to make Eva McWhinney uncomfortable. 'Geraldine was a lovely person. Professional, kind, good at her job... I can't imagine why anyone would want to hurt her.' Eva's face clouded. 'You don't think that Alec had something to do with her death?'

'I don't think anything yet, Eva. I don't have enough information to indulge in conjecture.' Grant took a moment to think, and her brow creased into a frown. 'Do you have a contact number or address for Alec?'

'I'm afraid not. But all of Geraldine's things are in the guest room. You're welcome to look in there, to see if you can find anything.'

'Thank you, I will. We need to break the news to him.' And question him about the previous evening's events, but there was no need to mention that to Eva. 'Would it be possible for me to do that now? The sooner we can contact him, the sooner we can let him know what's happened.'

'Of course.' Eva rose and crossed the room to head out into the hallway.

As DCI Grant followed in her wake, it suddenly struck her why Eva McWhinney's face had seemed so familiar.

And it had nothing at all to do with her resemblance to

any famous Hitchcock blonde.

\*

'And you're absolutely certain it was Hemlock Row?' There was a rising note of panic in David Lancefield's voice. 'Off the western end of Northumberland Street?'

Stella returned her husband's gaze with a narrowing of sharp, green eyes. 'David, darling, I have lived in Edinburgh long enough to know where Hemlock Row is. I walk down Northumberland Street on my way home at the end of every yoga class.' She dropped onto the plush drawing room sofa beside Kathryn and turned to her guest with a shake of the head. 'Has David looked after you in my absence, Kathryn? I hope he served you a decent breakfast?'

'We had a lovely breakfast, thank you. He's looked after me very well.' Kathryn turned warm, hazel eyes towards David as she spoke, hoping to reassure him, and not just about his qualifications as a host. 'I think David might want to know a little more about what's going on at Hemlock Row.'

'There isn't much more to tell. There was a police cordon across the end of Hemlock Row, and a whole line of police cars parked up on Northumberland Street. They had tied the entrance to the Row up with that blue and white tape stuff that they use to keep the great unwashed public at a distance.' Stella spoke in a mellow tone, but behind the soft façade, an acerbic wit was straining at the leash. 'I did stop and "ask a policeman", as the saying goes, but he wasn't prepared to say very much. Only that there had been a "police incident" and he wasn't at liberty to release any information to the public at this stage.' She glanced back at David. 'I did mention to him that a friend of my husband's lived in Hemlock Row and that you would be concerned, but he wouldn't budge.'

'I must call Eva and make sure that she's alright.'

David, anxious, braced his hands against the arms of his chair and pushed himself to his feet. 'There are only three houses in the row, and they all belong to her.' His breathing was shallow, and the words came out in fits and starts. 'She's bound to have been affected by this.'

Stella watched as he made his way across the room and passed through the doorway into the hall, and then she turned again to Kathryn. 'I couldn't tell David the whole story.' She lowered her voice. 'You can see how distressed he is already.' She flicked the sharp, green eyes towards the door, as if checking that he was still out of earshot. 'The policeman wouldn't tell me anything, but there were a number of residents standing around in Northumberland Street, talking about the situation. You know how people will gossip.' She wrinkled her nose. 'And thank God that they do.' She rested a hand on Kathryn's arm, an unexpected gesture of warm familiarity that would have been unthinkable just a few months earlier. 'A young woman has been murdered, in the lane behind Hemlock Row.'

Kathryn's mouth felt suddenly dry. 'Not Eva?'

'I don't know. No name has been given.' Stella flicked her eyes to the door for a second time. 'I knew David would dash to call her if I told him there had been some sort of problem. I thought it best to let him find out for himself.' She drew in a breath, and then said, 'I told you that he was besotted with the girl. He thinks that she is Lucy reincarnate. If something has happened to her, it will be like losing Lucy all over again.'

'Then let's hope it isn't Eva.' *For all our sakes.* Kathryn took hold of Stella's hand. 'Do they know how the woman died?' She could hardly dare to ask.

'I don't think so and I don't believe they have the killer.' Stella looked down at Kathryn's hand, wrapped around her own. But where she once might have pulled away, the gesture seemed to give her comfort. 'It's never going to go away, is it, Kathryn? This pall of death that hangs around the Lancefield family. It's never going to go away, as long as Richard insists on trying to dredge up distant cousins that the family doesn't need. For God's sake, why can the man not just let things rest now? All that dreadful business with Dennis Speed and Emma Needham, and now this. Can he truly not see the damage that he's doing?'

Kathryn squeezed Stella's hand. 'You're jumping to conclusions. The crime might have nothing at all to do with the Lancefields. The victim might be a complete stranger.'

'But if it's Eva, it will break poor David's heart. He didn't want to inherit the family's estates, and he didn't want his father to invent a family for him.' A solitary tear made its way down Stella's gaunt cheek and dripped from her chin onto the collar of her soft, jersey tunic. 'But he's agreed to Richard's demands and he's going to take on the estates. And now that Marcus has been spared a prison sentence, he will be able to look after things in St Felix. And cousin Barbara in Liverpool is always there for David if he wants someone else in the family to talk to. I've even agreed to spend more time at Salvation Hall, although God knows I can't abide the place. Why on earth can't Richard just be thankful for the family he has, and be content with that?'

Why, indeed? It would have been far too easy to blame it simply on an old man's intransigence. But Kathryn was spared the need to find an answer at all. She looked up as the door to the drawing room swung open. 'David? What's happened?'

He leaned against the doorframe. 'I managed to get through on the phone. Eva is safe.' He blew out a breath to steady his breathing. 'I'm afraid it's her house guest. The poor girl has been murdered, in the lane behind Hemlock Row. The police are there now.' He braced himself and then crossed the drawing room to return to his armchair. 'Eva said that she hopes we will still visit her at Hemlock

Row this afternoon. She has spoken to the police officer in charge and the house itself is not a crime scene. She may need to take some time out, to answer questions for the police, and there may be an officer or two there to carry out a further search of the room that her friend was using.' David rubbed at his forehead with a finger. 'But if that doesn't inconvenience us, she will look forward to seeing us at one o'clock, as originally planned.' He leaned back, relieved, and closed his eyes.

Kathryn turned to look at Stella, and as she did so Stella whispered to her. 'What did I tell you, Kathryn?' She leaned a little closer to her guest and hissed another, solitary word.

'*Besotted.*'

\*

Richard dropped Samson's lead gently to the floor and rested his walking stick against the wall of the church. A large, lightweight bag hung loosely across his body – an ingenious idea of Nancy's, so that he might carry the stick, the lead and a small bouquet of flowers – and he lifted the flowers from it slowly, being careful not to crush any of the soft, delicate petals. 'Roses and carnations this time, my dear.' He mumbled the words as he bent cautiously forward to place the bouquet beside the late Emma Needham's memorial. 'I promised that you would not be forgotten.'

He straightened his back with a sigh. Never forgotten? The girl should never have lost her life in the first place, and the erection of the small monument to her memory, a delicate marble angel embellishing the tomb of his granddaughter Lucy, seemed inadequate beyond words. But there was little else he could do now. Murdered by her partner, Jason Speed, Emma had suffered such an unspeakable act of betrayal that even now Richard could scarcely bear to think about it. And as to the way in which

Jason had desecrated Lucy's grave; what a damned bloody mess it had all been. The boy hadn't even been related to the Lancefields.

The old man banished the thought and reached behind to retrieve his stick. At least Marcus was home now, and that was some relief. Richard turned his eyes a little to the left, to the headstone erected for Lucy, and smiled at it. 'Well, Lucy, Marcus is home again and we are delighted to have him back. He's quite well, my pet, perhaps just a little jaded around the edges by his ordeal.' A soft chuckle escaped Richard's lips. 'Of course, I meant the ordeal of facing his trial, not of being billeted with his mother.' There was no question that the harpy had softened a little over the past few months, but it was still a struggle for Richard to consider her kindly. 'Oh, forgive me, my dear. I know I shouldn't harbour unkind thoughts about Stella. But old habits die hard.'

He drove his stick into the soft ground beside the grave and leaned on it. 'Anyway, Marcus is going to keep to his side of the bargain and make a fresh start on St Felix. And we have found another cousin for your father, up in Edinburgh. I know it's hard to believe, but she lives just a twenty-minute walk away from his home. So close, all the time, and we never knew.' He looked down at Samson, sitting patiently beside the marble slab. 'Your father says she has the Lancefield nose, but I haven't yet seen for myself. I have that pleasure to come. Kathryn is meeting with her today and I will hear all the gossip this evening. I have high hopes of the connection this time. There is no question that she is a legitimate member of the family, and she seems well-disposed to the connection.'

He frowned and cast a glance across to the corner of the churchyard. 'I'm not sure that I have the heart to say a word to Philip today.' Perhaps his memories of Philip and their friendship were fading. Or perhaps it was just his guilty conscience robbing him of words. Either way, Marcus was his priority now.

He pursed his thin lips and pulled at his walking stick, freeing it from the damp, claggy earth. 'Well, Lucy, I'm going to head home now. There's a chill in the air and Samson and I feel it all too acutely.' He bent forward to pick up the end of the dog's lead. 'We'll see you again soon, my pet.' He straightened and turned on his heel, tugging the dog gently behind him, and began to walk slowly down the path, away from the church. His breathing was laboured now, the cold February air nipping meanly at his lungs, and he halted beside the lychgate to steady his breath.

Beyond the churchyard the pavement was empty, but across the road, an all-too-familiar figure was making purposefully for the front door of the village inn, and Richard shrank back a little to avoid being seen. Zak Smith, his hands sunk deep into the pockets of his rough, woollen coat, his face obscured by its upturned collar, almost tripped over the doorstep in his rush to get inside.

There had been a time when Smith had been suspected of Emma Needham's murder, but they had all been wrong about that. And a time when his sister, Becca, the Lancefield's erstwhile housekeeper, had tried to warn Richard that Jason Speed was not to be trusted. The girl had been right, of course, but Richard had been too unwilling, too proud, perhaps even too arrogant to listen. In return for what he perceived to be her impudence, he had taken away both her job and her home, but there had been too much bitterness on both sides now to take her back.

He let out a sigh and stepped forward through the lychgate. 'Come along, dog. It's time we were back home.' He didn't know, yet, whether news of Marcus's release had stretched as far as The Lancefield Arms. But he wasn't going to linger in the village to find out.

# 5

DCI Grant swigged back the dregs of her filter coffee and surveyed the bottom of the empty mug with a disappointed eye. It was her second shot of caffeine in the space of forty minutes and if DS Pearson didn't turn up soon she would have to nip up to the canteen for a third.

She clattered the mug down onto the desk and turned her attention to the mobile phone beside it. The screen was blank, dark and elusive, and she prodded at it with a nicotine-stained finger to coax it into action, then swiped across the screen to unlock the screen saver. There were no incoming texts to read and no missed calls.

She tapped an impatient finger on the table. What the hell was taking him so long? It was almost forty minutes since the first lead had come in, the result of a long morning's door-to-door questioning. There was no denying that the information gathered presented only the thinnest of possibilities. But a lead was a lead, it was better than nothing. An elderly woman in Northumberland Street had been woken before midnight by a vehicle revving its engine. Annoyed by the disturbance, and determined to chastise the culprit, she had risen from her bed and opened the curtains just in time to see a dark blue van speed out of the lane at the back of Hemlock Row.

It had been too much to hope that she might have caught sight of the numberplate; she had only just been able to make out the colour of the vehicle as it flew under the street light on the corner. But the timing, approximately ten forty-five, had possibilities and Pearson was on a mission to secure footage from the city's nearest CCTV cameras. The worst-case scenario would be evidence that would eliminate it from their enquiries. And the best case? Grant could hardly dare to hope.

A brisk rap at the door of her office dragged her attention back into the room, and she glanced up sharply to see the door open and Pearson's smiling face appear in the gap. 'Our best chance for a sighting is the camera on Queen Street. I've put in a request, and we should have the footage by close of business today.' He rolled into the room and let the door swing shut behind him. 'I'll stay behind this evening to look at it. It shouldn't take too long, there won't have been that much traffic around at that time of night.'

Grant waited as he sank onto the visitor's chair at the other side of the desk. 'Was she a reliable witness?'

'The officer who took the statement seemed to think so.'

'So why did no one else mention it?'

'Not everyone is irritated by the sound of an engine revving. Most people probably wouldn't have noticed it.' Pearson leaned an elbow on the edge of the desk. 'We're going door-to-door again this afternoon, to ask about the van. It might jog somebody's memory.' He thought for a moment and then asked, 'What did you make of Eva McWhinney, ma'am?'

What, indeed? 'She's cool, isn't she?' Grant's lips curled into a smile. 'I didn't realise that you had a yen for the Grace Kelly type.'

Pearson's youthful cheeks reddened. 'That house is something, isn't it?' It was a clumsy attempt at deflection. 'It's a big place for a single woman. How on earth can she afford it?'

'She doesn't have to. She inherited it.' The same question had occurred to Grant but, unlike the diffident Pearson, she hadn't been too shy to ask. 'She told me that the house had been in the family since it was built.' The inspector leaned back in her seat and steepled her fingers. 'She gave me a tour of the house, and she had no issue with me looking at the room that Geraldine Morton was using. I had a good look out of all the windows to the rear of the house. None of them give a decent view of the mews. The lane is narrow and the wall at the back of the houses is too high; it overshadows the lane completely. Even if Eva had heard something, she couldn't have seen anything, at least not out of the windows.' Grant rested her chin on her fingers. 'Could you see Eva McWhinney as a suspect?'

The question caught the sergeant by surprise. Incomprehension flitted across his face, followed swiftly by incredulity. 'You are joking?'

'Am I?' Grant wasn't so sure. 'We've got to start somewhere, Ross. And what have we got to work with so far? A young woman's body, and a dark blue van that may or may not be a lead. The victim was a hard-working doctor at the infirmary.' Grant cast her eyes down to a sheaf of papers on her desk. 'Early indications suggest that she was a talented medic, popular with her colleagues. There is no obvious motive for the killing at this stage. There was no evidence of her being interfered with, and her handbag was found beside the body, complete with keys, purse, phone, credit cards and anything else that might have been worth stealing. And apart from her colleagues the only two people we can tie her to are Eva McWhinney and the boyfriend.'

'Alec Henderson?'

Grant grunted. 'We still haven't managed to get hold of him. I found an address and a phone number for him at Hemlock Row while I was searching the guest room, and I sent DC Chapman down to break the news and get the measure of him. But no one answered the door. Chapman has tried calling him but there's no answer. He's probably at work. According to Eva, he's a freelance journalist and he doesn't have a regular base apart from his flat. So he could be anywhere. All we've been able to do is leave a message asking for him to make contact.'

'Has Eva met him?'

'No. I wondered about that. Is there some sort of connection between the two of them? Or am I just clutching at straws?' It wouldn't be the first time. 'By the way, she was expecting a couple of visitors to the house this afternoon, a cousin and a friend of his. I agreed it could go ahead providing it doesn't get in our way.'

'As you see fit, ma'am.' Pearson sat back and folded his arms. 'So, notwithstanding the lead on the blue van, what are we going to do next?'

Grant shrugged. 'Wait for the pathologist's report. Wait for the CCTV footage. Keep trying to get hold of Alec Henderson.' She blew out an impatient sigh. 'Oh, to hell with it, Ross. There's something we're missing here and we have to keep the momentum going. I think we should go back to Hemlock Row and speak to Eva McWhinney again.'

\*

'I'm so pleased that you were still willing to come.' Eva led David and Kathryn along the hallway and into the large, sunlit drawing room. 'Of course, I'm heartbroken by Geraldine's death. If I'm honest, I'm still trying to come to terms with it.' She gestured towards the sumptuous blood-red velvet sofa before settling herself onto the chaise-longue. 'But I'm hoping that your visit will take my mind off it.'

How many times had Kathryn faced that sentiment since first encountering the Lancefield family? As many times as there had been unexpected deaths. She put the thought to the back of her mind as she sat down on the sofa beside David. 'As long as it's not an inconvenience.' She turned her head to look around the room. 'Eva, this house is magnificent. And it's astonishing that your family have retained the ownership since it was built.' Her gaze alighted on the painting above the fireplace, the study of Hemlock Row. 'It hasn't changed at all, has it?'

'Well, the iron railings at the front have been replaced, I think. The ones in the painting have a pointed finial and the current ones have a fleur-de-lys. But everything else seems to have remained intact.' Eva smiled. 'Much of the furniture is original too. I believe that a small number of items in the house were shipped back from St Felix, mostly the mahogany pieces.' She pointed to an impressive, glass-fronted china cabinet against the wall. 'One or two of the porcelain pieces in there are reputed to have come from the island, but I have no way of verifying that because they were made by English potteries. And there are some oils hanging in the dining room, including portraits of James and Charlotte McWhinney.'

'Now those I would be very interested to see.' Kathryn turned to David. 'Won't Richard be delighted when he hears about this?' She turned back to Eva. 'Do you enjoy living here, with all this history?'

'Enjoy it? I love it. And I feel very lucky to have inherited it. James must have been a man of some vision, to invest in his small piece of land in the New Town.'

'Do you know why it was named Hemlock Row?'

'Yes, but I'm afraid it's a rather mundane tale. This whole area was waste ground, and the plot of land that James purchased was covered in hemlock. No one else was prepared to touch it because it was poisonous, so he must have been prepared to take a risk or two.'

And that was an understatement. Kathryn cast a sideways glance at David and saw him give an almost-imperceptible shake of the head. Now was not the time to discuss McWhinney's risk-taking further. Instead, she leaned forward a little, towards Eva. 'I hope this isn't an awkward question, but can I ask how you felt when you received Richard's letter of introduction?' She gave a low, self-deprecating laugh. 'I only ask because... well, I suppose it's my fault that the family connection came to light. I was the one who traced you, from the information I had about James and Charlotte McWhinney.'

Eva hesitated and appeared to give the question some thought. And then she gave a gracious smile. 'I suppose I was intrigued at first. And then I was delighted. As I've already explained to David, I don't have much in the way of family. I lost my parents in a car accident several years ago and I don't have any siblings or first cousins. So receiving an invitation to connect, realising that I had some unexpected family, was a lovely surprise.' She stood up and crossed the room to a small, walnut writing desk. 'I do have a very distant cousin in London, his name is Laurence Payne.'

'Is he a relative on your father's side?'

'I believe so.' Eva turned to look at David. 'Of course, that doesn't necessarily mean that he's a Lancefield, does it? I'm not quite sure where he fits in. He and his family were always on my parents' Christmas card list, and we have continued sending cards to each other every year, just with little scribbled messages inside.' She turned back to the writing desk and bent down to pull open the bottom drawer. 'It's funny, isn't it, how we hang on to these tenuous connections?' She extracted something dark and heavy from the drawer. 'Now, this is something that I think will be of interest.' She nudged the drawer shut with her knee and turned back towards the sofa. 'The McWhinney family Bible. It was begun by James and Charlotte when they married and the details of all births, marriages and deaths are recorded in the pages at the front.'

Kathryn rolled her eyes. 'It took me days and days to piece together your line of the family, Eva. And all the time it was written in the front of a family Bible?'

'Ah yes, but you didn't know it was here, did you?' Eva stepped across to the sofa and handed the tome to Kathryn. 'Assuming that you have a camera on your phone, perhaps you might like to photograph the first few pages? To validate your research.'

It was an offer that Kathryn couldn't refuse. She took

hold of the Bible and balanced it on her knee. 'You don't keep it boxed up, or in some sort of protective case?' She ran a finger gently across the embossed leather cover. 'It's so old. Aren't you worried that something might happen to it?'

'Good heavens, no.' Eva appeared to find the idea amusing. She dropped down onto the chaise. 'It's just the family Bible. It's always been in that drawer. It's just a fact of McWhinney life.'

And yet it was so precious. Kathryn placed a fingernail under the cover and prised it open. The names of multitudinous McWhinneys were listed in the opening pages: their births, their marriages, their deaths. And their eventual occupations. Kathryn squinted down at the page. 'Surgeon, general practitioner, surgeon, surgeon... all the way to yourself. Eva McWhinney, cardiologist.' She flicked her eyes up towards Eva. 'Like father, like daughter?'

'I'm afraid so.' Sadness had crept into Eva's voice. 'There was no male heir to keep up the tradition, so it had to be me.'

'And the traditions must always be upheld.' David finally broke his silence. 'There is only me, now, to uphold the Lancefield family traditions. I know how it feels to carry the burden of a father's expectations. At least, I hope, I didn't place that burden on my daughter.'

Kathryn caught her breath and looked up from the family Bible. David was gazing at Eva as he spoke, and for the first time, Kathryn realised that his expression was one of utter enthralment. And now she understood why Stella had been so concerned; David was, indeed, besotted with his cousin, Eva McWhinney.

And, unless Kathryn was mistaken, Eva appeared to be returning his gaze with an equal display of affection.

*

DCI Price extended a cautious hand to Marcus Drake,

unsure that the gesture would be reciprocated. 'I do appreciate you agreeing to speak with me.' To his relief, Marcus took his hand and shook it firmly. 'May I sit?' He gestured to the large, Chesterfield sofa behind him.

'Why not? Salvation Hall isn't my home, so it's not really in my gift.' Marcus sat down in an adjacent armchair. 'I suppose you've come to talk to me about the verdict?'

'Not exactly.' They were in the drawing room, a vast expanse of luxurious space far beyond the needs of a quiet, discreet conversation. The policeman, given the choice, would have preferred a brief word over the casual comfort of a pint. But his position was a difficult one: he had been the senior investigating officer in the murder case against Marcus Drake, and he was the close, and growing closer, personal friend of the Lancefield family's consultant genealogist. He leaned back against the sofa's solid cushions. 'I can't say it came as a surprise. At least, not to me.' If he was honest with himself, Price had always known that Richard Lancefield would find a way to prevent his ward from enduring the hardship and humiliation of a prison sentence.

'You expected me to receive a suspended sentence?'

'I expected you to receive a guilty verdict because of your plea. But you gave us every assistance during the case, and I had every confidence that Richard would use whatever means were at his disposal to find a way to ship you out to St Felix at the earliest opportunity. I did think you might serve three to six months, so I wasn't quite prepared for you to walk away from the courtroom. But the legal argument was a sound one, and there are no grounds for us to challenge it.'

Marcus turned his head to look out of the drawing room window. 'To be honest, I expected to serve at least some time in prison. But I won't deny it's a relief to be free.' He turned back to Price. 'Richard arranged for me to have a brief holiday on Burgh Island. That's why I only returned to Salvation Hall yesterday.'

'Did you enjoy it?'

'Of course not. He booked me into some dusty, antiquated five-star place full of retired politicians and blue-rinsed dowagers.' Marcus sighed. 'But his heart is in the right place. And it did me good to get some peace and quiet. It gave me time to think.'

'And will you be heading to St Felix?'

'Yes. I'll be flying out on Monday if Nancy can secure the flights today.'

Well, thank God for that. 'I think it's probably for the best.' Price tried not to look too relieved. 'While you were in Edinburgh, did anyone tell you that Becca Smith had been sacked from her post of housekeeper at Salvation Hall?'

'Ah, so that's why you came. To talk to me about the Smith family and their harassment campaign.' Marcus nodded to himself. 'Yes, I've been told about it. It's one of the reasons Richard sent me to Burgh Island. He wanted me out of the way until Becca's anger had subsided.'

'You think it will subside?' Now that was optimistic. 'She's taken your release very badly, Marcus, as have the rest of her family. They're keeping a lid on it at the moment, but I can't promise that will last for very long.' And, truth be told, Price didn't have the police budget to offer Marcus any kind of protection. 'Still, if you're off to St Felix on Monday you won't have to keep your head down for too long. Becca and her family know that we're watching them. I don't think they will try anything foolish over the next few days.'

'I have no intention of going into Penwithen village, and if leave Salvation Hall I'll either take a taxi or hitch a lift with Nancy. Frankly, right now I don't feel like doing anything very much other than licking my wounds and contemplating a future without Lucy.'

Price felt a sudden pang of compassion. He had become so accustomed to seeing the young man in front of him as a murder suspect that he had almost forgotten that Marcus had suffered a bereavement. 'I've never said it before, but for what it's worth I am sorry for your loss. And I do hope that things work out for you when you get to St Felix.'

'Thank you.' Marcus fidgeted in his seat. 'Was there anything else, Inspector Price?'

The pang of compassion made way for an unexpected pang of remorse. It wasn't like Price to kick a man when he was down. But if he didn't take the opportunity now, he might never have the chance to ask again. 'I wanted to ask if you had remembered anything else about the moment you came across Philip McKeith leaning over Lucy's body.'

Marcus drew in a sharp breath, and then he closed his eyes with a knowing smile. 'I've already told you, inspector. When I found Philip leaning over Lucy's body I thought he was killing her, and I tried to stop him. I will always regret that I tried too hard.'

'And nothing else?'

'I know you don't believe me and I'm sorry that I have to disappoint you.' Marcus opened his eyes and fixed them on the policeman's face. 'I cannot tell you with any certainty whether Philip murdered Lucy because I cannot tell you with any certainty that she was dead before I killed him. But I can tell you this.' He leaned forward in his seat. 'I knew what Lucy was, and I knew what Lucy did. And I still loved her. Enough to promise you now that it wasn't me who killed her.'

# 6

An insidious drizzle had descended over Edinburgh's cobbled streets.

Kathryn had been game to take a brisk walk back from Hemlock Row to Palmerston Place despite the rain, hoping to clear her head, but David had insisted on a taxi. Now, confined reluctantly on the stiff back seat of a bone-rattling black cab, she turned thoughtful eyes away from her companion to gaze out of the window at the passing granite landscape.

Another city. Another Lancefield. Another death.

That the death in question hadn't been the death of a Lancefield scarcely seemed to matter. There had been something almost theatrical about the three of them – Eva, David and Kathryn – sitting in the drawing room at Hemlock Row, politely sipping afternoon tea and discussing the lives of long-dead ancestors, as if completely impervious to the murder investigation raging in the mews lane behind the house. The curtain had come down on the performance with the arrival of DCI Grant, and her request to re-examine Geraldine's room. Eva had been keen for David and Kathryn to remain while the examination took place, but the detective had looked askance at the suggestion. It was David who had saved the day, soothing the sting of their sudden departure with an impromptu invitation for Eva to join them for supper.

'It's quite remarkable, isn't it?' David's voice broke in across Kathryn's musings. 'To think that I've been living just twenty minutes' walk away from Eva and her family home for nearly twenty years, and I didn't even know that Lancefield descendants were living in Edinburgh.' He leaned into the corner of the cab, swaying slightly as the driver navigated yet another narrow junction. 'And won't my father be delighted when we tell him that there might be yet another cousin on the horizon, apart from Eva?'

'You mean Laurence Payne?' The name had been vaguely familiar to Kathryn. 'I might have seen the name Payne crop up in one or two documents already as I've examined the family papers. It will certainly save me some work if he does turn out to be a Lancefield descendant.' Eva hadn't been too sure. 'I know that Richard will be delighted when he hears about the contents of Hemlock Row, especially the family Bible and the painting of Charlotte McWhinney.'

'Though not so delighted to hear of the murder of Eva's housemate.' David was clearly troubled by the thought. 'I wondered if it might be pragmatic to keep the news from him, at least until a little more is known about the circumstances.' He lifted an eyebrow in Kathryn's direction. 'But you will tell Detective Chief Inspector Price, I suppose?'

'How can I not tell him?' But then again, how could she? It wasn't the sort of thing you could drop casually into a conversation. "Oh, by the way, Ennor, there's been another murder that appears to have some connection to the family." She brooded on the thought for a moment, imagining Ennor's response. Would it be incredulity or unease? Probably a bit of both, knowing Ennor. But either way, she knew he wouldn't let the matter drop until he knew all of the facts; until he'd convinced himself that there was no possible connection, and no risk to any of the remaining Lancefields. Not that there would be a great deal he could do about it when the crime had been committed in Edinburgh and outside his sphere of influence. She offered David an enigmatic smile. 'I wouldn't want him to hear the news from someone else. I don't think he'd be too pleased if I kept it from him.'

David was eyeing her now with gentle amusement.

'The two of you have grown quite close of late. Does he know that your divorce is almost complete?'

The candid question caught Kathryn off guard and a blush appeared in her cheeks. 'I hadn't got around to telling him yet.' She hoped that David wasn't going to ask her why. It would be better to change the subject. 'Eva said that she was taking some time out from work, didn't she? Until the police investigation had moved away from Hemlock Row? I wondered if you had thought of inviting her down to Salvation Hall this weekend.'

'To Salvation Hall?'

'Yes, we could suggest it to her this evening. Do you think Richard would consider it? We could invite her to the farewell supper for Marcus.'

David's brow wrinkled. 'You're plotting something.'

'Good heavens, no.' Kathryn frowned. 'Well, perhaps a little something. Don't you think it would be nice for her to meet Marcus before he heads off to St Felix? And wouldn't it help to take her mind off Geraldine's death? I know she seems rather calm and collected about it all, but it must have unsettled her.'

'Would she be willing to keep a diplomatic silence about the murder? So as not to upset my father, and spoil the celebration?'

'I don't know, but we have nothing to lose by asking her. I could make some enquiries about travel arrangements this afternoon. If there is a spare seat on our flight she could travel with us to Newquay. I think it would be worth checking before we extend the invitation.' The taxi made a sudden lurch to the left and Kathryn steadied herself against the door, dipping her head to look out of the window. They had turned into Palmerston Place. 'We're nearly home.' She turned back to David. 'What do you think?'

'I think it's a marvellous idea. I'm sure that my father would be delighted, and it would give her an opportunity to see Salvation Hall. Would she have to ask the police for permission to travel?'

'I can't see any reason why. At the end of the day, she was only Geraldine's friend, and she didn't witness the crime. And it's not as if the police consider her to be a suspect, is it?'

\*

'You don't seriously consider her a suspect?' DS Pearson leaned against the bedroom wall and folded his arms across his chest to steady himself. 'Could you honestly see Eva McWhinney strangling her friend?'

'She didn't seem too keen to let us take another look at this room, did she?' Grant kept her voice low, for fear of being overheard. 'When I came up here earlier today, she told me that Geraldine had been staying at Hemlock Row for almost three weeks. But there isn't much here in the way of personal effects, is there? For a stay of three or four weeks, if that's what was planned?' The policewoman cast her eyes around the room, and they alighted on a hook on the back of the bedroom door. 'There's a dressing gown, right enough, and a few bits of clothing hanging in the wardrobe.' She swivelled her eyes towards a nearby dressing table. 'A toilet bag, a cosmetic bag, a few bits of jewellery…'

'I got the impression that she had been going back to her own flat pretty regularly. Perhaps she was only keeping the bare minimum here. Maybe that was more convenient for her.' Pearson grinned. 'But you're not really interested in that, are you? Looking at this room was just an excuse to come back to Hemlock Row.'

'Of course it was an excuse to come back.' Grant muttered under her breath. 'Look, we've already agreed that we don't have a suspect or a motive yet, but Eva McWhinney and Alec Henderson are the closest we have to either. We know the motive wasn't theft, because her handbag was lying beside the body.' Grant scanned the room, a swift practised glance with narrowed eyes. 'I just hoped we might find something in the room to give us a steer.' She pulled a pair of latex gloves from the pocket of her coat and stretched them over her hands. 'What about a wee look in here?' She stepped closer to the dressing table and pulled on the top drawer. 'Empty.' She slammed it shut and repeated the exercise with the middle and lower drawers. 'Nothing in here at all.' She stepped over to the bed and examined the small, ornate bedside cabinet. 'Nothing on the top.' The cabinet had one shallow drawer and she pulled on the handle and bent down to peer into it. 'And nothing in here either.'

'What were you expecting to find?'

'How the hell should I know?' Grant, exasperated, slammed the drawer shut. 'Maybe I'm just looking for inspiration. Or a lucky break.' Or a miracle. She put a hand up to her head and rubbed at her temple. 'I want a thorough examination of this room, Ross. And an update on where we are with Alec Henderson.'

Pearson nodded and pushed himself away from the wall. 'I'll pop down to my car to make the calls.' He stretched out a hand to open the bedroom door and then wavered, turning his head towards her. 'Ma'am?'

She had begun to examine the wardrobe but something in his tone alerted her, and she looked up as he slowly opened the door. Eva was standing at the top of the stairs, her head tilted, her face a pale, inscrutable mask. Grant licked her lips and then smiled. 'Ah, Miss McWhinney. DS Pearson was just on his way to find you.' She extended the smile to the sergeant. 'She's here now, Ross, so if you wanted to pop downstairs and make those calls…'

He took the hint with practised ease, edging past Eva to access the stairs. Eva watched him descend the first few steps and then turned to pass through the open doorway. 'You wanted to speak to me?'

'Yes, if you could spare me a couple of minutes.' Grant pulled off the latex gloves and shoved them back into her pocket. 'We've been told that Geraldine's death occurred sometime between ten thirty and half-past midnight. We've also had a report of a dark blue transit van revving its engine and pulling out of the lane behind Hemlock Row at around ten forty-five.' Grant paused to let the information sink in. 'Can you remember hearing anything that might fit in with that?'

'I'm afraid not. As I've already explained, I was in the drawing room at the front of the house. The curtains were drawn, and the television was on. I was watching a film that didn't finish until well after midnight.' Eva looked suddenly troubled. 'You say she died last night? So she lay out there undiscovered all night?'

'I'm afraid so.' Grant softened her tone. 'You told me that she hadn't known Alec Henderson very long, but that she might have been going to stay over at his flat last night. We have to assume that she made her way back to Hemlock Row instead.' The policewoman chose her words carefully. 'Do you think it's possible that she was more interested in the relationship progressing than Alec Henderson might have been? That perhaps she had hoped to stay the night, but been disappointed?'

Eva dismissed the idea with a shrug. 'I don't think there was an intimate reason for her wanting to stay the night with him if that's what you're suggesting. I think she was more concerned about general safety and just hoping for a place to crash. She didn't want to risk travelling home if she had been drinking more than usual. We all have to be so careful these days.'

'I see.' It sounded plausible enough. And it would be interesting to see if Alec Henderson corroborated the theory. 'I'm sorry if our appearance this afternoon was inconvenient, Eva. It was very gracious of your cousin and his friend to make way for us.' Certainly, their response to Grant and Pearson's arrival had been more gracious than Eva's. 'Do you mind telling me their names, and where they're from?'

For a moment it looked as though Eva minded very much. And then she relaxed a little and said 'David Lancefield and Kathryn Clifton. David lives here in Edinburgh, and Kathryn is visiting him from Cornwall.'

'Thank you.' Grant observed the young woman closely. 'Did either of them know Geraldine?'

'No. It was their first visit to Hemlock Row. And their visit has no relevance at all to Geraldine's death.'

*Was that right?*

DCI Grant gave a diplomatic nod of the head. She would keep the thought to herself for now, but as far as she was concerned there was only one person who was going to decide whether or not that visit had any relevance to Geraldine Morton's death.

And it certainly wasn't Eva McWhinney.

\*

The barmaid at The Lancefield Arms wasn't for turning.

She gave Zak Smith her best scowl and then turned away to lift a small, glass tumbler from the shelf behind the bar. 'I've nothing to say to you.' She rammed the glass up against the gin optic, rattling a wrist full of thin, gold bangles. 'You don't deserve a girlfriend like me.'

Undeterred, Zak folded his arms on the bar. 'You don't mean that.' He watched as she added tonic to the measure of gin. 'You know you love me really.'

'I know no such thing.' She swigged at the gin. 'You were out all night. All bloody night.' She downed the rest of the glass in one. 'I was worried sick.'

'I told you yesterday morning that I was going to play poker with the lads. And you'll be glad that I did. I won a packet. There'll be a nice little treat in it for you when they pay up.'

'I don't want your dodgy money, thank you. I'm quite happy earning money of my own.' She sniffed her disapproval. 'And you don't stay out all night playing poker.'

'You do if you don't want to get it in the neck for waking your girlfriend up in the middle of the night. You're always banging on about how you need your beauty sleep.' There was an almost-finished glass of ale in front of him, and he downed the dregs and waved the glass towards her. 'Be a love, and put another one in there.'

Amber Kimbrall sneered at him and turned her eyes towards the end of the bar. 'Harry, there's a bloke down here wants a pint, when you're ready.'

She began to walk away, but Zak flung a hand across the bar to grab her arm. 'Don't be like that. I thought you'd be pleased.'

'You thought I'd be pleased?' She wrenched her arm free of his grip. 'Where's the evidence that you were playing poker and won? And where the hell have you been all day today? I haven't heard a word from you. Four times I've tried to call and you didn't answer your phone. I've been worried sick.'

'I came in at lunchtime to see you, but you weren't here.'

'You know I don't work Thursday lunchtimes.'

'I forgot.' The lie came easily to him, as all lies did. 'But I'm here now, aren't I?' He rolled his eyes. 'Look, I played poker until about two o'clock in the morning and I thought, I can't wake Amber up now, so I went round to Becca's and I slept on the couch.'

'You woke your sister up?'

'She's not as touchy as you about that sort of thing. She's used to it, having four brothers.' He grinned. 'Anyway, I had a full book of work on today. I had a Toyota estate coming in for a full service first thing this morning, so I went straight to the garage from Becca's.' He stretched out his hand a second time and ran an oil-stained finger affectionately down her arm. 'I took a couple of IOUs for my winnings. They'll be paying out later in the week. I'll take you out for dinner in Penzance if you like.

Pick a fancy place, somewhere with a good wine list.'

'And you think that's all it takes to make it up to me?'

His face softened. 'No, that's the bit that comes after. When we're on our own.'

'Is it?' Amber leaned over the bar, enveloping him in a cloud of musky perfume. 'Would you like to hear what I think?' She ran a finger softly across his cheek. 'I think you're a lying piece of shit.' She straightened her back and turned swiftly towards a customer at the other end of the bar. 'Yes, lover, another pint?'

Zak turned his head, watching through dark lashes as she drifted towards the man with a smile that should have been meant for him. She was beautiful when she was angry. It was almost worth making her angry just for the sheer joy of seeing it. But right now, he would rather know she was on side.

He cast a forlorn glance into his still-empty glass and then turned his head to look across the lounge bar. If no one was going to pour him a pint, he might as well play the fruit machine. He slid off the bar stool and ambled towards it, fishing in his pocket for change as he went. The search rewarded him with slim pickings, and he rattled the four pound coins into the machine one after another. He jabbed at the play button with an impatient finger, muttering as the reels spun round. 'Two oranges and a cherry? What good is that?' He jabbed again at the button. 'A bell, an orange and a melon?' He turned disgruntled eyes towards the bar. Amber had finished serving the other customer and was leaning against the counter watching him, her face once more a stony mask of disapproval.

He pressed the play button for a third time and the reels spun noisily around before landing on a straight run of three melons. The machine burst into life and a handful of pound coins rattled noisily into the drawer at the front. Zak turned his head again to look at Amber, nodding to her with a self-satisfied grin, and then bent down to scoop up his winnings.

He was just beginning to slot the coins back into the fruit machine when his mobile phone began to ring. He fished it out of the rear pocket of his jeans, glanced at the display, and then shot a furtive glance back towards the bar. 'I told you not to call me today.' He pressed the phone to his ear as he spoke, his voice an urgent whisper. 'I'm in The Lancefield Arms and Amber's watching me.' He spun on his heel, turning his face towards the door so that Amber couldn't see. 'Can't it wait until tomorrow?'

Apparently not. And when the caller spoke, he couldn't fail to understand the urgency.

It was all he could do to disconnect the call. And he could still feel Amber Kimbrall's shrewd, brown eyes burning into the flesh of his back as he lumbered out of the bar into the cold night air, without so much as a backward glance.

# 7

Kathryn relaxed into the armchair in the corner of the guest room and balanced the mobile phone in the crook of her neck. 'I'm back at Palmerston Place now, so I just thought I'd give you a quick call before supper.' She pulled her feet up onto the footstool at the end of the bed. 'How was your day?'

'Pretty boring, all things considered. I went over to Salvation Hall this afternoon, to have a chat with Marcus.'

'And that was boring?'

'Okay, maybe boring was the wrong choice of word. Let's say it was uneventful. Marcus tells me that he's leaving for St Felix on Monday, and he'll keep his head down until then. So hopefully, there won't be any more unpleasantness before he leaves.'

'Does Becca Smith know that he's been released?'

'I would think the whole world knows. But if Marcus has the sense to keep his head down, and Becca has the sense to give him a wide berth, then hopefully things will stay calm. I've enough on my plate building the case against Jason Speed without the Smith clan kicking off again. I've had enough of Becca's family to last me a lifetime.'

'And enough of the Lancefields?'

'If you must know, then, yes. Enough of the Lancefields.' The declaration came out just a little too forcefully. 'I'm sorry, Kathryn, but I just want things to calm down, for everyone's sake. No more murders, no more investigations. It will be a few months yet before Jason comes to trial, but until then I'm looking forward to my life becoming a Lancefield and Smith-free zone.' *If only.*

'But enough of my fantasies. How has your day been?'

'Very enjoyable. David took me to Hemlock Row, as planned, to introduce me to Eva.'

'And how did that go?'

'Very well. The house is stunning, and she had some wonderful family heirlooms to show us.'

'And does she look like Lucy Lancefield?'

Ah, the burning question. 'Yes, I'm afraid she does.' Uncomfortably so. 'It will be interesting to see how Richard reacts when he sees her photograph. David has invited her to supper this evening, and he's planning to invite her to Penwithen for the weekend. We thought it might be nice for her to meet Marcus before he travels to St Felix.' Kathryn paused, and added, 'I'm hoping that she'll bring the family Bible with her, for Richard to see.'

The silence at the end of the line might almost have been disapproving. Or perhaps Ennor was just rendered momentarily speechless by the news. Eventually, he coughed to clear his throat. 'I'm sorry, did I miss something here? You're planning to invite a girl who looks like Lucy Lancefield to spend the weekend at Salvation Hall, to meet with Marcus Drake?'

'Yes.'

'She looks like his murdered fiancée, and you're planning to introduce them?'

'It's not what you think.'

'It's not what I think that counts.' Ennor's anger was growing. 'Have you thought about the distress that meeting Eva might cause him? And what about Becca Smith? Have you any idea how she is going to react if she sees someone who looks like Lucy Lancefield? Who looks like the woman that her partner was having an affair with? The woman he was supposed to have murdered?' Ennor's frustration exploded at the end of the line. 'For pity's sake, Kathryn, whatever are you thinking of?'

'I'm thinking of keeping her safe.'

Now the silence at the end of the line was unmistakably

brittle, and the words that cut into it were brusque. 'Tell me.'

Kathryn opened her eyes and fixed them on the ceiling. 'Eva had a work colleague staying with her, a young woman called Geraldine Morton. And Geraldine was found murdered early this morning, in a lane at the back of Hemlock Row.' She waited for the news to sink in. 'I'm sure it's just a coincidence. The girl has nothing to do with the family. But she and Eva were very similar in appearance; both slim, both in their thirties, both with shoulder-length blonde hair.'

'So the girl who died looked like Eva?'

'Yes.'

'And Eva looks like Lucy?'

'Ennor…'

'Was there anything at all in the circumstances of this girl's death, apart from her resemblance to Eva and the fact that she was staying in Eva's home, that might suggest that Eva herself could be at risk?'

'Eva's very upset by her friend's death. I thought that inviting her to Penwithen would be a way of taking her mind off it.' Kathryn hesitated, and then added, 'And a way of keeping her out of harm's way until the murder has been investigated, and proven to be nothing to do with the Lancefield family.'

'You haven't answered my question.'

Only because she couldn't bring herself to answer it. 'I know I'm being ridiculous. I know this can't have anything to do with the family.' She was rambling now, grasping at words to justify her fears and excuse her reasonings. 'Apart from anything else, even David didn't know that there was a member of the family living in Edinburgh, and he's been living here for over twenty years.'

Ennor fell silent again. And then slowly, he said, 'She was strangled, wasn't she?'

'She was a colleague of Eva's at the infirmary, and she was staying at Hemlock Row while her flat was being renovated. She went out to meet with a boyfriend, and…'

'Kathryn, just tell me.'

There was no other alternative. Kathryn closed her eyes again and spoke softly into the phone. 'Yes, she was strangled. And the killer used her own scarf to do it.'

\*

Geraldine Morton's boyfriend lived in a spacious and tastefully-furnished flat on the first floor of an austere Pitt Street tenement.

As DCI Grant took a seat at the dining table to the rear of a high-ceilinged lounge, she cast an appreciative eye around the room. 'Have you lived here long?'

'A little over two years. I know the outside of the building doesn't have much to commend it, but that's the thing about Edinburgh tenements, isn't it? Even the ones that promise so little on the outside can have lots of potential on the inside. This one still had all its original fireplaces and pine panelling. And anyway, I like the location.' Alec Henderson sank onto the chair opposite. 'Are you sure I can't offer you a coffee?'

'No, I'm fine, thanks. I had one just before I left the station.' Grant turned the appreciative eye towards him. He was tall and athletic, with chiselled features and a shock of thick, black hair. Little wonder that Geraldine Morton had been hoping to stay the night. 'I'm sorry that we had to break the news of Geraldine's death to you over the phone.' Grant had been packing up for the day when word came through that Henderson had finally made contact. 'And I'm sorry to descend on you at home like this. But you'll understand that in a murder enquiry, time is of the essence.'

'Of course, anything I can do to help.'

The policewoman clasped her hands together and rested them on the table. 'My colleague, DC Pearson, has explained to you that Geraldine was found this morning in the mews lane behind Hemlock Row. But we believe that she died last night, and we need to establish her movements in the hours before her death.' Grant spoke softly and tried to sound reassuring. 'We know that she was staying with a friend while her flat was being renovated, but the friend thought that Geraldine had planned to stay here with you last night.'

'That was certainly the original plan. She was going to come straight down here after her shift at the hospital, to share a takeaway and a bottle of wine. But a friend of mine gave me tickets for a concert at the Usher Hall. He'd bought them as a birthday surprise for his wife, but she'd gone down with influenza during the day and didn't feel well enough to go.' Henderson snuffled a quiet laugh. 'To be honest, I don't think either of us was that keen; it was a bit high-brow for our tastes. Rachmaninov.' He made it sound like a disease. 'But it seemed a shame to waste the tickets, so we arranged to meet at the West End instead. We just had time to grab a pizza before the show started, and then afterwards we popped into a pub on Lothian Road for a quick drink.'

'And how long were you in there?'

'Only about half an hour. We left at about quarter past ten.' He hunched forward with a sigh. 'We walked up to Princes Street together and I wanted to flag down a taxi to take her back to Hemlock Row. But she said she was happy to walk. The town was quite busy and the streets are well lit. And it would only have taken her about fifteen minutes.' He looked down at his hands. 'I wish to God that I'd insisted on her taking a taxi.'

Grant nodded, a sympathetic bob of the head. 'Where exactly did you leave her?'

'At the corner of Princes Street and Frederick Street. I flagged down a taxi for myself and kissed her goodnight. She turned and waved to me as she walked off down Frederick Street.' Henderson swallowed hard. 'I hadn't known her that long, just five or six weeks. But it was going well. We had a lot in common.' He looked up at Grant. 'Can I ask what happened to her?'

'I'm afraid she was strangled.'

'Was she...?' He couldn't get the words out. 'Was she...?'

'It wasn't a sexual assault, if that's what you're going to ask me.'

His shoulders seemed to sink under the relief. 'Then why?'

'We don't know yet, Alec.' Grant watched his face as she spoke. 'It wasn't robbery. Her handbag was found beside her, and anything we might expect to be stolen was still in it. We did notice, when we searched the bag, that her mobile phone was switched off. I don't suppose you know why that might have been?'

'Yes.' He nodded. 'We both turned our phones off before the concert started and I don't remember either of us switching them back on afterwards. We were too busy chatting. I think I switched mine on when I got home.'

'And what time was that?'

'Sometime just before eleven.' He flinched, stung by an unexpected thought. 'You'll want me to verify that somehow, I suppose?'

'I'm sorry. It's just routine.'

'There's no need to apologise. I may have the receipt from the taxi in my wallet. Would that be any good?' His mouth curved with a boyish smile. 'I collect receipts for anything I can claim back against tax.' He stiffened. 'Only the legitimate expenses, of course.'

Grant returned his smile. 'I'm not interested in your financial affairs, Alec. I just want to know about Geraldine.' And where you were last night. 'The receipt will be better than nothing.' And it might lead her to the taxi driver. 'I suppose it goes without saying that Geraldine didn't have any enemies? Anyone who might have had a grudge against her?'

'A grudge?' He met the question with a blank stare.

'Geraldine was a kind, gentle, unassuming soul. I couldn't imagine anyone wanting anything but the best for her.' His eyes looked suddenly moist. 'Is there anything I can do, Inspector Grant? To help you find the killer?'

'I'd be grateful if you could let me know if you remember anything else relevant about your time with Geraldine yesterday evening.' The detective dug a hand into the pocket of her coat and pulled out a business card. 'You'll find me on this number, or there is an email address if you prefer that.'

He took the card from her and studied it. 'Detective Chief Inspector Alyson Grant.'

'That's me.' She stood up and held out a hand. 'Thank you for your time.'

For a moment he just stared at her hand, and then he rose to his feet and took hold of it. 'You're welcome. And if there's anything else I can do. Anything else at all.'

There was one other thing. Grant tried to suppress a wry smile and failed. 'I know it's a ridiculous thing to ask a journalist, but I'd be grateful if you'd keep this conversation to yourself. Our investigation is at a very delicate stage. I wouldn't like to see it blown off course by any unnecessary speculation in the press.'

\*

Richard watched as Nancy lifted a velvet cushion from the other end of the small damask-covered sofa. She balanced it on her lap and curled her fingers tightly around its edge, her face a picture of petulance, her cheeks hollowed beneath the fine, angular cheekbones, her full lips squeezed into a pout.

He rested his elbows on the arms of his chair and steepled his fingers under his chin. 'I can't see that it makes all that much difference. It's only a matter of contacting the caterers and asking them to provide for an extra person.'

'It's too short notice. They require seventy-two hours for any changes to the booking.'

'Nonsense. If they wish to retain our custom, they will accede to our request.' He spoke to her gently, as if admonishing a child. 'Now, what is this querulous display really about?'

Her scowl deepened. 'I don't understand why you have to keep doing this, Richard. I don't like to see you being taken advantage of.'

He bridled at the suggestion. 'And who, pray, do you suggest is taking advantage? David is my son, and therefore entitled to my support and patronage. Marcus was engaged to my granddaughter and has done the family a significant service. In return, it is my decision to send him to St Felix and employ him on the Woodlands Estate. Becca Smith may have taken advantage of me, as you put it, in the past. But she no longer works at Salvation Hall, and I provide support to her child simply because Frankie is my goddaughter, and the child of my late dear friend, Philip.' Richard watched Nancy's face as he spoke. 'Kathryn, then?'

'Of course not.'

'Then I don't understand.'

'You're funding Jason Speed's legal representation, and he isn't even a member of the family.'

'Oh, come now.' Richard clicked his teeth. 'I'm funding Jason's representation because we led him to believe that he was a member of the family. But for that, he would not have murdered his father or his partner.' The old man smiled, a perceptive curve of the lips. 'This is not about Jason Speed. This is about Eva McWhinney.'

Nancy growled. 'I don't understand this fascination you have with people who are related to you so distantly that they may as well not be related at all.'

'It is not for you to understand.' It had been a mistake then, to invite her to the Dower House. He should have taken David's video call by himself. 'Where is Marcus this evening?'

'He's taken a taxi into Penzance, to have supper with Ian Mitchell. He wanted to spend some time with him before going out to St Felix.'

'If he returns before ten o'clock, you can let him know that I wish to speak to him here at the Dower House. Otherwise, I will speak to him in the morning.' Richard lifted a gnarled finger towards a small writing desk in the corner of the room. 'In the meantime, perhaps you would be good enough to put the laptop away. I won't be needing it again this evening. David is going to send a text message to my mobile phone later, to let me know whether or not Eva has accepted our invitation. I will let you know in the morning whether to notify any changes to the caterers. And now that will be all.'

It was an unmistakable dismissal. Nancy blinked, and her lower lip began to tremble. 'Richard, can I…?'

'No, you cannot. Whatever it is.' He was losing patience with her now. 'We are done for today.'

She bit on her lip to steady it and pushed herself up from the sofa, turning to walk slowly out of the room. But she paused at the doorway to glance over her shoulder. 'I'll be in the library for the rest of the evening if you need me, working on my own family tree. Kathryn left me some lines of enquiry to follow up before she travelled up to Edinburgh.' Nancy snuffled back a tear. 'We are all one family at Woodlands, Richard. My family as well as yours.'

'Thank you, Nancy. I do not need reminding how far my family extends.'

He felt a twinge of regret as she walked out into the hallway. She was beginning to rebel, and he couldn't help wondering if she already knew the truth: that she was the child of his illegitimate daughter, the grandchild he could never bring himself to acknowledge.

He rested his head wearily against the wing of the armchair. In truth it made no difference whether she knew or not. The line between spirit and defiance was a fine one, and however much he loved Nancy he had little use for disloyalty. The girl had wanted for nothing with a comfortable home, a good education, and the opportunity to live and work with him at Salvation Hall. What more did she expect?

She had never been insolent towards him before, but something now was giving her the courage. And whatever it was he had to put a stop to it, and put a stop to it quickly before any more damage was done.

# 8

'I didn't expect David and Stella to go to so much trouble.' Eva sipped thoughtfully on her gin and tonic.' I thought I was just coming to Palmerston Place for a bowl of pasta and a glass of wine.' She was sitting in an armchair beside the fireplace and she rested her hand, still holding the glass, on the chair's arm. 'I saw the dining room when David brought me down the hallway to the drawing room. The table looked as though it might have been set for royalty.'

'Ah, but you're something much more important than royalty. You're another distant cousin for the family.' Kathryn couldn't help but tease. 'You're to be cosseted and feted.' She was nursing a freshly-mixed martini and she raised it in a toast. 'Here's to the latest addition to the Lancefield clan.' And, please, God, let this be the last one. 'I know it must sound like I'm making light of the situation, but David is so happy to have met you. I think it's just his and Stella's way of trying to make you feel welcome.'

Eva sipped again on the gin. 'I find it all very strange, to be honest. All those years we have lived so close without knowing. And now, here I am in David's home, enjoying his company and meeting his wife.' She smiled. 'Stella is quite a character, isn't she?'

'I suppose she is. I'd only met her once or twice before I came to stay this week, and I can't say that we got on particularly well. I think she was suspicious of my motives in helping Richard to document the family's heritage. But she seems to have mellowed since the last time I saw her. She has certainly been a very welcoming hostess.'

'She didn't seem hugely enthusiastic when David invited me to Penwithen for the weekend.'

Kathryn could hardly be honest about the reason. At least not at this stage of their acquaintanceship. 'Give her time, Eva. She is very protective of David. It's taken her months just to get used to me.'

'And is she also protective of Marcus?'

'Could you blame her for that?' It was a difficult question to answer. 'At least David was honest with you about Marcus and Lucy. He kept nothing back.' Perhaps it was time to change the subject. 'Richard will be so excited when he hears that you've accepted the invitation to visit Penwithen. Do you think the police will stand in your way?'

'I can't see why they would. It's not as if I saw what happened to Geraldine, and I've given them all the information I can about her. Of course, I've promised them access to the house if they need it, so I will need to discuss that with them.' Eva hesitated. And then she said, 'They still have no idea why she was targeted. I've been told this afternoon that they're interested in a dark blue van that was seen leaving Hemlock Row around the time that she was killed. I didn't hear or see it myself, but a neighbour did.' Eva drew in a breath. 'It seems such a long shot to me. Geraldine was a lovely person, very kind and thoughtful. I can't imagine she had an enemy in the world.'

'Forgive my asking, but did you talk to her about the letter you received from Richard? Or the fact that you had connections to the Lancefields?'

'Yes, I told her about it. Why wouldn't I?'

Kathryn stared down into her glass. 'I just wondered if she might have told anyone else about it.'

'I don't know. But I didn't ask her to keep it to herself. Kathryn, is there something that you're not telling me?'

Where could she begin? 'David told you about Marcus on Wednesday, didn't he, when you met for lunch? He told you about Lucy and Philip, and the court case.'

'Yes, he told me. But I didn't discuss any of that with Geraldine. I spoke to her briefly on the phone late on Wednesday afternoon, when she called to say that she might be away overnight. But why would that have any relevance in the matter of her murder?' Eva's eyes narrowed. 'For what it's worth, I think the last few months must have been a very sad and difficult time for David and his family. But it doesn't make any difference to me, Kathryn. I'm taking this turn of events for what it is. David has lost his daughter, and Richard is hoping to find an extended family to support David. And David is absolutely charming. I feel very lucky to have met him, and I hope that I can be of some help to him when he comes to take over the estate.'

It was a pretty speech. 'You need to repeat that sentiment to Richard when you meet him. He'll be delighted. Especially as you have an interest of your own in the family's heritage.'

'It would be difficult not to, growing up in Hemlock Row. It's always been a part of the McWhinney family.' Eva smiled and looked almost relieved that the conversation had changed direction. 'Do you have any idea, Kathryn, why the two lines of the family came to be divided? I know that James McWhinney practised medicine during his time on St Felix, and the family Bible shows that he married Charlotte Lancefield while he was out there. But they came back to Scotland just a year or two later, and there is nothing in the Bible that suggests much of a connection with the Lancefield family after that.'

Out of the frying pan and into the fire. Kathryn drew in a thoughtful breath and blew it out again slowly. 'Yes, I think I do know why the two lines separated. I've been able to work it out from the plantation records for the Woodlands Estate, and from a number of letters that passed between various family members at the time.' And it wasn't the most heart-warming of stories. 'With a family like the Lancefields, and their connections to the darker side of Caribbean history, I'm afraid it's inevitable that there will be…' Kathryn chose her words carefully. 'It's inevitable that there will be a darker side to their personal family history. Slavery was a brutal business. And not for the faint-hearted.'

Eva stared down into her gin and tonic. 'There has always been a rumour in the family that James McWhinney did something daring to further his career. My parents and my grandparents were aware of it, but it was something that wasn't talked about. I got the impression that it was something which might not have been ethical.'

That would be putting it mildly. 'You said yourself that your ancestor was a risk-taker, Eva. And I think that he took risks to further his career, risks which did not please Charlotte's family.'

'And that's why they came back to Edinburgh?'

'I believe so.' But now wasn't the best time to discuss it. 'With respect, I think David wants this evening to be something of a celebration. And I don't want to spoil that by raking up the past. But I promise that I will tell you what I've discovered. I haven't shared the full story with David or Richard yet, but with David's approval I will share it with you both tomorrow.'

\*

Ennor Price swivelled gently in his chair and considered the view from his study window with unfocused, almost-unseeing eyes. The window was impressive, tall and arched, and on a clear night, he could see both the Cornish sea and Cornish sky in welcome equal measures. But tonight the view was obscured by a covering of low, persistent cloud that mirrored the fogginess of his thinking.

Today should have been the end of the Marcus Drake affair, though Price wasn't naïve enough to think that everyone would have considered Drake's conviction a success. It had come as no surprise to him that Marcus might never see the inside of a prison cell for the manslaughter of Philip McKeith. But he knew that Becca Smith had expected something better, and he knew that she wouldn't take the news of a suspended sentence calmly in her stride.

It was all to the good that Richard Lancefield was planning to ship the errant Marcus off to St Felix before anyone in the Smith family laid eyes on him. But still, there was no question in Price's mind that Becca's family would strike against the Lancefields in revenge.

And he couldn't help wondering now whether maybe, just maybe, they already had.

He drew his eyes away from the window and focused them on the desktop computer to his left. The computer was switched on, but idle, and he prodded at the keyboard with a reluctant finger. The screen woke up with a blink. 'Geraldine Morton Edinburgh Murder.' He repeated the words to himself as he typed them into a search engine, and then bent his head forward to stare at the screen as a whole raft of matches appeared.

He plumped for the top one, a local evening newspaper report, and narrowed his eyes to focus as its account of the crime filled the screen. 'Talented medic... murdered... New Town...' He whispered the key points to himself as he skimmed through the text. 'Infirmary... late last night... strangled with a scarf.' And the critical phrase from any policeman's point of view: 'motive so far unclear.'

He leaned back from the screen and lifted his eyes to stare out again through the study window. The cloud had parted a little and in the distance now, beyond the night-time outline of rooftops and chimneys, he could just make out tiny flickers of light from the familiar gathering of boats moored up in the harbour. 'Motive so far unclear.' He repeated the phrase to himself, but it didn't feel any better the second time around, and he turned back to the screen, rattling the mouse against his desk to scroll down through the rest of the article.

*Oh, for pity's sake…*

A small, grainy photograph had rolled up into view, a picture of the victim taken only last year. She was young. She was pretty. She was blonde.

And she was an eighty per cent match for the late and unlamented Lucy Lancefield.

'And Eva looks even more like Lucy than this?'

Price let go of the mouse and flopped back into his chair, folding his arms as he went. An uncomfortable tingling had broken out across the back of his neck, the prickling of a policeman's instinct, his nerves dancing into life to alert him to something that this time he really didn't want to believe.

Somewhere up in Edinburgh, a pathology report was being written. It would confirm that the girl had been strangled with the scarf she was wearing. That the fabric had cut into the flesh of her neck, scarring her skin as it went. Fibres from the scarf would probably be found embedded underneath her fingernails, where she had tried to pull the ligature away from her throat.

There would be no chance of fingerprints on a murder weapon made of fabric. But there would be signs of a scuffle where the murder took place, dirt in the fibres of her clothing that would indicate just where her body had fallen.

He closed his eyes and bowed his head. It was Lucy Lancefield all over again. And Emma Needham not long after her. Three girls, all with some connection to the Lancefield family, all strangled with the scarf they were wearing. He could hardly believe it was possible.

It couldn't be possible.

If nothing else, Lucy's suspected murderer was dead and Emma Needham's killer was being held on remand, awaiting a trial date for her murder.

*It couldn't be possible.*

Two murders connected to the Lancefield family were enough for any detective. Four, if you included Philip McKeith and Dennis Speed. As far as Ennor Price was concerned, he'd dealt with his quota of Lancefield family tragedies. This one could stay firmly on someone else's patch.

He opened his eyes to stare again at the screen. 'Any information... contact DCI Alyson Grant.' The name was coupled with a dedicated contact phone number and he stretched out a hand to pick up a pen. 'I hope you're prepared for what could be coming down the line, DCI Grant.' He scribbled her number on the pad beside his computer. 'Because Bulldog Drummond wasn't prepared when Dennis Speed went under a bus.' He dropped the pen and stretched out a hand to retrieve his mobile phone from the desk. 'And as for Eva McWhinney...' He began to scroll through the phone's directory in search of a familiar number. '...I don't care what Kathryn has to say about it. You can keep her in Scotland. There's no way in hell I'm having a Lucy Lancefield lookalike on the loose down here in Cornwall.'

\*

DCI Grant pulled the cigarette from her lips and balanced it between the nicotine-stained fingers of her left hand. Her last indulgence of the day had been interrupted by the persistent ringing of her mobile phone, and it was with more than a little irritation that she reached out with her free hand to scoop up the phone and answer the call.

'Ross? What have you got for me?' She cast a disappointed glance at what was left of the cigarette and then leaned forward to the coffee table to stub it out on the edge of an overflowing ashtray. 'It had better be good.'

'We've had a result with the blue van.' He sounded annoyingly perky for someone who'd been on duty for nearly sixteen hours. 'I know it's late, ma'am, but I thought you'd want to know.'

'Define "result".'

'We've examined the footage from the three CCTV cameras nearest to Hemlock Row, for the hours before and after the estimated time of death. There was nothing for the hour before on any of them, and nothing for the hour after on the footage for West George Street or West St Andrew Street. But it was picked up on the Queen Street camera, heading east, and we can see it moving into the right-hand lane, as if it was going to head up towards Princes Street. I've put in a request for the footage from cameras at the east end of Princes Street, North Bridge and Leith Walk, to see if we can track where it went after that.'

'Do you think it was heading south or east?'

'We think the ultimate destination was south. The van was a Ford and we managed to make out the first six digits of the number plate, so we did a trace. But I don't understand the result. It's a hire van belonging to a small rental firm, and they're not located in this area. Like, seriously not in this area.' DS Pearson paused, and Grant could imagine his expression; the familiar air of bemusement that settled across his features when some irksome or incongruent fact was taxing his brain. 'The hire firm is based in Cornwall, at an address on the outskirts of Truro.'

'Cornwall?' Grant coughed out her amusement. 'I think you should have knocked off at teatime, Ross. Why on earth would someone hire a van to drive all the way from Truro to Edinburgh to commit a random murder?'

'Well, that's the peculiar thing, ma'am. The hire firm has an out-of-hours number, so we've already managed to touch base with them, and they couldn't have been more helpful. They had the name of the hirer for us in something under an hour, and there appears to be a link to Edinburgh.'

The inspector shivered, a tiny, unexpected thrill of anticipation. 'Has the van been returned to them yet?'

'No, it's not due to be returned until Saturday. But I have a name and address for the hirer, and we can put out a request for him to be interviewed.' There was a pause, and then a rustle of paper down the phone line as Pearson inspected his notebook. 'I've got the details here, ma'am. The hirer's name is Marcus Drake. And the address he gave for the booking was Salvation Hall, Penwithen.'

# 9

'Then you didn't get back in time to see Richard yesterday evening?' Nancy Woodlands, busy frying bacon in the kitchen at Salvation Hall, threw the question over her shoulder without an accompanying glance.

'No. I saw that note you'd left for me.' She had slipped it under his bedroom door. 'But I didn't get back until after eleven. Ian insisted on Irish coffees after dinner, and I didn't have the heart to say no.' Truth be told, Marcus didn't have the heart for anything much at all. 'Do you know why Richard wanted to speak to me?'

'He didn't say. But I'm guessing that he wanted to let you know that David has invited Eva McWhinney to your farewell supper tomorrow evening. She's travelling down with the rest of them.' Nancy half-turned her head, her lip curled into a mischievous smile. 'Aren't you a lucky boy?'

'They're bringing her down to Cornwall?' Marcus puffed out his cheeks and turned his head away from the kitchen table. 'Is that a good idea? Won't that just aggravate the Smith family even further?'

'Only if they hear about it.' Nancy pulled the frying pan from the hob and tipped the bacon onto a serving dish beside a pile of grilled tomatoes. 'I take it that you didn't meet her when you were staying up in Edinburgh?'

'Of course not. David didn't meet her himself until this week. He wasn't going to risk scaring her off by introducing me before the court case was settled. But I suppose things are different now.' Now that it's safe, Marcus thought. Now that I'm no longer at risk of going to jail and being an even bigger embarrassment to the family.

'Perhaps he was just being pragmatic.'

'Maybe.' Marcus shrugged. 'I don't really know anything about her. You probably know more than I do.'

'You think?' Nancy picked up the serving dish and turned on her heel, stepping towards the table with a knowing smile. 'I did learn a little yesterday evening when Richard and David had their video call. I sat in with Richard.' She placed the dish gently down on the table. 'She sounds a paragon of virtue.' There was a bitter tinge to Nancy's voice. 'It's rather unfair, don't you think, letting her gate-crash your party? It's meant to be a special occasion for the family.'

'What's unfair about it, given that I don't particularly want the party in the first place? I'm only going through with it because I don't want to offend Richard. Anyway, all I have to do is grit my teeth until it's over, and then make myself scarce to St Felix.'

'Well, I don't think it's a good idea.' Nancy pulled a chair away from the table and sat down, pushing out a petulant lip as she went. 'Don't you mind that we're constantly being side-lined?'

'Side-lined from what?'

'From the family. I don't understand why Richard has to keep digging up these long-lost relatives. He doesn't need any more family. He has us.'

'It's for David.'

'David has us.'

'It's not a competition, Nancy.' Marcus stretched out a hand to pick a piece of crispy bacon from the serving dish with his fingers. 'Neither of us are blood relatives to Richard and David. And in any case, I won't be here, will I? I'll be on St Felix.'

'And sooner than you think. They did have flights available for Monday. We leave from Exeter nice and early, to pick up a connection at Gatwick. So, you'd better get your bags packed.' She lifted a small plate from the table and held it out towards him. 'And I hope you're going to develop better table manners before we get there. You'll be expected to set an example.'

'Will I?' He dropped the piece of bacon onto the plate. 'I suppose if I don't it will reflect badly on you as my babysitter.'

The suggestion appeared to amuse her. 'You won't need a babysitter. Once my mother has her hands on you, you won't even have time to remember that I'm there. She's making plans already to introduce you to anyone and everyone on the island. All the workers on the Woodlands Estate, the neighbours…' Nancy leaned forward and lowered her voice to a whisper. 'I hear she even has one or two unmarried ladies lined up to show you the island.'

'I hope you're joking.'

'Oh, trust me, I'm not. You're not a visitor to St Felix, Marcus. You're an event. Unmarried, eligible, and with a patron like Richard Lancefield? The queue of girls will be halfway around Quintard Bay by now.'

'And they'll all be wasting their time.' Marcus took the plate from her hand and placed it on the table. 'Both you and your mother seem to have forgotten one very important point.' He picked up a fork from beside the plate and skewered the piece of bacon with it. 'You both seem to have forgotten that I'm still grieving for Lucy.'

\*

Price stared down at the blank sheet of paper on his desk. 'Who made the call?' The question was a restrained one, considering the caller was responsible for lifting his blood pressure and further shattering his chances of a quieter life.

Tom Parkinson leaned against the wall of the office. 'It was a DS Ross Pearson. The murder took place on Wednesday evening, and so far this is the only lead they have.'

Price jerked his head and raised his eyes to look at the sergeant. 'To be absolutely clear about this, you took a call this morning from a DS Ross Pearson, asking if we could assist him by tracing and interviewing Marcus Drake about the hire of a van that might have been used in a murder?' The policeman puffed out an indignant breath. 'The same Marcus Drake that has been on Ross Pearson's patch for the best part of five months, and who has just walked free from a murder charge?'

If Parkinson felt any sympathy with his senior officer's exasperation, he didn't let it show. 'The victim was found yesterday morning, in a residential street in the centre of Edinburgh. The area they call the New Town.' He eased himself away from the wall and pulled a notebook from his pocket. 'This blue van is the only lead they have at the moment.' He opened the notebook and glanced at his notes. 'They estimate it left Edinburgh sometime between ten forty-five and midnight.'

'And this DS Pearson, he's working with a DCI Alyson Grant?'

Parkinson's eyes narrowed. 'How the hell did you know that?'

'Second sight.' Price swivelled gently in his chair. 'The victim has connections with the Lancefields.' He lifted a pen from his desk, turning it around between his fingers as he spoke. 'Kathryn told me about the murder yesterday evening. You know she's in Edinburgh to meet another of these distant Lancefield cousins? The dead girl was lodging with the cousin. Her body was found in the alleyway behind the cousin's house.'

'You would think that the old man would have learned his lesson by now.' The sergeant stepped forward and sat down on the chair next to Price's desk. 'But this couldn't have anything to do with Marcus Drake, could it? He only came back to Penwithen from Burgh Island on Wednesday evening, and you spoke to him yourself at Salvation Hall yesterday. He can't possibly be the killer.'

'It doesn't mean that he couldn't have hired the van for someone else to drive.'

'But why on earth would he do that? What would be the motive?' Parkinson shook his head. 'Anyway, he wouldn't be stupid enough to give his real name, would he? The trail would lead straight back to him.'

There was another possibility. 'It could be the Smiths, up to their old tricks again? Hiring the van in Marcus's name, to pin the murder on him.'

'Surely even they wouldn't go that far? And who would have driven it, all the way up to Edinburgh and back again? It must be a twelve-hour stretch each way.'

'Not if you stick to the motorway network and use the M5 and M6. I've done it in just under ten hours.'

'Well, it doesn't make any sense to me.'

'It doesn't make any sense to me either. Yet.' Price dropped the pen onto the desk. 'But I suppose none of that matters at this point. We'll have to take this DS Pearson at his word, find the van and impound it. You've got the registration and the details of the firm it was hired from?'

'Yes. It wasn't one of the big nationals. They traced it to an independent business in Truro.'

'Then get over there now and speak to them. I'll put in a call to DCI Grant. I was planning to do that anyway. I want to see how much she knows about the Lancefields and Marcus, and fill in the blanks for her.'

'And what about Marcus himself?'

'For that matter, what about Richard and David? Their home was given as the address, wasn't it?' Price wanted to say "What about Kathryn?" And more to the point "What about my relationship with Kathryn?" Instead, he said, 'I'll go over to the hall and speak to him. Let's catch up later this morning and see what we've got.'

Parkinson nodded and pushed himself up from the chair, turning to leave the room. And then he cast a glance over his shoulder at Price. 'Is it starting again, boss?'

'Not if I have anything to do with it. Whatever it is that's going on, we need to shut it down.' Price nodded to himself. 'And we need to shut it down now.'

\*

Kathryn slid a simple, hand-drawn family tree across the kitchen table towards David. 'Now that Stella has gone out, can I take the opportunity to tell you more about the McWhinney affair?'

'I take it that Stella wouldn't be impressed by what you have to tell me?' David gave a whimsical smile as he glanced down at the document. 'What power she holds over all of us. Now even you are pussyfooting around her sensitivities.'

'Me? Hardly.' Kathryn's cheeks dimpled with feigned innocence. 'But it's such a relief that she is warming to the idea of supporting you with the estates, I don't want to do anything that might encourage her to do a U-turn.' Kathryn tapped a finger on the family tree. 'This shows the date of James and Charlotte's marriage, and the names and birth dates of their children. They were married on St Felix in 1802, but all of the children were born in Edinburgh after their return.'

'Did the family disapprove of the match?'

'I haven't found any evidence to suggest that, at least not at the time of the wedding. I believe that a substantial dowry was bestowed on the couple by Benedict Lancefield, and members of the family attended the ceremony. And McWhinney had been the Lancefields' medical man for something close to two years by the time the marriage took place. They'd had plenty of time to get the measure of him.'

'Would he have worked full time on the estate?'

'Not at first. I think he was initially engaged to provide medical services to Woodlands on an ad hoc basis. But James appears to have persuaded Benedict that the plantation would benefit from having its own hospital. That it would be a sound investment.'

'And Benedict agreed?'

'Yes. Of course "hospital" is rather a grand term for what was probably just an outbuilding with a few beds in it. Up to this point, medical care on the plantation appears to have been quite an amateurish affair. The estate documents make reference to a lying-in room and a midwife, a boy who could draw teeth and a herbalist who used herbs and preparations to treat minor ailments. The plantation appears to have had its own medicinal garden. They only engaged the services of a doctor for more serious complaints.'

'I suppose I should be relieved that they cared enough to take care of the slaves' medical needs.'

Kathryn gave a rueful smile. 'It wasn't a compassionate act, David, it was to protect their investment. Slaves were a valuable commodity and it was in the Lancefields' interests to look after them.' She consulted her notes. 'In 1799, the plantation suffered a serious outbreak of yaws – that's a nasty tropical disease – and several slaves were lost. As a result, Benedict decided to take McWhinney's advice and improve the medical provision on the estate. He arranged to build the hospital and to pay a retainer for the doctor to make himself available for up to three days a week. On the other days of the week, McWhinney would be free to work for other plantations.'

'Was he a good doctor?'

'He had good credentials, he trained at the Edinburgh Medical School, but I don't think he had a great deal of practical experience. He was newly qualified, he was cheap and keen, and he presented excellent references. And there is a suggestion that he was a handsome, charming man. I've found at least one piece of correspondence between Charlotte and her sister Maria, saying that she felt lucky to have made such a well-favoured match. His income was modest, so the only conclusion I could draw was that he was well-favoured in some other way. I'm guessing that it was physically.'

David's brow creased. 'So if the family approved of the marriage and McWhinney was a decent medical man, why on earth was there a rift?'

'It's explained in some of the family's correspondence.' Kathryn licked a finger and began to leaf through a small collection of papers on the table in front of her. 'In 1803, Benedict Lancefield and his wife Eugenie decided to return to England for a prolonged visit.' She pulled a document from the set. 'It was agreed that the Woodlands manager and the overseer would deal with the day-to-day running of the estate and that McWhinney and Charlotte would act on behalf of the family in Benedict's absence. They would be Benedict's eyes and ears, to ensure that the Lancefields' decent practices were followed. But McWhinney had ideas of his own, and Benedict's absence gave him the opportunity to try some of them out.' Kathryn slid the document across the table towards David. 'James McWhinney was a great admirer of a doctor employed on a Jamaican plantation, a man called John Quier who had conducted medical experiments on the slaves in his care.'

'Experiments?' David picked up the document and glared at it. 'Please don't tell me that McWhinney ran experiments on human beings.'

The news had been bound to upset him. 'I think he saw it as a means of furthering his medical career and standing. And he was, I think, intrigued by the possibilities.' She pointed at the document. 'You're looking at a copy of a letter from Benedict Lancefield to his brother Richard, in which he says McWhinney had asked for permission to run experiments of his own, a request which Benedict had denied. In fact, he had asked McWhinney to never mention it again.'

'And with Benedict and his wife out of the way in England, McWhinney saw his opportunity and took it? Dare I ask what kind of experiments he ran?'

'I'm still curating the relevant documents, but I believe he was interested in a new, untested vaccine for smallpox.'

It was a lie to spare David's feelings, of course, though Kathryn knew she couldn't keep the truth from him forever. 'I'm afraid the experiments went very badly and a number of slaves died. There is evidence that Charlotte was distraught at the outcome. She sought advice from a nearby plantation owner, and sent a letter to her brother Benedict in England, to tell him what had happened. Benedict held her partly responsible for the affair, and sent instructions to his attorney on St Felix to have the couple removed from Woodlands, by force if necessary.'

'So, Charlotte was removed from her home? Was that when the couple returned to Edinburgh?'

'I believe so. Benedict never forgave Charlotte for her failure to control her husband and he banished her from the family. Ironically, on their return to Edinburgh, McWhinney was applauded for his courage in daring to conduct the experiments in the hope of progressing medical knowledge. He went on to carve out quite a career for himself, and the family lived a fairly affluent life.'

'And what of Charlotte?'

'I've found letters between Charlotte and her sister Maria in London, and her brother Richard in Liverpool. Those letters suggest that her marriage was a happy one, but that Benedict never forgave her.'

David grimaced. 'I don't suppose I should be surprised by this sorry tale. Nothing really shocks me after the horrors of *The Redemption*. But still…' He tapped a finger on the document in front of him. 'Do you think Eva knows about these experiments, Kathryn? Do you think she knows that her family's wealth was built on them?'

'I don't believe she does. But I suppose the only way to know for sure is for us to ask her.'

## 10

The Penwithen bakery occupied a neat, double-fronted building in the village, directly across the road from the church of St Felicity's.

Nancy walked slowly up to the left-hand window and glanced through it to examine the baskets of homemade bread and pastries. 'Olive bread, focaccia, pain au chocolat...' She murmured under her breath, raising her eyes just a shade higher than the display. The shop within appeared to be reassuringly empty.

She smiled to herself, a smirk of self-assurance, and then bent down to loop Samson's lead over a hook beside the door. 'Now, you be good. I won't be long, and I'll bring you a biscuit.' She waited until the dog, well-accustomed to the drill, had settled himself down on the pavement and then she stretched out a purposeful hand to push firmly on the door.

The bell above the door frame rang with a familiar, brassy chime and a small, neat, middle-aged woman emerged from a doorway behind the counter. 'Good morning.' She tossed the cheerful greeting into the air, wiping her hands down her apron as she spoke. 'What can I do for you?' She flicked friendly eyes up to the face of the customer by the counter and then checked herself. 'Oh, it's you.' The friendly eyes took on a wary look. 'Well, we are honoured this morning. I thought you were taking your orders by delivery these days.' She ran her hands down the apron a second time, smoothing away imaginary wrinkles. 'Now that our Becca's not at the hall to run your errands.'

It had been one of Becca Smith's responsibilities as

housekeeper at Salvation Hall to collect the regular, daily bakery order. But Becca was no longer the housekeeper, and Nancy was in no mood for an argument. 'We need a few extras this weekend, Emily, and it was no inconvenience for me to call in and pick them up. David and Stella are coming down for the weekend, and Kathryn will be with them. And they are bringing another guest.'

Emily's smile frosted further. 'And I suppose that guest would be Marcus Drake?' The news of his release must have travelled fast. But then it would.

'The guest is a distant cousin of the family. She's travelling down from Edinburgh with them to visit Richard. He's very excited about it.' Nancy stepped closer to the counter and swept her eyes over its offerings. 'I'll take two loaves of olive bread, please.' She watched as Emily pulled a crisp paper bag from under the counter. 'How is Becca?'

'She's alright.' Emily picked up a set of tongs and used them to lift a loaf from the basket at the end of the counter. 'All things considered.' She dropped the loaf into the bag and then flipped it over by the corners with an expert's ease, twisting them tightly to hold the bread in the bag.

'It must be difficult for her, knowing that Marcus didn't go to prison. But at least he was found guilty of Philip's murder.'

'You mean his manslaughter.' Emily grunted the correction as she bagged a second loaf and placed it down on the counter. 'No disrespect, Nancy, but I would prefer not to discuss it.' She fixed the girl with a defiant eye. 'Anything else?'

'I'll take four steak pasties and two lamb.' Nancy fluttered a hand across the counter. 'Is that rosemary focaccia? I'll take one of those as well.' She tilted her head. 'Have you seen Becca since the trial?'

'Of course I have. I called in to see her when I heard the result. Just to tell her how sorry I was.' Emily's cheeks flushed as she bagged the pasties. 'You'll be pleased, of course.'

'Me? Why would you think that?'

The baker glanced up sharply from the task in hand and narrowed one eye suspiciously. 'Why wouldn't you be?'

'I am human, Emily. I do understand how Becca must be feeling. You seem to forget that I worked quite closely with her.'

Unconvinced, Emily placed the pasties down on the counter beside the bread. 'So, who is this cousin who's coming to visit?'

'Her name is Eva, and she's a doctor at the Edinburgh Royal Infirmary.' Nancy lifted a loaf from the counter. 'I wonder if I might ask you to do me a small favour while I'm here? Could you pass a message on to Becca for me?' She placed the loaf gently in her shopping basket. 'Could you let her know that, although I understand how disappointed she must be with the outcome of the case against Marcus, it wouldn't be a good idea for her to take her anger out on the family again. For her own sake, and for Frankie's, I would ask her to think about Richard for once.' She lifted the second loaf from the counter. 'Richard is an old man, and he's very keen for Eva's visit to go well. And although he's forgiven Becca and Zak for the harassment campaign they conducted against the family after Philip's death, he hasn't forgotten it. And I don't think he would be so forgiving if it were to start up again.'

A flash of righteous indignation lit Emily's eyes, and Nancy responded with an almost imperceptible shake of the head. 'I wouldn't, Emily.' She glanced over the woman's shoulder, to the shelves of neatly-baked pastries that lined the wall. 'I'll take half a dozen strawberry tarts, and half a dozen mille-feuille. Can you box them up for me, please, with a carrying string?' She turned her head to look through the window at the ever-patient Samson. 'I'll have my hands full walking back to the hall.'

Emily opened her mouth to speak and then thought better of it. She pulled an empty cake box from beneath the counter and turned towards the pastry shelves, her shoulders heaving. 'Half a dozen strawberry tarts.' She hissed the order through gritted teeth. 'And half a dozen mille-feuille.'

Behind her back, Nancy smiled; a supercilious curve of the lips, any pretence of warmth now gone. 'And just one more thing: a shortbread biscuit for Samson. I won't need a bag for that. You can charge it all up to our account, please, Emily. I'll pop back at the end of the month to settle up with you.' She lifted the lamb pasties from the counter and placed them in her basket. 'And you won't forget to pass on my message to Becca, will you? I would hate for there to be any misunderstanding.'

\*

'So, you think it's possible that Geraldine Morton was murdered by mistake? That the killer mistook her for Eva McWhinney?' DCI Grant exhaled noisily down the phone line. 'Well, I won't deny that there was a strong resemblance between the two women. But what would be the motive for murdering Eva?'

Price closed his eyes and leaned back in his chair. 'When I saw the photograph of the dead girl on the internet yesterday evening, I thought someone was walking over my grave.' Or perhaps over Lucy Lancefield's grave. 'The motive could be a hate campaign against the Lancefield family.'

'A hate campaign?' Grant fell silent, mulling the idea over. Eventually, she said, 'In retaliation for Marcus Drake walking free?' She didn't sound convinced. 'As far as I'm aware, Marcus resided with his family in Palmerston Place for several months and we never had a hint of trouble. He fulfilled all his bail conditions and there were no reports of any activity against him. If the Smith family were happy to travel all the way up to Edinburgh to vent their spleen, why not come up here earlier and take a shot at Marcus himself?'

The answer to that question was simple, at least as far as Price was concerned. 'They truly believed that he was going down for Philip McKeith's murder. He'd admitted the crime, there was no reason for them not to expect a custodial sentence.'

'So why didn't he get one?'

'Technically, he did. But the Lancefield family have influence. Significant influence. I can't prove it, but we all know that the "old-boy network" works in mysterious ways.'

'Are you suggesting that the sentence handed down was questionable?'

'No. That's the point. These guys know just how to play the game. The sentence was within the prescribed guidelines for the crime committed. And the Smith family were just too innocent to see it coming.' Much like Price himself. 'But they live by their passions, and since Marcus was released I've been waiting for them to make a move. I thought they were biding their time, but maybe I was wrong.'

'And the fact that the van was hired in Marcus Drake's name? Where does that figure in your theory?'

'We don't know yet. My sergeant is already on his way to Truro to question the van hire firm. Just because it was hired in his name doesn't mean that he hired it, let alone that he was driving it. And until it's confirmed to me that there is evidence to prove Marcus hired it, I'm inclined to think that someone is setting him up.'

Grant fell silent again. And then she clicked her teeth. 'And suppose he was being framed by the Smith family, what would they get out of that?'

'Revenge. Maybe they see it as a way of putting him back through the legal system, having him charged with a murder that he didn't commit. They're not exactly deep thinkers. They wouldn't consider the risks or the ways in which such a plan might go wrong.'

'Well, if they were targeting Eva McWhinney and hit on Geraldine Morton by mistake, I would say their plan went spectacularly wrong.' Grant snorted a contemptuous laugh. 'Did Marcus ever meet either of those girls?'

'Not to the best of my knowledge. It goes without saying that I have a pretty close connection to the Lancefields, and I have it on very good authority that he didn't meet either of them.'

'This connection between Eva and the Lancefields. It's a bit unusual, isn't it? An old man searching out long-lost cousins?'

'That's one way of putting it. But there's no law against it, is there?'

Obviously none that Grant could think of, judging by the silence at the end of the line. Eventually, she said, 'That blue van is the only potential lead we have at the moment and I'll be honest with you, DCI Price, this isn't where I expected it to take us. How soon can you get back to me on the hire firm?'

'Hopefully within the next couple of hours. When we end this call, I'm going over to Salvation Hall to speak to Marcus, and then I'm meeting with DS Parkinson to get an update on the van. In the meantime, I would advise you to have a word with David Lancefield and Kathryn Clifton while they're still in Edinburgh. They're planning to travel back to Cornwall tomorrow, along with David's wife Stella.'

'That's Drake's mother?'

'Yes. And they've invited Eva to come down here for the weekend.'

A gasp of astonished laughter burst down the phone line. 'Am I hearing this?' Grant was incredulous. 'My investigation is at a critical stage. I don't want a key witness swanning off to the other end of the country.'

'I know she's your key witness. But it's also my belief that she's a potential victim and she needs protection. Do you have the budget for that?'

'No. Do you?'

'No. But I have a back-door way to keep an eye on her.' He picked a pen up from his desk and twizzled it between his fingers. 'When Kathryn told me yesterday evening that Eva was planning to come to Cornwall, I'll admit I was dead set against it. But now I've slept on it, maybe it isn't such a bad idea after all. I count Kathryn Clifton as a friend and that gives me access to Salvation Hall on a personal, as well as a professional basis. I think, given the circumstances, and with Kathryn's encouragement, the family will give me access to the hall on an informal basis over the weekend, just to keep an eye on things.'

'But if you're right, and the Smith family are behind Geraldine's murder, then surely Eva would be safer in Scotland? Travelling to Cornwall would put her at greater risk than she faces now?'

Price held his tongue and let Grant think about it.

And then she let out another little splutter of Celtic incredulity. 'My God, Price, you're not letting her come to Cornwall for her safety. You're suggesting that we use her as bait.'

\*

David Lancefield had been waiting in the Crab and Lobster for almost twenty minutes by the time Stella arrived. He dropped his newspaper onto the table as she approached, and stood to greet her. 'Stella, darling, you look marvellous.' He held out a hand. 'As always.' He smiled as she tapped his hand playfully with her fingers, and then leaned back in his chair. 'I've already ordered for us, but I asked the waitress not to serve coffee until you arrived.' He turned his head, in search of the girl who had taken the order, nodding as his eyes found her. 'Ah good, she's seen me.' He swivelled his eyes back to Stella. 'And how was the salon this morning?'

'Bleak.' Stella slipped off her coat and draped it over the back of an adjacent chair before sitting. 'There had been a mix-up with my booking and Jordan only had time to do my cut. I had to make do with a junior stylist for the highlights.' She leaned across the table. 'Tell me the colour isn't too harsh.'

'The colour is fine.' He tilted his head. 'If anything, I think the shade is a little warmer than usual. It complements your skin tone beautifully.' In truth, he could scarcely tell that anything had happened to Stella's hair at all in the few short hours since he'd last seen her, but he could hardly admit to that. 'At least they were able to fit you in today.'

She studied his face and then, reassured, she pointed to the empty chair beside him. 'Isn't Kathryn joining us for lunch?'

'We had quite a long and difficult chat about the family this morning. She wanted to take a walk to clear her head. She knows we'll be here until one thirty if she changes her mind.' He turned his head to look out of the window. 'I think she's feeling a little morose. She told me this morning that she feels she is divorcing more than her husband. She is divorcing that part of her life that was spent in Edinburgh.'

Stella rolled her eyes. 'You have to romanticise everything, don't you?'

'Yes, of course.' He could see no point in denying it. 'It makes life more pleasurable.'

'Do you think that taking Eva down to Penwithen will be pleasurable?'

'Why wouldn't I?' The sudden change of direction caught David unawares. 'I rather hoped that you had formed a favourable impression of her after last night's supper. She was a charming guest. You said so yourself.'

'I know I did.' Stella rested her hands on the table. 'She has lovely manners, and she seems to be very quick-witted. But I'm worried that you're going to get hurt.'

'Hurt?' The notion puzzled him. 'In what way could Eva possibly hurt me?'

'She looks so much like Lucy.'

'I know she does.' But that didn't answer his question. 'Stella, I'm not a fool. And that isn't why I've grown fond of her. It's because she's a breath of fresh air. She doesn't stand in judgement of my family and its origins.'

Stella's eyes flew up to his face. 'Are you comparing her to me?'

'Of course not. But if we are to take on the estates after my father dies, we must at least make our peace with the past. Kathryn says we have to own it before we can bring about change, and I am beginning to understand what she means. We have a wonderful opportunity here. Marcus has agreed to go out to St Felix to learn the ropes at Woodlands, and he will be on the spot should we need to make any changes there. Kathryn will assist us, I'm sure, with any changes that we need to make at Penwithen. And cousin Barbara will always be on hand to bring a sense of balance to our undertakings.'

'And Eva... what will Eva bring to the party?' Stella didn't wait for him to answer. 'David, your family's heritage is tainted. It's not fair to expect my son to manage a plantation estate that your family should never have owned. And I will admit that cousin Barbara is a sweetheart, but she makes no secret of her disdain over the way the Lancefields made their money.'

'Barbara is entitled to her opinions. And, happily, her opinions don't appear to get in the way of her willingness to provide support to the family.' David could feel his irritation growing. 'Kathryn also has strong feelings about our family's line of business, but she doesn't let it prevent her from seeing its possibilities for the future.'

'Kathryn can't change the course of history. The

Lancefield heritage is tainted, David. And introducing a Lucy substitute into the mix isn't going to change that.'

David winced, stung by the suggestion. 'I don't want to quarrel about it, Stella. My mind is made up. Eva is coming to Salvation Hall to meet my father, and to meet Marcus.'

His wife regarded him with a defiant eye. 'And how do you think The Girl is going to take to this new addition to the Lancefield family?'

'I do wish you wouldn't use that dreadful nickname. Nancy deserves better.' David pursed his lips. 'I can't see any reason why Eva's visit would cause Nancy a problem.'

'Hasn't it occurred to you that, since Lucy's death, The Girl has achieved the privileged position of being the only young woman in Richard's life?'

'Apart from Kathryn.'

'Kathryn has a sensible head on her shoulders, and doesn't seek to wield any power within the family.'

'And you think that Nancy does?'

'Of course she does. She considers herself to be a part of the family, despite only being Richard's secretary. If Richard is as besotted with Eva as you are, just think of the trouble it will cause.'

It wasn't something that David had considered. He would have to ask Kathryn's opinion on the subject. But in the meantime, the decision was his. 'Eva is coming to Penwithen. The flight is booked and we will collect her from Hemlock Row on our way to the airport tomorrow.'

'Always assuming that the police will permit her to leave.'

'Indeed.' David snapped out the word, his patience nearing its limit.

But Stella was not for turning. 'Well, I think you're asking for trouble. And when the brown stuff hits the fan in Penwithen, when Nancy sets eyes on Eva and begins to rock the boat, don't say that I didn't try to warn you.'

# 11

'And you believe that Eva was the intended target?' Marcus Drake's face had paled at the news of Geraldine Morton's murder, a spontaneous reaction which Price very much doubted could be feigned. 'Does Richard know about this?'

'I don't believe so.' They were sitting in the drawing room at Salvation Hall and the policeman, perched awkwardly as always on the edge of the sofa, looked down at his fingers. 'I certainly haven't mentioned it to him, and neither has Kathryn.'

'But David knows about it? And my mother?'

'Yes. But if you're wondering why they haven't shared the news with you, I think they were trying to spare you the upset, coming so quickly after your trial.'

'While you're not so worried about sparing my feelings?' Marcus laughed wearily under his breath. 'I don't suppose I can blame you for that. In fact, I appreciate your honesty.' He tugged on his ear. 'At least this time you can't put me in the frame for the murder. I've been here at Salvation Hall since I left Burgh Island and I have a handful of witnesses to prove it.'

Price felt his heart sink. 'I'm afraid things are a little more complicated than that.' He looked up at Marcus as he spoke. 'I'm afraid evidence has come to light which may implicate you in Geraldine's death.'

'Implicate me?' The words hardly seemed to have registered. Marcus's face fell blank and in reply, he stared not *at* Price, but through him, as if the answer to the conundrum lay beyond. And then he laughed again, louder this time, a snort of genuine amusement. 'What will they think of next?' He waited for the policeman to answer. And then the penny dropped. 'You're not joking, are you?'

The detective answered him with a frown. 'Where is Richard this morning?'

'He's in the Dower House, dealing with some paperwork.'

Then they couldn't be overheard. 'Look, Marcus, I'm trying to be discreet about this. I don't want to upset Richard. And for what it's worth, I don't want to cause you any trouble after everything you've been through. But I had to come here to speak to you because I need two things from you: I need your alibi for Wednesday evening when the murder took place; and I need confirmation that you haven't rented a blue Ford Transit van from a firm called Trennick Rentals, in Truro.'

Marcus growled. 'I'm due to fly to St Felix first thing on Monday morning. Is this ridiculous turn of events going to stop me?'

Stop him from what? From running away? Price kept the thought to himself. 'I hope not. Not if you can give me the answers that I need to eliminate you from the enquiry.' And if he could satisfy DCI Grant with sufficient evidence that both the alibi and the denial of any knowledge of the blue van were genuine.

The young man slumped back in his seat. 'I was here on Wednesday evening. I had supper with Richard in the Dower House, and Nancy cooked for us. We had a lot to discuss, and I was there until very late in the evening.'

'And Richard and Nancy can corroborate that?'

'Of course.'

'And the van?'

'I have never heard of Trennick Rentals. Are you suggesting that the van was hired in my name?'

'Yes.'

'Well, assuming that you're able to provide some sort of evidence of that, you'll be able to provide confirmation of how it was paid for. At that point, if a debit or credit card in my name was used to secure the booking, I'll be more than happy to provide you with bank or credit card statements to disprove the evidence.' Marcus growled. 'Always assuming that none of my accounts have been accessed fraudulently. In which case, I'll be reporting it to you as theft and asking you to investigate the crime.' There was a bitter inflexion in his voice.

And Price could hardly blame him for that. 'I am sorry that this has happened, Marcus.'

'I'm sure you are, Inspector Price.' Marcus drew in a world-weary breath. 'But I have to ask, ludicrous though it is, why you think I might have been involved in the murder of a woman that I don't know?'

'I didn't say that I thought you were involved. If anything, I think someone wants us to think that you were involved. And I've already told you that I believe Eva was the intended target, which suggests a link to the Lancefield family.' Or a strike against the Lancefield family. 'As to who the actual killer might be… well, there's no telling how long it will take us to work that out. But it will be a whole lot easier once we've eliminated you from our enquiries. And make no mistake, Marcus, we will work it out.'

\*

DCI Grant's return to Hemlock Row had been met with a lukewarm reception, and it had been touch and go whether Eva McWhinney would invite her into the house. Now, on the other side of the front door, she found herself leaning against the wall in the hallway, wondering why the young woman was so reluctant to invite her through to the drawing room to sit in comfort. 'I'm sorry if I've come at an inconvenient time, but you'll understand that with a murder investigation, the sooner we can establish all the relevant facts the better.'

'Of course.' Eva gave a non-committal smile. 'But I'm

not sure what else you think I can tell you.' There was an impatient edge to her words. 'And I haven't remembered anything else that might be relevant since you came back yesterday to speak to me.'

The inspector returned Eva's smile with little enthusiasm. The time for social niceties was fast running out, and Alyson Grant didn't pride herself on her patience. 'Actually, I've come to ask you if the name "Marcus Drake" means anything to you.'

Evidently it did. Eva's clear, blue eyes momentarily widened and then narrowed again with suspicion. 'What does this have to do with Geraldine?'

Grant ignored the question. 'Have you ever met Marcus Drake? Has he ever been here to Hemlock Row, either with or without his stepfather?'

'No. But before you ask, I do know what's been happening to him over the last few months. David Lancefield didn't hide that from me. But I understood it to be a purely domestic matter. I was told that Marcus was engaged to David's daughter Lucy and that Lucy was having an affair. David was quite open with me. He told me that Lucy was murdered by her lover and that Marcus killed the lover.' Eva hesitated, and then said, 'I suppose it sounds rather sordid. But don't they say that crimes of passion happen even in the best of families?' She gave a fleeting, almost challenging smile. 'Are you going to tell me that wasn't the case? That David lied to me?'

'No.' Grant, still leaning against the wall, folded her arms to steady herself. 'That all sounds pretty much the way I heard it. Can I ask when David Lancefield told you this?'

'When I met him for lunch on Wednesday. It was our first face-to-face meeting, although we'd spoken before on the phone.'

'And how long had you been in contact by phone?'

'About six weeks.'

'So, in fact, David Lancefield did keep that from you.

For six weeks.'

Eva lowered her chin. 'I can see why you would say that. But for what it's worth, I felt quite sorry for him. We'd only been seated in the restaurant for a few minutes before he sort of blurted it out, as if he was desperate to get it out in the open. He told me that Marcus had been found guilty of manslaughter, but had avoided a prison sentence. He said that Marcus was very embarrassed about the situation and had left Edinburgh for a short holiday, but that he wouldn't be returning. So it wasn't likely that I would meet him.'

'But that's changed, now that you've been invited to Penwithen to spend the weekend with the family?'

A deep, crimson flush made its way across Eva's neck. 'How did you know about that?'

Another question for Grant to ignore. 'I wouldn't normally take very kindly to a key witness in a murder investigation disappearing off to the other end of the country, but in this case, I'm prepared to make an exception. But I'd like you to be careful, Eva. There is something about this Lancefield family that doesn't stack up.' She glanced down the hallway at nothing in particular. 'Tell me…' She looked back at Eva. '…has your cousin ever mentioned Dennis Speed and Emma Needham?' Apparently not, judging by the flicker of uncertainty that appeared in the young woman's eyes. 'Did you know that the Lancefields have reached out to other distant cousins in the last six months?'

'Yes. I believe they have connected with a cousin in Liverpool, her name is Barbara. David tells me that she's now in regular contact with the family, and he hopes to introduce us. Unless you're going to tell me there is some reason that I shouldn't meet with her?'

Another question for Grant to ignore. 'Has David told you that the family have been on the receiving end of a hate campaign because of what Marcus Drake did?'

The flush in Eva's neck began to spread upwards

towards her cheeks. 'Have you come here just to try to frighten me, Inspector Grant?'

'On the contrary, Eva. I'm trying to protect you. I'm trying to understand just how much you know about this family that has wheedled its way into your life. And how truthful they have been with you. They've invited you to stay at their home in Cornwall, but they haven't shared with you some very pertinent information that might lead you to decline the invitation. I want you to be in full possession of the facts before you travel to Penwithen.'

'Are you suggesting that I might come to harm in some way because I'm related to the Lancefields?'

Grant considered the question. Was that what she was suggesting? There was no question that DCI Price, down in Penzance, would like them both to think so. 'I think I'm suggesting that the Lancefields haven't been completely open and honest with you.'

'I see. And what on earth does any of this have to do with Geraldine's death? Isn't your remit to find her killer? Shouldn't you be focusing on that, rather than picking holes in my family?'

'I am focusing on that, Eva. Geraldine was connected to you because she was staying at Hemlock Row as your guest. You are connected to the Lancefields because they reached out to you as a distant cousin.' Grant sucked in a breath. 'And a blue van that we're trying to eliminate from our enquiries, a van that was seen leaving Hemlock Row shortly after Geraldine's murder, was hired in Cornwall at the beginning of the week, from a firm less than twenty miles away from Penwithen.'

The high flush of colour drained completely from Eva McWhinney's face, and a look of unmistakable dismay settled across her fine features. For a moment, it looked like she might cry. She swayed gently on her heels and then sent an awkward smile in the detective's direction. 'I suppose this is the point at which I ask the obvious question, isn't it? Just who are Dennis Speed and Emma

Needham?'

*

'And you want me to break that piece of news to David and Stella?' Kathryn, alone in the kitchen at Palmerston Place, snapped the words into her mobile phone. 'You want me to be the one to tell them?'

'Yes, please.'

'And you've already spoken to Marcus, and he denies it?'

'Well, he was hardly likely to admit it, was he?' Ennor sounded almost amused by the suggestion.

'Does Richard know about this?'

'He will by now. Marcus was going to tell him.'

Kathryn cursed under her breath. 'Ennor, we haven't even told Richard about Geraldine's murder.'

'I know. But he's not a child, Kathryn. In fact, despite his age, Richard Lancefield is one of the most steely and resilient individuals I've ever encountered.'

'So you say.' She made no attempt to disguise her annoyance. 'I don't suppose it makes any difference now.' She placed an elbow on the glass table top and rested her chin on her upturned hand. 'I met DCI Grant yesterday, you know. She came to Hemlock Row when David and I were there. Does she really believe that Marcus is somehow responsible for Geraldine's death?' She wanted to ask 'Do you believe, it, Ennor?' But it was a question too far.

'Grant is only doing what any sensible SIO would do. She's following the only lead she has.' Ennor hesitated, and then he said, 'I would like both you and David to have a word with her, if you would. I'd like her to have a first-hand explanation of why the Lancefields are trying to rustle up distant cousins. I tried to explain it to her myself, but I don't think she believed me.'

'So, you would like me to make it sound like an

everyday occurrence?'

'I just think that if David explains the family's point of view, and you are there to back him up, she will see that there's nothing suspicious about it. Grant strikes me as a "belt and braces" sort of copper. You see some romantic notion of the Lancefields reaching out to find their family, but all she sees is an attractive young woman on the receiving end of an unsolicited approach from a stranger; a stranger whose family has already experienced more than its fair share of murders.'

'Are the police going to prevent Eva from travelling to Penwithen with us this weekend?'

'No, that's the good news. I've persuaded Grant that it would be a good idea for the visit to go ahead. She was going to speak to Eva at lunchtime, to let her know.' Ennor hesitated again, and then said, 'There's something else. I'd like you to persuade Richard to invite me to Salvation Hall at the weekend. So that I can be on hand if anything kicks off.'

'And just what, exactly, do you expect to kick off?'

'Possibly Becca Smith. Or one of her brothers.'

'Becca Smith?' He was going too fast. 'You think that the Smith family are responsible for hiring that van?'

'Let's just say that I'm exploring the possibility.' Ennor spoke softly at the end of the line. 'I thought you would at least be pleased that I don't consider Marcus a suspect in Geraldine Morton's murder.'

'How on earth could he be a suspect for a murder committed hundreds of miles away? And what would be the motive?'

'I can't answer either of those questions. Which is probably why I don't consider him a suspect. But I do think that someone is trying to frame him. I still think that the wrong girl was murdered and that Marcus was supposed to take the blame.' Ennor sighed; a long, slow breath that carried all his frustrations down the phone line. 'Kathryn, I thought it was going to be over soon. I thought that once Marcus was on his way to St Felix, there would only be Jason Speed's trial to deal with. And then everything would settle down. I thought that David would be content with his two new cousins and that Becca Smith and her clan would eventually back off and leave the Lancefields alone.'

'Instead of which you're looking at another murder.'

'And the risk of yet more malicious interventions from the Smiths.' Ennor was beginning to sound despondent. 'In fact, the only thing cheering me up at the moment is the knowledge that you're coming back to Penwithen on Saturday. I never thought I'd say this, but I've missed my regular history lesson this week. You never did tell me exactly why the McWhinneys distanced themselves from the Lancefields.'

'They didn't. If anything, it was the other way around. They had to relocate back to Edinburgh because Benedict Lancefield turned them off the Woodlands Estate, and wouldn't have anything to do with them.'

'I can't imagine that McWhinney would have lost much sleep over that.'

'Probably not, although the fault was on his side. He was banished from the plantation for conducting unethical medical experiments on slaves that belonged to the Lancefields.'

There was silence at the end of the line. And then Ennor spluttered an incredulous laugh. 'Kathryn, you never cease to amaze me. Did Benedict Lancefield object to that because it was a crime against humanity? Or was he just trying to protect the family's profit margins again?'

Kathryn scowled down at her phone. 'Did I ever tell you that you can be absolutely despicable?'

'Yes, of course you did. More than once.' Ennor's voice softened. 'Do you have any idea just how much I'm looking forward to you coming back to Cornwall so that you can tell me all over again?'

# 12

Zak Smith was already in The Lancefield Arms, sitting at a table in the window and nursing a half-finished pint of ale. He barely looked up as his sister approached, instead wrapping his hand around the glass in readiness to lift it to his lips. 'Alright, Becs? What's the panic?'

'There is no panic. I've got news.' She flopped onto the chair opposite, dropping her shoulder bag to the floor as she wriggled her knees under the table. 'The Lancefields have another cousin coming to stay at the hall. Can you believe it?' She was lit up, her voice a semi-tone or two higher than normal, her eyes wide with the thrill of gossip. 'She's called Eva McSomething. I can't remember the name exactly. And they're bringing her down for the weekend.'

If Becca expected her brother to rise to the bait, she could only have been disappointed. Zak turned his dark eyes distractedly down into his pint and then lifted the glass to his lips and drank, savouring the flavour before he swallowed. 'And you dragged me all the way over here from Penzance, just to tell me that?'

His sister pouted. 'I thought you would want to know.'

'Why? Because you want me to cause trouble for Old Man Lancefield again?' He stared down into his glass. 'They're nothing to do with us now. Marcus Drake has walked free, and you're just going to have to get used to it.'

'But, Zak…'

He held up a hand to stop her. 'Enough. I've got more on my mind to worry about than the Lancefields.'

The curt dismissal left Becca momentarily speechless. She rose in her seat and folded her hands primly on the edge of the table. 'Something's wrong.'

Zak screwed up his nose and jerked his head towards the bar. 'Amber's on my case. I'm in the dog house. Again.'

Becca turned to look at the bar to see Amber Kimbrall busy pulling a pint for a customer, her plump and pretty face set firm in an uncharacteristic mask of concentration. Or perhaps just working hard to avoid catching anyone in particular's eye. 'Have you two had a fight?'

'You could put it like that.' Zak kept his eyes firmly fixed on the ale. 'I was out all Wednesday night playing poker and she's accused me of playing away.'

His sister grumbled under her breath. 'Is that all? Can't you just ask one of your mates to set her straight?'

'I'd love to.' He bit mischievously on his lip. 'But it would be a bit tricky.'

'Why?'

'Because I *was* playing away.'

It took a moment for the confession to register, and then Becca kicked her brother roundly under the table. 'You bloody idiot. Amber's the best thing that ever happened to you. You can't afford to blow it.' She twisted her lips into a curl of disdain. 'Who was it? Some little tart that you picked up in the pub?'

'She wasn't a tart, she was a bit of class. I picked her up in the Embassy Club and went back to her place for a drink. I didn't mean for it to happen. It just got a bit out of hand.' He leaned across the table. 'There's nothing in it. I won't be seeing her again.' He winced. 'The thing is, Becs, I told Amber that I spent the night on your couch.'

'You did what?'

'It was the only thing I could think of to throw her off the scent.'

'Did she believe you?'

'Of course not. But that's where you come in, isn't it?' His lips twisted into a crooked smile. 'You just need to back me up, little sister.'

'But I don't want to lie to Amber. She's a mate. Why should I lie to her?'

'Because I'm your favourite brother. And that's more important than being a mate.' He grinned into his glass and then swigged on what was left of the ale. 'Come on, Becs. You can do that for me, can't you?'

'I still don't see why I should.'

'Alright then. Because being a mate is just as important as being your favourite brother. You love us both and you want us to be happy. You know we're good together. You just said so yourself.'

Becca studied her fingers and then dared to look at his face. His lips were still smiling but his dark, grey eyes were tired, his usual roguish spark dulled by some so-far-unshared secret. 'Okay.' She whispered the word slowly as she cast an uncertain glance back across the bar in Amber's direction. 'If it's that important to you, and you think it will put things right with Amber, then I'll do it. But if I do, you'll owe me.' She turned her attention back to Zak, fixing him with a determined gaze. 'I mean it, Zak. You'll owe me, and you'll owe me big time.'

\*

The booking clerk at Trennick Rentals was a tall, platinum blonde with perfect teeth and an unseasonable tan. She took a moment to consider DS Parkinson's opening gambit, studying his face with sharp, intelligent eyes, and then offered him a manufactured smile. 'We're not worried about the van. It's not due back until Saturday.' She licked an index finger and used it to leaf through a hand-written ledger. 'If I remember rightly…' She nodded to herself, running the manicured finger down the page. 'Yes, here it is. The van was booked in person and paid for in advance. In cash.'

'In cash?' The sergeant's heart sank. 'You are joking?'

She smiled up at him. 'I don't make jokes about money,

pet.'

'Is it legal to pay for a hire vehicle in cash? Don't you have some duty of care to ensure that it's legitimate money?' It was a question to which he should have known the answer, considering the number of anti-money-laundering courses he'd taken. Perhaps he should have paid better attention. 'And what if the van isn't returned, or it comes back damaged?' He rested an arm casually on the counter. 'How do you recover your losses without taking a charge on a credit or debit card?'

The blonde gave him a withering look. 'We're not some corporate multi-national, we're a back-street van-hire firm. Most of our customers are local tradesmen. They come to us because their van is off the road and they need to keep the business ticking over. Some of our customers don't even have credit cards. They just need to be mobile so they can earn a living.' She sniffed. 'We're just filling a gap in the market, Sergeant Parkinson.'

It was the first time he'd heard it called that. 'So, this Marcus Drake came in, in person, and hired the van. Was he a local tradesman?'

'I dunno. He hasn't hired from us before.'

'Did he look like a tradesman?'

'I didn't say that he was a tradesman. Only that we serve tradesmen.'

'But he gave his address as Salvation Hall, didn't he? You must have heard of the place. Did he look like the sort of person who might live there?' Parkinson pointed down at the ledger. 'Did he give you any evidence to confirm his address?'

'I can't remember.'

'Don't you keep a record? It's in the book, surely?'

'Not necessarily.'

'Then what about his driving licence?'

The woman shrugged. 'I can't remember that either.'

'Surely you made sure he had a clean licence before you gave him the keys?'

Now she laughed, a soft ripple of genuine amusement. 'He was just the person arranging the hire. It doesn't mean that he was the one who was going to drive the van.' She nodded to herself. 'Now I think about it, he didn't collect the van himself. It was another young man who came in to collect it.'

'And you just gave the keys to this other young man?'

She smiled again. 'We try to be helpful.'

Parkinson snarled under his breath. If this was her idea of being helpful…

He pulled a leather-backed notebook from the inside pocket of his jacket and leafed through it to pull out a small photograph. 'Is this the young man who hired the van?'

She watched as he placed the picture down on the counter, and then leaned over to examine it. 'No, that's not him.' She sounded confident.

'What about this one?' He produced a second photograph and placed it on the counter beside the first.

'I don't know. He looks sort of familiar, but I can't say he had anything to do with the van.'

Irritated, Parkinson tapped a finger on the counter. 'Did either of these men collect the van?'

'No, it was a younger man. Gentle and softly spoken, with lovely eyes.' She almost sighed. 'Rather shy. And very dishy.'

'And you'll be expecting him to return the van on Saturday?' The policeman scooped up the photographs and slid them back between the pages of his notebook. 'What happens if he doesn't turn up? Aren't you worried about losing the van?'

'Not really. If the van doesn't come back, we'll send someone round to the hirer's address to see what's happened to it. It doesn't happen very often, mind. The people we deal with generally know that it wouldn't be a good idea to walk off with one of our vans. And if they get that wrong, they don't make the mistake a second time.'

Now that was something Parkinson would like to see – a two-bit, backstreet, van-hire outfit sending the boys round to Salvation Hall. He pushed the notebook back into his pocket. 'I'll probably pop back on Saturday, to see if I can catch the hirer when he returns the van. Would you have any objection to that?'

'Not if it's in the name of a good cause.'

'Good. I'll be reading up on the latest money-laundering and vehicle hire regulations before I come. Perhaps we could share notes.'

She pushed out one last smile, dimpling her cheeks. 'That would be most helpful, Sergeant Parkinson, I could do with a refresher course. If you give us a call before you set off, I'll make sure the kettle is on.'

\*

Kathryn cast an appreciative glance around the orangery to the rear of Hemlock Row, taking in the superb collection of exotic plants which lined its shelves and benches. 'I hope you're going to take some photographs of the house and its contents to Penwithen, to share with Richard. He's a very keen orchid grower, you know.'

'So David tells me. Though I'm not sure I would be able to compete with him.' Eva, seated on a generous Lloyd Loom sofa in the centre of the room, leaned forward to a small table and set about pouring Earl Grey tea into china cups. 'Is it true that he wins prizes at all the local shows?'

'It is. Or at least, it used to be true. He used to grow prize specimens in partnership with Philip McKeith. I'm afraid he's lost his appetite for the competitive side of things now.' There was no need for her to explain why. 'But he's still very keen on the growing. He has a dedicated orchid house behind the hall and he spends a great deal of time in there, alone with his orchids.'

'He must be lonely.' Eva lifted a cup and saucer from

the table and offered it to Kathryn. 'Alone with his plants and his memories.'

Kathryn smiled as she accepted the offering. 'That's the funny thing. I don't think that he is. It's very warm and humid in there, almost as hot as the Caribbean, and I think it makes him feel at home. I think that the heat and the plants evoke happy memories for him, and I think that stops him from feeling lonely.' She picked up a slice of lemon from a dish on the table, dropping it thoughtfully into her cup. 'His memories of St Felix bring him comfort.'

'Then I'd better take some photographs this evening, and see if I can add to that comfort.' Eva lifted her cup and saucer from the table. 'I wanted to ask you about the family Bible too. I know it's cumbersome, but I'd be pleased to box it up and take it to Penwithen if you think he might like to see it.'

'I'm sure he would love to see it, Eva. But that's not the reason you invited me back to Hemlock Row this afternoon, is it? To ask about adding to Richard's memories?' The invitation had been an unexpected one; the call made directly to Kathryn's mobile phone, the request for her to spare an hour of her time alone and unaccompanied. Unexpected, though perhaps in the light of Kathryn's earlier conversation with Ennor, not wholly unreasonable. And it presented an opportunity that Kathryn felt she could ill-afford to turn down. 'Can I ask why you didn't want David to join us?'

Eva blushed. 'I didn't want to embarrass him. And I wanted to be able to speak frankly about the Lancefield family to someone who knows them.' She stared down into her cup. 'DCI Grant came to see me this morning. And she told me about Dennis Speed and Emma Needham. That they were murdered.'

'I see. And did she clarify for you that those murders were nothing to do with Richard and David? That Jason Speed was hardly known to the family?'

'She did. And I can accept that the murders must have been devastating for the family, and I can accept that David and Richard were in no way to blame for what happened. They couldn't possibly have foreseen that Jason was illegitimate, let alone that he might be a killer. But I don't understand why David withheld the information from me. It doesn't make any sense. He told me about Philip and Lucy, and about Marcus. And I've accepted that it was a domestic matter.'

'Eva, are you worried about meeting Marcus, now that he's been found guilty of manslaughter?'

'Worried?' Eva's nose wrinkled 'No. It was a crime of passion, wasn't it? He must have loved Lucy to try to protect her like that. And it takes courage to admit to your crime and face up to the punishment.' She shook her head. 'No, this has nothing to do with Marcus. I'm more worried that David kept something from me. That he didn't tell me about Dennis and Emma.'

'Do you think, perhaps, it might be because he couldn't find a way to tell you? It was incredibly difficult for him. Not so much the matter of Dennis's death, but Emma's. Emma and Jason were staying in Penwithen when it happened. They had arrived unannounced, and David and Richard decided to put them up for the night in the Lancefield Arms, the pub in the village, rather than inviting them to stay at Salvation Hall.' Kathryn softened her tone. 'It was David who found Emma's body in the village churchyard. And I think he still blames himself for Emma's death. He thinks that she might still be alive if he had offered to accommodate them at the hall.'

'So you don't think that the Lancefield family is cursed?'

'Cursed? This is the twenty-first century, Eva. I do hope that was just a figure of speech?'

'Four murders related to the Lancefield family in the last six months. And now my friend Geraldine has been murdered, just weeks after David and Richard reached out to me.' Eva turned anxious eyes to Kathryn. 'Am I at risk here, Kathryn?'

'At risk?'

'I'm asking if you think it's safe for me to stay at Salvation Hall?'

'Safe? Of course it's safe. David and Richard wouldn't invite you if they thought you would be at risk.'

'Have you ever felt at risk there, Kathryn?'

'Good heavens, no.'

*Good heavens, no.* And that was the truth.

Wasn't it?

Kathryn opened her mouth to speak, to tell Eva that she, before anyone, had listened to Marcus Drake confess to the murder of Philip McKeith; to tell her that she had, with David, walked up to the village church to confront Jason Speed about his illegitimacy and to prevent a third murder – the murder of his cousin Barbara Gee – from taking place. And even then, she had never felt at risk. But what would be the point?

Instead, she gave a reassuring smile. 'If it makes you feel more comfortable, I usually stay at a hotel in Penzance when I'm in Cornwall, but only because I choose to keep a professional distance from the family when I'm working during the week. This weekend, I'm going to stay at Salvation Hall. And I wouldn't do that if I thought there was any risk to my safety.'

'And what about the Smith family?'

'The Smiths?'

'DCI Grant also told me about their hate campaign against the Lancefield family.'

Kathryn's smile faded. 'That, I'm afraid, is true. The Smith family did make Richard's and David's lives a misery for a while. But that stopped after Emma Needham died.'

'And is likely to start up again now that Marcus has walked free.'

'Not necessarily. The police in Cornwall have made it pretty clear to them that any resumption of hostilities against the family will be dealt with swiftly and severely. And in any case, any anger on their part would be directed at Marcus, and he will be leaving the country on Monday.' Kathryn let out a sigh. 'Don't you want to visit Penwithen, Eva?'

'Yes, of course I do. I want to meet Richard, and I want to meet Marcus. Just as I want to see Salvation Hall for myself. I want it more than anything. But surely you can understand that I don't want to risk my life to do it?'

## 13

Marcus found Richard Lancefield in the orchid house.

'I'm sorry to disturb you.' He closed the door of the glass house behind him and leaned against the door frame. 'But I needed to speak to you.'

'There is no need to apologise for seeking me out, my boy. You'll be on your way to the Caribbean in a day or two so the more time we spend together, the better.' The old man swept a hand across the dusty surface of the potting bench and peered down at his gloved fingers. 'I seem to make more mess than ever these days.' He stretched up to a shelf to retrieve a small, soft brush to sweep the bench. 'You'd better take a seat. We can talk while I work. It's almost dark and I don't want to leave the place in a mess.' He turned to Marcus with a questioning eye. 'How do you find the temperature in here? It's always too warm for Kathryn. But it's a pale comparison to the heat you'll find at Woodlands.'

Marcus sat down on the shabby wicker chair beside the door. 'It's fine.'

'Good.' Richard skimmed the brush across the potting bench as he spoke, sending tiny swirls of dusty compost into the air. 'Of course, it will be sunny in St Felix and at this time of year it will be an intense, dry heat.' He smiled to himself. 'It's a pity that I won't be able to come out and visit you.' The smile was followed by a sigh of resignation. 'I do envy you. Are your travel preparations going well?'

'Preparations? I suppose so. Although just talking about heat has made me realise that I probably don't have the right clothes. And I need new sunglasses, books to read, a new laptop…' Marcus relaxed a little and folded his arms. 'I sound as though I'm going on holiday, but it's a change of life and now I think about it, maybe I don't feel prepared for it.'

'How do you feel?'

'Like I'm running away. I know I haven't been imprisoned, but I've had my freedom curtailed for nearly six months. The freedom to make my own choices, to travel where I please, even to think about what the future is going to hold without Lucy.'

Richard dropped the brush onto the potting bench. There was a small wooden stool underneath, and he pulled it out and sank onto it, holding onto the bench to steady himself. 'My boy, this trip to St Felix is not meant to be another kind of prison sentence. And I do not seek to take your freedom away from you. Perhaps you are right to think of it as a holiday, at least to begin with. Take it lightly. Feel your way around Woodlands, get to know its people and its nooks and crannies. Make it your playground, if you can. Or your sanctuary. I had hoped it might be an opportunity for you to forget what's gone before and make a fresh start. To have some space away from Salvation Hall and the life that will never be, so that you can consider the life to come. The life that you want to come.'

'I thought you wanted me to stay out there for years and learn to run the estate?'

'Well, that might be what I want. But we can't all have what we want, can we? Not even me.' He chuckled softly at the thought. 'I know I'm an old fool. And perhaps there is a part of me that is being shamelessly vicarious here. A young man, with his whole life ahead of him, and the opportunity to make a life on a paradise island with nothing to hold him back from finding his destiny... that might have been me, Marcus. But it was denied to me because of my responsibilities. I had my time on St Felix, but my destiny was to return to Penwithen, to marry, to provide the family with an heir and to run the estates from

Salvation Hall. Perhaps part of me is foolish enough to think that you would want the very things that I had wanted, but I hope I would never impose that on you. If you don't want to go to St Felix, if you don't feel ready, or have already made up your mind that it's not for you, then please just say so. Just speak up, my boy, and the flights will be cancelled.'

'I don't want to let you down.'

'You will only do that if you don't speak the truth. But perhaps we might achieve a compromise? Go out there for a month and take it as an opportunity to reflect on your future. And then you and I will talk. We will have one of these magnificent video calls that modern technology makes possible, and share a glass of rum at a distance, and you can tell me your decision. Stay or go. Or even stay another month, and another, and another until you know your mind.' Richard lifted his hand and rubbed his brow with a finger. 'There is another consideration here, of course. This isn't just about what you and I might want. There are others to consider, people who might not take too kindly to your staying in Penwithen.'

'You're thinking about the Smith family.'

'Aren't you?'

Marcus lowered his eyes. 'No. There's something else. I'm wondering if I'll have the opportunity to travel on Monday. There's something you don't know. Something that you haven't been told.'

'Is there?' The old man laughed softly again. 'Are we talking about the murder of Geraldine Morton?' His eyes creased as he watched Marcus's face. 'Oh, I know all about that. I'm sure you all have my best interests at heart, keeping it from me in case it distressed me. But old Mayhew in Penzance knows my constitution better than that. He knows I can still deal with bad news. He heard about it yesterday from a connection up in Edinburgh, and he called to let me know.'

'But David and Kathryn...'

'Tush, my boy. If it pleases David and Kathryn to think that my feelings need to be spared, I can only take that as a kindness.' Richard raised a quizzical eyebrow. 'Of course, if there has been a development that has escaped old Mayhew's attention…'

'The police are trying to trace a dark blue van that was seen speeding away from Hemlock Row around the time that Geraldine Morton was murdered.'

'And why might that stop you from travelling to St Felix?'

'Inspector Price tells me that the van was hired from a firm in Truro. And it was booked in my name, giving Salvation Hall as my address.'

The old man's rheumy eyes narrowed. 'How was the van paid for?'

'I don't know. The inspector is still looking into that.'

'Did you hire the van, Marcus?'

'Good God, no. The inspector thinks that someone is trying to frame me. There is no other explanation.' Marcus pushed himself to his feet. 'Someone is trying to frame me for a murder that I didn't commit. I don't know who, and I don't know why, but I can certainly hazard a guess. And I can tell you now, Richard, that I'm not going through the legal process again for this family. I don't know what the hell is going on here, but I do know that it's nothing to do with me.'

\*

'But if the van was paid for in cash, there's no audit trail back to the person who hired it.' Price took a bite from the pristine, newly-unwrapped Mars bar and turned his head to gaze out of the Audi's window. They were parked on the shoreline at Marazion and the car park was empty, save for the mobile coffee van, its welcome reappearance a half-hearted nod to the fast-approaching spring tourist season. Another few weeks and the place would be heaving with day-trippers and the first smattering of off-season holidaymakers; a small price to pay for the opportunity of a decent Americano, a bar of chocolate and a quiet place to discuss a murder case. He turned back to look at Parkinson. 'Is that even legal?'

'I'm looking into it. It must be a breach of money laundering regulations, if nothing else. They have a duty of care to know where the cash is coming from.' The sergeant tapped his fingers on the steering wheel. 'Something else to add to the workload.'

'At least now, we know that Marcus couldn't have collected it, because he was still on Burgh Island at the time.'

'Someone could have paid for it and collected it on his behalf.'

'But what would be the motive? There would be nothing in it for him. How could he benefit from the death of a girl he didn't know?' Price bit again on the Mars bar and considered his own question. Then he said, 'Even if I'm right, and the real target was Eva McWhinney, her death wouldn't benefit him in any way.'

'Perhaps he sees her as a threat. She could be another candidate for Richard Lancefield's attention, and she's a fully paid-up member of the Lancefield family, while Drake is only David's stepson.'

'I don't believe that Richard would let Marcus leave the family circle now. He's taken the rap for Philip McKeith's murder and he's being rewarded with the opportunity to run the Woodlands Plantation. He's too useful to the family, and I think he knows that. No…' Ennor stretched out a hand to retrieve his coffee from the shelf above the dashboard. 'This van is nothing to do with him.' He sipped on the coffee. 'You didn't get a positive identification of Zak Smith?'

'No. I showed her the photograph and she thought he looked familiar, but she couldn't place him. She didn't recognise Marcus either. Which confirms that neither of them hired or collected the van. She couldn't remember what the man who hired the van looked like, but she said the man who collected it was young and fair-haired.' Parkinson chuckled. 'She said he was good-looking, with gentle eyes.'

'Zak's brother, Robin?'

'That was my thinking. I've tried to find him this afternoon, but he's disappeared to Devon with his girlfriend. They're supposed to be visiting her aunt in Torquay. I've got a call out to try and track him down.'

'Is it possible, then, that Zak could have arranged for someone else to hire the van and Robin could have collected it? Have you tried Zak for an alibi yet?'

'No, that's my next task. When we've finished here, I'm going over to The Lancefield Arms. If Zak isn't in there, I'll try Amber Kimbrall. She's usually his alibi anyway.' Parkinson's eyes lit with a wry smile. 'She never learns.' He folded his arms and shifted in his seat. 'How did you get on with Marcus?'

'As you would expect, he denied all knowledge. But he looked worried. He's not stupid, Tom. He knows someone is trying to frame him, and he knows the Smith family are most likely at the bottom of it.' The policeman sipped on his coffee. 'Got any plans for the weekend?'

'We're taking Ella to a birthday party tomorrow. Amy's niece is turning five, so we'll be up to our kneecaps in balloons and trifle.' Parkinson's smile softened at the thought, caught momentarily off-guard by the sudden change in the conversation. And then the smile faded. 'But you weren't asking from a place of avuncular interest, were you?'

Inscrutability settled across the inspector's face. 'Eva McWhinney is coming down to Penwithen to visit Richard Lancefield. I've cleared it with DCI Grant, and I've arranged to have access to the hall while she's here, just to be on the safe side.'

'Do you think she's at risk?'

'Don't you?' Price stared into his almost empty coffee cup. 'She's going to be within twenty miles of the place where that van was hired. If the van was relevant to the murder, and Eva was the intended target, she'll be right in the murderer's home territory.'

'And you want us to be on hand, in case it all kicks off?' Parkinson frowned. 'I thought we didn't have any overtime budget left for this month?'

Price raised the coffee cup to his lips and grinned. 'We don't.'

\*

'Was Eva very disappointed in me?' David pushed his gloved hands into the pockets of his coat as he spoke. 'I didn't intend any malice in not telling her about Dennis and Emma. But it was difficult enough telling her about Marcus. You can understand that I was afraid I'd frighten her off?'

Kathryn, walking beside him, slipped her arm into his. 'She wasn't disappointed. She just wanted to know the facts.' It wasn't a complete lie, just a gentle bending of the truth to save his feelings. But the next bit wouldn't be so easy. Nor the bit to come after that. 'DCI Grant has told her about the Smiths, and their behaviour towards the family. And she's warned her that the Smiths might cause trouble if she visits Salvation Hall.'

'Has it put her off?'

'No, of course not.' Thank goodness. 'Eva's made of sterner stuff than that. I don't even think she plans to mention it to you now that I've given her a more rounded explanation.' They were walking north along Palmerston Place, their pace brisk, their destination a small hotel on the edge of the Dean Village. 'I'm glad that Stella decided to stay at home and pack this evening. It's given me an opportunity to talk to you about something else in private.'

'Something you wouldn't want Stella to hear?' They had

reached the junction with Douglas Crescent and David halted at the kerb, turning his head to look over Kathryn's shoulder. 'There's nothing coming.' He stepped out into the road, Kathryn's arm still firmly threaded through his own. 'Is this something you're going to tell me while we're walking, or would it be advisable to wait until we both have a stiff drink in front of us?'

'I'm going to tell you now. And there's no easy way for me to say it. Just remember that things are never quite what they seem.' Kathryn squeezed David's arm. 'The investigation into Geraldine Morton's murder has thrown up a possible connection to Marcus.'

David Lancefield stopped abruptly. 'But that's ridiculous. We've only just secured his release. He's scarcely had time to draw a breath, let alone commit another murder.'

'The police are investigating a van that was hired in Truro, and driven to Edinburgh. The van was hired in the name of Marcus Drake, and the hirer gave his address as Salvation Hall.'

David's face glazed as he took in the news, and then he lowered his chin. 'Have you any idea of the effect that this will have on Stella?'

'Of course I do. And I also know how it must make you feel, and how Marcus must be feeling. Why do you think I wanted to speak to you in private?' Kathryn drew back her arm and pushed her hands into the pockets of her coat, turning on her heel to walk on towards the Dean Village. 'Ennor is involved in the investigation. He thinks that the Smith family may be trying to frame Marcus. And I'm inclined to agree with him.'

Behind her, David was slowly following in her wake. 'We have made the mistake once before of blaming Becca Smith's family for a murder that had nothing to do with them. I won't let that happen again.'

'Can you think of an alternative?'

'I wish I could.' He drew in an angry breath. 'Why on

earth would the Smith family murder Geraldine Morton and try to pin the crime on Marcus? What had Geraldine ever done to them?'

He would realise in a moment. Or perhaps he needed a gentle nudge. 'There was quite a resemblance between the two girls, wasn't there?'

'A resemblance?' The point seemed lost on him, and then his eyes widened. 'Kathryn, this changes everything. We cannot take Eva to Penwithen when there might be a risk to her safety. It would be better for her to stay here in Edinburgh.'

'Ennor won't let anything happen to her. And Eva is determined to travel to Salvation Hall to meet Richard.'

'Could we postpone her visit until Marcus is safely despatched to St Felix?'

'And what difference would that make?'

'Well, if the Smith family's aim is to frame Marcus for a crime he didn't commit, it will be too late if he's already gone to the Caribbean.' David stretched out a hand and took hold of Kathryn's arm. 'Kathryn, what on earth am I saying? This has to stop now. This madness of digging up stray members of the family. We are putting innocent people's lives at risk. My father will have to accept that we are the family. With you and I running a trust to secure the estates, and Marcus covering things in St Felix, we can manage. Stella will support us, and cousin Barbara and we have Nancy. It is enough. It is more than enough.'

'So what do you suggest? That we put Eva back in the bottle and forget about her? Is that being fair to Eva?' Kathryn could feel her temper rising. 'Can you just forget about her?'

'Of course I can't. But I don't want any harm to come to her. I can't face the possibility of another innocent life lost because of a connection to the family.' He groaned. 'And she looks so much like Lucy. If anything happened to her, it would be like losing my daughter all over again.'

They had reached the corner of Belford Road. 'David,

nothing is going to happen to Eva. That van might have nothing to do with Geraldine's murder. And it almost certainly has nothing to do with Marcus. Ennor has promised me that they will look into it today, and he's promised to be with us at Salvation Hall over the weekend. It will be unofficial, but he will be on hand as much or as little as we want him there.' Kathryn turned to face him. 'Do you really think anyone would make an attempt on her life while she's in the family's private home, with a detective chief inspector as a private bodyguard?'

# 14

'Aren't you meant to be on the other side of that counter?' Tom Parkinson, weary from a day full of frustrations, tried to sound cheerful as he made his way across the bar at The Lancefield Arms. 'I could be off duty for the next twenty minutes and in need of a kind word and a pint.'

Amber Kimbrall, perched on a bar stool, turned her head slowly to acknowledge the policeman. ' I can manage the pint, Sergeant Parkinson, but I can't make any promises about the kind word.' She slid languorously off the stool and made her way slowly to the business side of the bar, the gold bangles at her wrist jangling as she reached up to a rack for a pint glass. 'Best ale?'

'Please.' Parkinson settled on the stool she had just vacated. 'It's quiet in here this evening.'

'It's quiet in here most evenings, but you won't hear me complaining about that.'

'Maybe not. But doesn't a business need at least a few customers to survive?'

'Not this one.' She jammed the glass under the ale tap and pulled down gently on the pump. 'The Arms has been making a loss for years. Richard Lancefield only keeps it open because he reckons that every village needs a pub. He thinks we should always be open in case anyone passing through needs a drink and a bite to eat.'

It sounded just like the sort of thing the old man would consider. 'Well, I suppose it pays your wages. And it gives me somewhere to question you about Zak's misdemeanours without having to take you down to the station.' Parkinson glanced around him. 'So where is he this evening? I thought this was his second home.'

Amber's pretty face clouded as she topped off the pint. 'Zak Smith is nothing to do with me. Not any more. If you want to know what he's been up to, I suggest you go into Penzance and try his garage.'

'I could do that, I suppose, but it would be a waste of good diesel driving all that way, just to hear the same story that you could give me now.' The policeman leaned on the bar. 'I need an alibi from him for Wednesday night. If I drive to Penzance, he'll just say "I was at Amber's all night". And then I'll come back here to Penwithen to ask you to corroborate the story, and you'll say "He was with me all night, Sergeant Parkinson" and I'll have wasted my time as well as the diesel.'

Amber fixed the sergeant with a stern gaze as she slid the pint of ale noiselessly across the bar. 'He'll get no alibi from me this time. Because he wasn't with me on Wednesday night.' She turned her hand upwards. 'That'll be three pounds and twenty-five pence, when you're ready.'

Parkinson stared at the upturned hand. 'Are you saying that you won't give Zak an alibi?'

'I can't give him an alibi if he wasn't with me, can I? That wouldn't be honest.'

'It's never stopped you before.'

'Well, it's stopping me now.' She flashed feisty, challenging eyes across the counter. 'If you bother to waste your time and your diesel, and get yourself over to Penzance, Zak Smith will tell you that he played poker on Wednesday night, stayed out too late, and spent what was left of the night on his sister's sofa so he didn't have to wake me up.'

'And you don't believe him?'

'Of course I don't believe him.'

'Does Becca back up his story?'

'I don't know, because I haven't asked her. And before you ask, the reason I haven't asked her is because I don't really care. Zak Smith is a lying, scheming toerag. He says he was sleeping on Becca's sofa, and I don't believe a word of it.'

'So where do you think he was?'

'Playing away, Sergeant Parkinson. Where do you think he was?'

Parkinson mulled the question over and then wrapped a hand around his pint. 'I honestly couldn't say.' He lifted the glass and sipped on the ale. Truth be told, if he told Amber Kimbrall where he thought Zak Smith was on Wednesday evening, she simply wouldn't believe him.

\*

The email from Price had only just landed in Grant's inbox, and she had wasted no time in examining it. The brief biography of Zak Smith and his catalogue of petty crimes had a photograph attached, an image that now filled the screen. 'Did you make a mistake then, pal?' She whispered the words as she stared hard at the picture. 'Were you in Edinburgh on Wednesday night, aiming for Eva McWhinney? Or does Ennor Price just have a vivid imagination?'

There was no denying that Smith was a good-looking young man. Probably in his thirties. Lean and keen, with piercing eyes that smiled almost mockingly at the camera from beneath a shock of wavy, black hair. He certainly looked the type to hire a van from a back-street operation, paying cash to avoid an audit trail, and it wouldn't be a stretch of the imagination to see him giving a false name and address for the pleasure of implicating an enemy.

But would he commit a murder? Would he strangle an unknown, defenceless young woman just for the hell of it? And would he drive over six hundred miles, twelve hundred, if you include the trek back home to Cornwall, to do it?

Grant leaned back in her chair, bouncing it gently on its casters, and folded her arms across her chest, her eyes still glued to the screen. She'd seen plenty of Zak Smiths in her time, and she could quite easily believe that this one was guilty of all the minor misdemeanours that DCI Price had laid at his door: harassment, deception, motoring offences... he'd even racked up a short stretch inside for poaching. But in Grant's experience, cocky little beggars like Smith liked to put on a performance. They took pleasure in flouting the rules in ways they could almost get away with. In fact, boasting to their mates that they had got away with it was part of the fun. Intimidating your enemies, point-scoring over the police, or depriving the landed gentry of their pheasants, all were things you could laugh about over a pint in the pub.

But boasting that he had got away with murder – with wilfully taking another human being's life – who the hell was going to be impressed by that?

Grant leaned forward again and clicked at her keyboard, minimising the photograph and enlarging the email from Price. If she remembered rightly, Smith's motive for harassing the Lancefield family was to exact some sort of revenge for the fact that Marcus Drake had murdered his sister's partner. Perhaps the boast here was that he had travelled all the way to Edinburgh to commit a murder that could be pinned on Marcus Drake.

But then why not just strike at Marcus Drake himself? If the desire for revenge ran that deep within Becca Smith's family, why not just cut to the chase and take Drake's life in return for Philip McKeith's? It just didn't make any sense. And it certainly didn't provide a cast-iron motive for Geraldine Morton's murder.

Grant heaved a sigh. It was time to get back to basics. She pulled a piece of paper from the in-tray on her desk and then rifled in the desk's top drawer for a pen. 'Just what have we got here?' She scrawled a starting point at the top of the page.

*A murdered medic, with no motive for the murder.*

Geraldine Morton's colleagues at the Royal Infirmary

had talked of a kind, studious, talented professional without the proverbial enemy in the world. DCI Grant herself had spoken to the girl's family in East Linton – loving parents and siblings who were quite clearly grieving Geraldine's loss and had no sense of any grievance against her that might lead to murder. So, what about…

*A murdered medic who resembled a colleague.*

Assuming that Eva McWhinney herself had no reason to want the murdered girl dead, they were left with the possibility of mistaken identity. That Geraldine had been murdered by mistake, that she had been unhappily in just the wrong place at just the wrong time, and taken for the friend who owned the house at Hemlock Row?

That friend was related to the Lancefield family of Penwithen, and there was no question at all that murder followed that family around. At the suggestion of Ennor Price, Grant had done a bit of digging into the Lancefields' murky past, discovering in the process that they made their fortune in the Caribbean and had strong and unpleasant links to slavery and the slave trade. Not that the fact was likely to have any bearing on Geraldine Morton's murder. No, if Geraldine had been mistaken for Eva, then a far more recent crime was likely to be at the bottom of it, a crime committed in Cornwall.

Grant hissed through her teeth and flung the pen down on the desk. 'I'm just back at Zak Smith and that bloody van. What the hell am I missing?' She counted out her thoughts on the fingers of her other hand. 'Nothing from her colleagues, nothing from her family, nothing from Eva McWhinney, nothing from the boyfriend…'

*Nothing from the boyfriend?*

Now that was an avenue she hadn't pursued. And while her imagination couldn't stretch far enough to link Alec Henderson with Zak Smith and the notion of murder for revenge, there might be some mileage in finding out what he knew about Eva McWhinney and her links to a very wealthy and notorious Cornish family.

And, more to the point, whether he or Geraldine Morton had ever heard the name of Marcus Drake.

\*

'I know who you are, of course, but I don't understand why you've come to see me?' Eva had been busy packing for the weekend when Alec Henderson turned up on the doorstep and, caught off guard, she had made the mistake of inviting him into the house. It hadn't occurred to her that Alec had even known where Geraldine was staying while her flat was being refurbished, but she could see now that, of course, he must have known. He would have known that as surely as she knew that Geraldine was building a relationship with a man who lived in Leith.

They were sitting in the drawing room at the front of the house, Eva on an armchair by the fireplace and Alec on the large, blood-red velvet sofa. In response to her question, he tilted his head. 'I've come to pay my respects, and to see how you are. Geraldine's death must have come as a shock.'

Of course it was a shock. What else could it possibly have been? 'That was very kind of you. But there was really no need.' She was still trying to fathom what might have led him so precisely to 3 Hemlock Row. 'How did you know where to find me? I didn't think it had been printed in the newspapers.'

'It wasn't. Geraldine told me where she was staying.'

'Oh, I see.' Eva sounded unconvinced. 'DCI Grant tells me that they had trouble tracking you down, Alec. To let you know about the murder.'

The suggestion didn't seem to disturb him. 'I was in Glasgow for most of the day, working on a commission, a piece about investment fraud. I'm hoping that one of the broadsheets will be interested in it. You never know.' He gave a self-deprecating laugh. 'Such is the life of an itinerant freelance journalist.' An awkward silence settled between them, and then he said, 'Geraldine was very fond of you, Eva. She often talked about you. You'd been friends for a very long time, I think?'

'As long as we worked together at the infirmary.' It was all the answer he was going to get. 'I do know that she was very fond of you, Alec, even though you hadn't known each other more than a few weeks. She told me that she enjoyed spending time with you. If anything, it should be me who is asking how you are. After all, you were getting on so well, and now you've lost her.' Eva rested her hands in her lap. 'Have you spoken to her family at all? They live out in East Linton, don't they?'

'Her family?' For the first time since arriving, he looked uncomfortable. 'No, I haven't spoken to them. I don't have any contact details for them. I'm not even sure if they were aware of our relationship.' He frowned. 'Did she have a large family?'

'Parents, and two brothers, I believe.' He didn't know anything about Geraldine's family, but he knew that she had been living at 3 Hemlock Row? 'I can give you their phone number. I'm sure they would be pleased to hear from you. If nothing else, you must have been the last person to speak to Geraldine, before…'

Another awkward silence settled across the room, and then Alec turned his head and nodded towards the window. 'Are those the original Georgian shutters?' He rolled his eyes towards the fireplace. 'And the original marble mantelpiece?' He whistled softly through his teeth. 'This is a beautiful house, Eva. Geraldine told me how much she enjoyed staying here. She said it's been in your family for centuries.'

'Did she?' Eva felt the muscles in her neck begin to stiffen.

'Yes. She said it could be traced back to the beginnings of the New Town, in the early nineteenth century.' He was looking at Eva with an expectant gaze. 'James McWhinney built it, would that be right? Just after he returned from the

Caribbean?'

Eva blinked, and this time her smile was inscrutable. 'I'm afraid I don't know. I can only tell you that this is my family home. I've never gone in for all that "family history" stuff. It's all the past, isn't it?' She saw a flicker of suspicion in his cool, grey eyes. He didn't believe her, and in truth, she probably hadn't expected him to. 'Will DCI Grant be speaking to you again, Alec?'

'Again?' He repeated the word as if he didn't understand the question. 'I shouldn't think so. I've already told her everything I can about my date with Geraldine on Wednesday evening.' His eyes narrowed. 'Have the police progressed any further with the investigation?'

'I'm afraid I don't know. I'm not in their confidence.' She no longer needed to wonder what he was doing at Hemlock Row. He was here to ask questions. To ask about the case, and to ask about her friendship with Geraldine.

And, for some inexplicable reason, he was here to ask about Hemlock Row.

# 15

'It's all arranged. The taxi is booked for six thirty to take us to the airport, and we're picking Eva up on the way.' Kathryn jammed the mobile phone into the crook of her neck as she spoke. 'David's car is still at Exeter Airport, so all we need to do when we get there is pile into it and be nice to each other.' She hauled her suitcase up onto the guest-room bed and flipped the lid open. 'The tricky bit will be getting all the luggage into it. I only have one small suitcase and David will be travelling light. But Stella looks to have packed for a month rather than a weekend, and Eva is planning to bring the family Bible with her as well as her luggage.'

'Did you tell David and Stella about the van?' Ennor sounded anxious at the end of the phone line, and not in the mood for small talk. 'Did you tell them about Marcus being implicated in Geraldine's murder?'

Kathryn picked up a small laundry bag from the bed. 'Yes, I told David. And he broke the news to Stella.' She pushed the laundry bag into the corner of the suitcase. 'I have to say that her reaction wasn't quite what I expected.'

'You mean the news didn't upset her?'

'Upset her? She was furious. Absolutely incandescent.' Kathryn unzipped the lining in the lid of the suitcase. 'If I were you, I'd be less worried about keeping the Smith family away from Eva, and more worried about keeping Stella away from the Smith family.'

'Thanks for the warning.' Ennor sounded almost amused by the notion. 'And what about DCI Grant? Did you and David manage to touch base with her?'

'Yes, sort of. David wasn't keen, so I called her on the

number you gave me, and I did my best to give her the background on Richard's quest to find more family. But I got the impression that she just found the whole situation ludicrous.' Kathryn slipped a small sheaf of papers into the suitcase lining and zipped the compartment closed. 'She's very twitchy about Eva leaving Edinburgh, you know. She asked me all manner of questions about you, and whether or not you could be trusted.'

'Excuse me?'

'I don't think she's any more impressed than I am with the idea of you using her witness as bait to catch a murderer. I think she'd feel more comfortable if you had some hard evidence to back up your theory that Eva was the intended victim. It makes her nervous that you're just acting on instinct.' Kathryn paused to draw in a breath. And then she said, 'DCI Grant asked me why you were so obsessed with the idea that being connected to the Lancefields is dangerous.'

'You mean five deaths wasn't enough evidence for her?'

'Four deaths, Ennor. There is no proof that Geraldine's murder was anything to do with the Lancefields.'

'No proof *yet*.' He sounded disappointed. 'I thought you had more faith in me, Kathryn. Do you think I've got this one wrong?'

'Truthfully? I just don't know what to think. I thought we were bringing Eva down to Penwithen to keep her safe. And as to the Smith family... I don't believe that Marcus had anything to do with the murder, and I can see how they might have tried to set him up. But there are still too many unknowns. How would the Smiths have even known about Eva? How would they have known where she lived? The only people who knew about her connection to the family were me and the Lancefields.'

'And Marcus.'

'Now you're being ridiculous. You admitted yourself that you didn't believe he had anything to do with it.'

'And Geraldine.'

'Geraldine?'

'Wouldn't Eva have mentioned it to her? The two girls were living together, after all.'

'Ennor, you're not making sense.'

'I'm not trying to. I'm just trying to show you that the Lancefields weren't the only people who knew about the connection. And in police work, that's the sort of fact that can lead to a breakthrough. If Geraldine knew about the connection, then who might she have told? Where might she have been when she told them? Who might have been listening in to their conversation?'

'Okay, I'll concede the point. But it still doesn't get us any closer to the truth, does it?' Kathryn let out a sigh. 'Ennor, it will be alright, won't it? You won't let anything happen to Eva?'

'Of course I won't let anything happen to her.' He sounded disappointed. 'You don't really think I'm using Eva as bait, do you? I don't expect the Smith family to make any attempt on her life while she's at Salvation Hall. Even they aren't that stupid. I'm just hoping that her arrival in Penwithen will shake them up enough for one of them to slip up. I want to see how they react. Word is bound to get out, if it hasn't already, that Eva is coming to stay. If she was the intended murder victim, and the Smith family had a hand in the murder, they'll see that the wrong woman was targeted. But that doesn't necessarily mean they'll try again. Apart from anything else, they don't have access to Salvation Hall since Becca was dismissed from her post. As long as Eva doesn't leave the house and grounds, there isn't any risk to her safety.'

He made it sound so simple, and yet…

Kathryn sank onto the bed next to the suitcase. 'And what if she wasn't the intended victim? What happens then?'

The brief silence at the end of the line suggested that Ennor Price hadn't considered that particular eventuality.

'I guess that she'll stay the weekend, go back to Edinburgh on Monday, and continue to help DCI Grant get to the bottom of Geraldine's murder.' He sounded uncertain. 'What time will you arrive tomorrow?'

'We should be at Salvation Hall by lunchtime. I was hoping that you would be there when we arrive. Richard is expecting you.'

'Then I'll be there. If you send me a text when you leave Exeter, I'll set off for Penwithen. I'll call into a couple of the village shops on my way. It won't do any harm for the Smith family to see me. I'll make it known that I'm spending the day at the hall visiting you. And I'll drop into the conversation that you're bringing Eva to visit Richard. One way or another the news has probably already reached them, but there's no harm in making sure.'

\*

'The van was well alight by the time the fire crew reached the layby.' PC Brownlee leaned on the side of his patrol car. 'They tell me it took them eight minutes to put the fire out completely, and they called it in to the station immediately after that. They suspected arson, and they gave us the registration to check. It matched with the dark blue Ford Transit that you've been looking for, but we couldn't get hold of DCI Price.'

'How long before you arrived on the scene?' DS Parkinson turned away as he spoke, looking back at the Audi parked a few metres behind Brownlee's patrol car. He flicked his key fob towards it, clicking the lock shut, and turned back to the uniformed officer. 'Was it still alight?'

'About ten minutes after the call came in and no, it wasn't. It was already out.' Brownlee nodded to himself. 'The fire crew are on the ball though. As soon as they heard the van was wanted in connection with a murder enquiry, they put the kid gloves on.'

Parkinson rocked on his heels as he surveyed the scene in front of him. Kid gloves or not, there was a risk that the crime scene had been significantly contaminated. But he could hardly blame the fire crew for that. 'Who called the brigade?'

'A young couple driving home to Helston. They'd been to the cinema in Penzance and saw the fire as they drove past. They parked farther up the road and made the call from a mobile phone.'

'Do we have contact details?'

Brownlee patted his jacket. 'In my notebook, sergeant. I'll take a statement tomorrow, if it will help.'

'Thanks.' Parkinson frowned. 'There was definitely no one in the vehicle?'

'No. But I'm told by the fire crew that whoever set it alight knew what they were doing. They suspect an accelerant was used, and the windows had been left open to let air flow through to fuel the flames. And they believe there is a set of keys on what's left of the floor, down near the brake pedal. They haven't touched anything though. They've done their best to keep the scene as clean as they could.' Brownlee cleared his throat. 'In a straightforward case of arson, the investigation would be left to me, but I suppose, this being relevant to a murder case…'

'It's still going to be left to you, at least for the moment. I don't have time for the finer details, so if you have the time to pick this one up, I'd be very grateful. I need you to liaise with the fire officer, and establish exactly how the fire was started. Have you called in for a forensic team yet?'

'No.'

'Then get onto it now. A scene like this deteriorates by the minute. We don't just need to know how the fire was started. We need to know who came here to start it, and how they got away.' Parkinson stepped away from the patrol car and began to walk down the layby towards what was left of the van, following the beam thrown by the headlamps of Brownlee's car. The February night air was tainted with the reek of smoke and chemicals, and he bent his head in a bid to avoid the stench. 'I have the details of the van's ownership. You don't need to worry about that for the moment, I'll let them know tomorrow that they won't be getting it back.' That news wasn't going to go down too well with the blonde at Trennick Rentals. But there's a silver lining in every cloud, he thought as he walked. At least now they wouldn't need to send the boys round to Salvation Hall, to ask Marcus Drake for the keys back.

## 16

Marcus watched in silence as Nancy cleared the breakfast dishes into the dishwasher.

She had a quiet, calm efficiency that never baulked at any kind of service demanded of her. As Richard's secretary and personal assistant, she might be forgiven for expecting to spend her time making appointments, dealing with correspondence and helping the old man to manage the affairs of his estates.

But there was so much more to Nancy Woodlands than her secretarial role might suggest. Ask her to prepare a meal, and she would tell you that she had a new recipe she was itching to try. Ask her to walk the dog, and she would tell you that she loved Samson, it was a pleasure to be out in the fresh air with him. Order flowers for Lucy's grave? She missed Lucy almost as much as the family did and would take the opportunity to order a floral tribute of her own while she was about it.

She didn't deal directly with the housework or laundry, of course. Since Becca's untimely departure from the hall, those pleasures had been delegated under Nancy's watchful eye to a carefully chosen and discreet local cleaning firm. The upkeep of the garden had been entrusted to a friend of a friend of Richard's, a man of advancing years who ran a small and specialist landscaping firm. And the redoubtable Mrs Peel, that willing and useful pair of hands in the village, was always on standby for anything that remotely resembled a domestic emergency. No, there was nothing much that fazed Nancy by the asking of it.

Except, perhaps, the need to provide an alibi for Marcus.

It occurred to Marcus now, as he watched her, that Nancy, as well as Richard, was in a position to provide him with an alibi for the night of Geraldine Morton's death. Just as she had provided him with an alibi for the time of Lucy's and Philip's murders all those months ago. The alibi then had been false, of course, and Nancy within her rights to confess to the sin and rescind it. Which was nothing more than Marcus would expect.

But it had never been lost on him that her confession came ahead of his own; that she alerted both the family and DCI Price to the fact before Marcus stepped up to confess.

And it had never been mentioned again. There had been no conversation between the two of them to clear the air, no attempt at an explanation by Nancy, no attempt by Marcus to reassure her that her decision to confess had been understood. He had arrived back at Salvation Hall on Wednesday of that week to be greeted by Nancy like an old, old friend who had never been away. But as each day passed, that rescinded alibi hung in the air between them, a reminder that Nancy's alibis were not to be relied upon without question.

A reminder that trust had been broken.

He felt a laugh begin to rise in the pit of his stomach, and he pinched his lips inwards too late to stifle it.

'What?' Nancy, busy now setting a coffee tray, heard the unbidden snuffle as it escaped his lips, and turned to glance at him over her shoulder.

'Nothing.' He pushed his chair back, swinging it up onto its back legs. But it wasn't nothing, was it? He was thinking about the dark blue van and the possibility that he was being framed for a murder that he didn't commit. Of course, Nancy knew about Geraldine Morton's murder. But she didn't know anything about the blue van, not least because both DCI Price and Richard Lancefield wanted Marcus to keep the information to himself.

But the irony was not lost on him that Nancy, once

again, was his alibi. And this time, she wouldn't be able to change her story. Because this time, the story was true. There would be no opportunity here to offer him a lifeline against a police investigation, only to draw it away in a heartbeat.

'Don't set a coffee cup for me, Nancy.' He lowered the chair to the ground and rested his hands on the kitchen table. 'I'm going into Truro with Ian this morning. One last shopping trip before I head off to St Felix.' Always assuming that he was still going to St Felix. 'I probably won't have the opportunity to do it tomorrow.'

Nancy raised her head and pouted at him. 'Well, I hope you're going to be back in time for Eva's arrival. They should be arriving here around lunchtime. I'll be setting you a place at the lunch table.'

'I'll be lunching in Truro with Ian. We're planning to be out all day.' One last burst of Cornish freedom. 'But I'll be back in plenty of time to dress for dinner.'

'And so I should hope.' She clicked her teeth in remonstration.

And suddenly Marcus realised that he was afraid of her. Not viscerally, gut-wrenchingly, physically afraid of her, of course. But afraid of her resolve; her ability to function as if everything between them was normal. Her ability to deal with the mundane, despite the presence of an oversized elephant in the room.

There was something about her that was deep; Lucy had noticed it, although Lucy had never been in awe of it. Nancy had a discomfiting ability to ignore those things that any mere mortal would be transfixed by. Like the ability to concentrate on the setting of a coffee tray, despite the presence of a convicted killer in the room while she was doing it.

'Nancy, you are still comfortable with the idea of escorting me out to St Felix?'

She lifted her head with a smile of genuine, unmistakable warmth. 'Of course I am, Marcus. Why wouldn't I be?' She tilted her head. 'That's the second time you've asked me that since you arrived back at the hall. Is there a reason why I shouldn't be comfortable?' Her words were reassuring, but there was just the merest hint in her voice of… mischief?

Did she already know then, about the dark blue Transit van, even though Marcus had been asked to keep it to himself? Even though Richard, David and Kathryn were faithfully keeping the secret?

She seemed to know everything else that was going on at Salvation Hall, it would hardly be a surprise if she knew that someone was trying to frame him for another murder.

\*

'I'm sorry I had to call you in on a Saturday, Ross, but there have been developments in the Morton case overnight.' Developments probably not significant enough to justify ruining Pearson's weekend as well as her own. But Grant didn't like the idea of her murder investigation playing out hundreds of miles away in Cornwall. It made her feel impotent when she needed to feel busy; made her feel redundant when she needed to feel that she was doing something useful to move the case forward. 'Did you have plans?'

'Nothing more important than the case, ma'am.' The ever-efficient sergeant was sitting to attention at the other side of her desk, like an eager puppy waiting for the ball to be thrown. 'Have you heard from DCI Price?'

'Yes, first thing this morning. They've found the van. It turned up last night in a layby just outside some place called Helston.'

'I have nothing on this weekend that couldn't wait, ma'am, if you'd like me to go down to Cornwall.'

'To Cornwall?' The suggestion threw her. But only because twenty years of policework had knocked some of the enthusiasm out of her. 'Thanks for the offer, Ross, but for now I think we need to leave DCI Price to deal with it.' Apart from anything else, Price knew his territory and his suspect far better than they did, and she didn't want to get in the way. 'They've sealed off the scene, pending a daylight inspection, and then they'll move the van to Penzance for a full forensic examination. But there isn't much left of it to examine. I'm told it was well alight by the time it was discovered, so there isn't much hope of any decent forensic evidence.'

'Well, at least now we know that the van made the journey from Edinburgh to Cornwall.'

'And that's what I'd like you to begin with. I've suggested to DCI Price that we try to track the van's route back. All the big service areas between here and Helston will have CCTV and the killer, always assuming that the killer was driving the blue van, couldn't have driven all that way without stopping to top up his fuel. He must have filled up at least once, possibly twice, depending on the model of the van and how much fuel he had left in the tank when he set off. And he would have needed other things during a ten-hour drive: coffee, maybe something to eat. We could catch him on CCTV at a service station, maybe even on a drive-through if he didn't need a comfort break at the same time.'

Pearson nodded. 'I'll get someone onto it straight away. We can start with half a dozen of the big service areas. There's no way we can look at them all, but we just need one sighting to put us on the right track.' He pulled a notebook and pen from his pocket. 'You said there were a couple of developments overnight?'

'Yes, the other one is firmly on our patch. Alec Henderson paid a visit to Eva McWhinney last night, and I want to know why. He turned up at Hemlock Row uninvited and unannounced, and started asking questions about the house and Eva's connections to the Lancefield family.' Grant's brow beetled forward. 'Eva was particularly concerned because he mentioned something about the history of the house, about its being built by a man called James McWhinney. He claimed to have got that information from Geraldine Morton, but Eva doesn't have any recollection of sharing that with Geraldine.'

'Did he make her feel uncomfortable?'

'He did, yes. Although I can't get my head around the fact that she invited the man into the house when he turned up.' After all, Eva had done everything possible to keep DCI Grant on the doorstep just the day before. 'The man's a bloody journalist. She might as well have invited a vampire over the threshold.'

If Pearson was unsettled by the comparison, he didn't let it show. 'Are you beginning to suspect that there is some sort of link between Henderson and Geraldine's murder? Or maybe between Henderson and the Lancefield family?'

'I don't know. But I want to speak to him today, and I want a witness with me when I do it.' Grant put a hand up to her lips to chew on her thumbnail. 'But first, I want some information rustling up on him. Let's dig a bit deeper into his background. And get someone to keep an eye on Hemlock Row while Eva is away in Cornwall.' There was a clock on the office wall, and the inspector glanced up at it. 'She'll be on her way to Exeter by now. I don't want Henderson snooping around while the house is empty.'

\*

David Lancefield's Mercedes coupe had been parked at Exeter airport for a week. The fact that the car was waiting for them when their flight landed had definitely been a bonus. But the notion that all four of them, plus luggage, would fit comfortably into such a compact vehicle had unquestionably been a triumph of hope over common sense.

And yet Eva, shoe-horned into the back seat along with Kathryn and an overspill of luggage, seemed in high spirits and determined to make the best of things. 'I've travelled in worse conditions. At least this car has decent headroom. My father had a passion for restoring Lotus sports cars, and he used to take me about in an Eclat; plenty of room for the adults in the front, and a back seat the size of a matchbox for the kid in the back.' She ran a finger around the canvas bag on her lap. 'It had a rear window that sloped down quite sharply and the taller I grew, the more ingenious I had to be about fitting in. By the time I was fifteen, I was reduced to sitting sideways with my back against the side window and my feet up on the seat in front of me.'

'Then it's a good job that you weren't claustrophobic.' Kathryn herself was beginning to feel nauseous thanks to the lack of space and air. 'Are you okay with that bag on your lap? It's not too heavy?'

'No, it's just the family Bible. In the end, I wasn't sure whether to bring it with me, or just take some photographs of it. But I wanted to share it with Richard, and digital photographs just wouldn't have done it justice.' She pointed at the bag on Kathryn's lap. 'How's your load?'

Kathryn rolled her eyes. 'I'll live. If I understand rightly, it contains gifts for Marcus to take with him to St Felix, and a bottle of Strathisla for Richard.' She raised an eyebrow. 'Stella knows that Richard is keen on his malt whisky, although these days the doctors think he should be reducing his consumption.' There was another bag between them on the car's seat, a nylon holdall, and Kathryn looked down at it. 'What's in the mystery bag?'

Eva beamed. 'It's another surprise for Richard, although I think you will find it interesting, too. It's something that's been in the family for generations.' She turned to look out of the car's window. 'How long will the journey to Penwithen take?'

'Just over a couple of hours. David is a very steady driver. He won't be speeding to get us there.' Which was all to the good. 'Have you ever been to Cornwall before?'

'No. And not just because it's at the other end of the country for me. To be honest, I just don't travel much. I'm far too busy at the hospital. Although I do take an occasional break up to a hydro in Perthshire. It's meant to be for fresh air and recreation, but I usually spend most of the time catching up on my sleep.'

It sounded to Kathryn like a lonely life. She wanted to ask if Eva had ever been married, or even had a long-term relationship. But their acquaintance was too short for such an intrusive line of questioning. Instead, she said, 'For what it's worth, we're all very pleased that you've decided to travel to Cornwall.'

'Ah, but this isn't a holiday, is it? This is a leap of faith.' Eva's eyes wandered towards the occupants of the car's front seats. 'Until Geraldine died, I don't suppose I ever realised how important it was to grasp those opportunities that life throws at us.'

'Even the unconventional ones?'

'Especially the unconventional ones.' Eva leaned a little closer towards Kathryn as she spoke. 'In any case, I never thought I would say this but I'm pleased to get away from Edinburgh for a few days. It's like your visit to Hemlock Row on Thursday. It's taking my mind off the police investigation.' She frowned. 'And of course, I'm hoping that you're going to tell me more about my illustrious ancestor while I'm spending time with you in Cornwall. Just what exactly did he do that was so contentious?'

Kathryn put a finger to her lips and signalled towards the passenger seat in front of her. 'I suppose any connection with slavery, and any success which came from that connection, could be considered contentious.' It was a deflection, a pragmatic attempt not to say too much in front of Stella. 'I was hoping to share more with you when we meet with Richard. It will kill two birds with one stone if I only have to tell the story once.'

'Twice.' David glanced up at the rear-view mirror with a wry smile. 'I have already heard the tale. It won't shock my father, very little does, but I think perhaps Kathryn is sensitive to Stella's views.'

Beside him in the passenger seat, Stella bristled. 'It's my understanding that the medical fraternity in Edinburgh has always had quite strong links to the Caribbean. The result of all those impoverished Scottish doctors trying to make their fortunes in a foreign land.'

'Good heavens, Stella.' David could hardly hide his surprise. 'Where did that come from?'

His wife gave him a lofty sideways glance. 'I've been reading up on the subject. Since you've agreed to take on the estates, I thought I should become a little more informed.' She tilted her head towards the back of the car. 'You must have known, Eva, that your family's wealth originated in the Caribbean? Given how much of the New Town was built on slave money?'

'I did know a little about it.' Eva cast a bemused glance at Kathryn as she spoke. 'Does it trouble you, Stella?'

'Trouble me? Good God, Eva, it horrifies me. It has always horrified me that David's family made their money from such misery. But to discover that some of Edinburgh's finest buildings only exist because of the profits from it?' Stella wriggled her shoulders and settled deeper into the soft, leather contours of the passenger seat, her lips pursed into a pejorative pout. 'But we can't always turn away from such things, can we?'

'No, I don't suppose we can.' Eva bit on her lip to stifle a smile. 'But perhaps we can do something to make amends. I understand from David that he has some ideas for a charitable foundation. Perhaps that's something that I could be involved in?'

The suggestion hung in the air, and then David's eyes moved again to the rear-view mirror. And if Kathryn didn't know better, she would have sworn that those eyes were brimming with tears.

# 17

Amber Kimbrall's cottage was at the end of an eighteenth-century row in Quintard Street, just around the corner from The Lancefield Arms.

She had been enjoying a leisurely breakfast when Becca Smith arrived, relishing the peace and quiet of a Saturday morning, and she had let the unexpected visitor in with poor grace. 'I hope you haven't come to bend my ear about that toerag you call a brother.'

Becca followed her into the small, neatly-furnished lounge and dropped her bag onto an armchair as she passed it. 'Aren't you worried about him?' She slumped, uninvited, onto the sofa.

'Worried?' Amber wrinkled her nose. 'What good would it do me to worry about him? He's obviously got himself involved with some little tart from the town, and we all know it wouldn't be the first time.' She gave a dismissive sniff. 'The only thing different about it this time is that I'm not interested in taking him back.' She stepped into the small kitchen behind the lounge. 'I suppose he's staying at yours?'

'No, I don't know where he is. That's why I've come to see you.' I've been ringing his mobile constantly since yesterday evening, but he's not answering.'

'So, he's at your mum's.'

'No, he's not. I've tried that. And Mum can't get through to him either. I wondered if you would try calling him? He might answer if he sees your number trying to get through.' Becca sounded hopeful. 'He's really sorry, Amber, for how he's behaved.'

'Zak doesn't know the meaning of the word sorry. I

know he's your brother, Becs, but he's gone too far this time.' Amber emerged from the kitchen, carrying a small white bowl. 'You won't mind if I have my breakfast.' It was a statement, not a question. 'I know your brother has been playing away, and lying to me about where he was just makes it worse.' She sat down on the sofa next to Becca. 'I know he wasn't staying at yours.' There would be little point in criticising the girl for letting herself be used. Amber knew that when it came to her siblings, Becca Smith knew nothing other than blind loyalty and unquestioning devotion.

'He was staying with me, Amber. Why would I lie about that? He turned up at two o'clock in the morning, and I let him sleep on the sofa. I could hardly turn him away, could I?'

'He wasn't staying with you last night though, was he? Why do you think he isn't answering his phone? Because he's with the same little tart he was with on Wednesday night. You know it, I know it…' Amber's voice trailed off, and she shook her head. 'I can't live like that, Becs. It's not fair.' She stared down into the cereal bowl. 'He came to see me on Thursday evening, in the pub, and he tried to turn on the charm. And I wasn't having any of it, so he sloped off to play the fruit machine, licking his wounds and wasting his money.' She blinked. 'But while he was there, his phone rang and he answered it. And he looked across at me…' She raised her eyes to the ceiling and felt the sting of an unbidden tear. 'And I knew then that there was somebody else. I saw the shifty way he looked at me.' She turned to look at Becca. 'Why can't you just tell me the truth?'

Becca groaned. 'Because I'm afraid of the truth.' She shuffled in her seat, wretched with her confession. 'And because he's my brother. I know he isn't perfect, Amber. Of all people, I should know that. When he asked me to lie for him, he admitted that he'd played away. But he wanted me to cover for him because he loves you.'

'Because he loves me?' Amber's face flushed red. 'I knew it. I knew the devious bastard was lying. And I knew that you were lying too.' Her tears were flowing freely now, and she brushed them away with the back of a hand. 'You know what? I don't want to hear any more.' She stood up and waved towards the door with the cereal bowl. 'Just go, Becca. Just get out of my house and leave me alone.'

'I can't. I'm worried about him.'

'Then more fool you. He doesn't deserve your concern. He's lied to me and made a liar out of you. Let his new woman sort it out. She's welcome to him.'

'But that's what I'm worried about, Amber. I don't think there is another woman. I know my brother, and I know when he's lying. And this time, it's like even his lie wasn't real. There's something that he isn't telling me, and I don't know what it is. But I think it's the reason he isn't answering his phone. I think he's got involved in something that's way out of his depth. And I'm worried that something bad is going to happen to him.'

\*

The receptionist at Trennick Rentals was busy filing invoices when Tom Parkinson arrived.

She looked up as he walked through the door, and clicked her teeth. 'I thought you were going to let me know when you were on your way. I could have had the kettle on.'

'I like to keep an element of mystery about me. It adds to the fun.' If only that were true. Even now, his wife's admonitions about missing her niece's birthday party were ringing in his ears. 'I thought you might be interested to know what happened to your van.'

The blonde frowned. 'I've already told you, the van won't be back in until later today.'

'The van won't be back in. Period.' He leaned an elbow

on the counter. 'We found it in a layby outside Helston last night. To be honest, it would probably be as well if you fished out the insurance documents.' Always assuming the van was insured. 'There isn't that much of it left to return.' He dug into his pocket and pulled out his mobile phone, placing it down on the counter in front of her.

She peered down at the image filling the screen and growled under her breath. 'Is that our bloody van?'

'It is if the registration plates are kosher.' He took back the phone and slid it into his pocket. 'I'm sorry I don't have better news for you. But at least you won't have to send the boys round to get it back.' There was a clock on the wall behind her, and he glanced up at it. 'It should be on the back of a truck by this afternoon, on its way to Truro nick for a full forensic examination.'

'You don't need a forensic examination to see what happened to it. Some bugger's torched it.' She growled again, an angry rumbling in her throat. 'Who the hell is going to pay for this? And who's going to pay for it to be transported back here? I hope you're not going to put it on the back of that truck until we're clear on who's paying the transportation costs?'

'There won't be any charge to you for taking it to police premises. And I promise you we'll look after what's left of it.'

She looked suddenly deflated. 'Do you have any idea what happened to it?'

'Apart from the obvious?' He shrugged. 'We think it's been destroyed to prevent us from establishing who hired it, and discovering who drove it all the way to Edinburgh to commit a murder.'

The blonde drew in a sharp breath. 'Our van was used in a murder?' She dismissed the thought with a laugh. 'No, I'm not buying that, pet.'

'I don't really care whether you buy it or not. Pet.' His tone was less friendly now. He pulled the phone from his pocket for a second time and swiped at the screen with the fingers of his free hand. 'I showed you a couple of pictures the last time I was here, and you didn't recognise either of the men. Do you recognise this one?' He held the phone out towards her.

Her eyes widened, and she nodded. 'That's the young man who collected it. Is he the one who destroyed it? He just didn't look the type.' She sounded disappointed.

Parkinson swiped again at the phone's screen. 'What about this one?' He turned the screen towards her again. 'Recognise him?'

She took the phone from him and lifted it to her eyes to take a better look. 'No. If you're asking about the man who paid for the rental, he was bigger than this. Thick set, darker hair.'

The sergeant tapped on the phone. 'Swipe left, to the next picture.'

She followed his instructions. 'That's him. That's the man who rented the van, and gave his name as Marcus Drake.' She spun her eyes back to Parkinson. 'You're not going to be able to pin the damage to our van on him, are you? The fire will have seen to that.' She frowned. 'But you know who he is.'

'Yes, we know who he is.' Parkinson took back his phone and slipped it into his pocket. 'And we're not examining the van to find out who hired it or who torched it. We're looking for a link between the hirer of the van, the murder in Edinburgh, and the arsonist who tried to stop us.'

She let out a laugh, a ripple of genuine amusement. And then she realised that Parkinson wasn't joking. 'I hope you're not trying to suggest…'

'I'm not trying to suggest anything. Now that we've identified the men who hired and collected the van, we need to bring them in for questioning. And we need to take a formal statement from you, to confirm that you recognise them. I'll arrange for a uniformed police officer to stop by this afternoon to take that statement. But in the meantime, do yourself a favour. Give someone a call and ask them to come and keep you company in the office. A colleague, a friend, even a family member if you have to.' He put a hand on her arm. 'And I'm not joking about that either. The man that we believe committed the murder and torched the van is still on the loose.'

\*

Richard Lancefield had welcomed his new cousin to Salvation Hall with the warmest of embraces, and a heart full of hope. She had barely alighted from David's car before the old man was beside her, his arms outstretched in greeting, the ever-faithful Samson trotting closely at his heels and barking his own staccato salutation.

Now, in the relative calm of the library, the old man was regarding the girl through rheumy, almost disbelieving eyes. With her thick, blonde hair coiled artfully up into a chignon, the fine, porcelain complexion, well-defined cheekbones and perfectly-groomed brows; he could almost have been looking at Lucy.

But there was one place where the resemblance ended, of course, one very important detail that could never have been conveyed by the photograph that David had shown him on their video call the previous evening.

And that was in the windows of the soul.

Lucy's eyes had been brown: sharp and searching, self-assured, and always full of challenge. But Eva's eyes? Those eyes were soft and grey, and almost overflowing with an unmistakable air of vulnerability. And he couldn't help wondering just where that vulnerability came from when Eva McWhinney had everything in life that a modern young woman could possibly need: an exquisite home and a distinguished career.

Unless, perhaps, she was lonely.

They were sitting side by side on the library's sofa, and he stretched out a gnarled hand and placed it gently on her arm. 'I couldn't be more pleased that you have come to visit us, Eva.' He turned his eyes up as he spoke, catching the attention of David, sitting just a few feet away in the captain's chair beside the desk. 'David tells me that the last few days have been quite distressing for you, and I am most sorry for the loss of your friend.'

'Thank you, Richard.' Eva smiled, a hesitant dimpling of the cheeks. 'I can't deny that it's been upsetting. But I am very pleased to be here.' Her expression spoke more of relief. 'Of course, it will be difficult to settle until they catch Geraldine's killer. Especially as there appears to be a connection between the killer and this part of the world.'

Her directness caught the old man by surprise. He blinked and looked again at David. And then he patted the arm beneath his hand. 'Your candour does you credit, my dear. As does the courage you have displayed by daring to venture into the lion's Cornish den. But we won't let anything happen to you. I want this weekend to be an event for all of us to remember, and to remember for the best of reasons.' And not the worst. 'Very soon, Nancy is going to bring us some coffee, and then David will take you up to the room we've prepared for you so that you can unpack and freshen up before lunch. It would please me greatly if we could lunch together here in the library, and take a little time to get to know each other. And then Samson and I will give you a tour of the house and gardens.'

'And will David be joining us?' Eva cast a questioning glance towards David.

'I'd be delighted. I believe that Stella intends to rest this afternoon. She found this morning's early start quite tiring.' David turned towards his father. 'Eva has brought the family Bible to show you, and some pictures of Hemlock Row.'

The old man beamed. 'Then we can immerse ourselves in my favourite pastime: examining the family's history and putting the pieces of our respective jigsaws together. I cannot tell you how much I am looking forward to learning more about Hemlock Row and its history.' He squeezed Eva's arm. 'If there is anything you need while you are here, my dear, anything at all, you have only to ask. The room that we've prepared for you is known as the Green Guest Room. It has its own bathroom and dressing room and a splendid view across the gardens towards St Felicity's. That's our lovely village church.' He inclined his head towards David. 'Perhaps you could take Eva up to her room now, and I will chase Nancy to bring the coffee?'

'Of course.' David rose to his feet and extended a hand towards Eva. 'It's on the first floor. I'll bring your overnight bag up to the room, but perhaps the family Bible and other bits and pieces can stay here in the library, for us to look at after lunch.'

Richard watched, entranced, as they left the room. And then he braced his hands on the sofa and pushed himself to his feet. Samson, curled in his basket beside the fireplace, lifted his head and pricked up his ears, but his master shook his head with a smile. 'Not yet, Samson. We'll take our fresh air when we show Eva around the gardens.' The dog's chin sank back onto his paws, and Richard laughed softly under his breath. 'Oh, dog, what would I do without you?' He walked slowly across to the grand, mahogany desk, the desk that had graced the library for the better part of three hundred years. and focused his attention on the small collection of framed photographs that hung above it.

The collage had been in place for many months now, hung at Kathryn's request as a reminder of why her work for the Lancefield family was so important. A photograph of Richard as a young man, relaxing on a sun-drenched beach on St Felix, was at the centre. Above it, a picture of David and Lucy relaxing on a holiday in the Mediterranean hung next to an image of Lucy, taken in the drawing room at Salvation Hall, her arms wrapped tightly around Marcus. And below it, a small but striking portrait of Nancy, her irrepressible energy shining out in the proud tilt of her head and the spirit in her eyes, had recently been joined by a photograph of cousin Barbara.

'We must ask Eva for a photograph to add to the collection. It would sit quite nicely to the left.' The thought pleased him, and then a sudden realisation struck. 'My word, there is no picture here of Stella.' He felt a sudden pang of shame. 'We must put that right today. And put it right with haste.' He turned his eyes upwards to look at the picture of Lucy and Marcus. 'It's only fair to include her in the family now.' As if he had to justify the decision. 'And my dear Lucy,' he reached across the desk and ran a finger down the simple, silver frame that bordered her image, 'I hope we'll have your blessing to hang a photograph of Eva here. I know that she could never replace you, my dear girl. But I do think she could be the balm to heal the pain of your loss.'

## 18

'So, Alec Henderson usually writes about financial affairs, including financial crime?' DCI Grant ran an experienced eye down the page of hand-written notes in front of her. 'But now he appears to be diversifying?' That was one way of putting it. In the last couple of hours, Ross Pearson had carried out the most thorough investigation he could manage into the freelance journalist's output. And there was no question in Grant's mind that Henderson had moved on from his original focus of digging up dirt on Edinburgh's banking and financial community, in favour of digging up dirt on hitherto respectable members of society. 'He's a bona fide muckraker.'

Pearson, hovering at the other side of her desk, pointed to the notes. 'He did a piece on Albie Andrews at the end of last year, and sold it to one of the broadsheets.'

Grant whistled. 'Andrews, the charity-boss-turned-paedophile?'

The sergeant blushed. 'Nothing's been proven, ma'am, as far as I'm aware. But Henderson's article has certainly pushed Mr Andrews into a corner.'

Into a corner, out of a job, and racking up the legal fees by the minute, if the rumours were true. 'What did Henderson get out of ruining somebody's reputation? A few hundred quid, maybe a thousand if he was lucky? Do you think he did it just for the money, or does he get some sort of kick out of exposing the great and the good? He doesn't strike me as the type to revel in a social conscience.' Grant chewed on her thumb. 'Do we know what he's working on at the moment? Do I need to be worried that the murder of Geraldine Morton is going to be his next big story?' She had asked him not to share any details of the case with any of his journalistic friends. It had never occurred to her that a grieving boyfriend, always assuming that he was grieving, might stoop low enough to write about the murder himself. 'Is that why he went to Hemlock Row yesterday evening? In search of a bit of colour to spice up a piece on Geraldine's death?'

Pearson sat down on the chair at the other side of the inspector's desk. 'Intending to write about it doesn't necessarily mean that he had anything to do with the murder though, does it?' The sergeant folded his arms across his chest. 'And in any case, didn't he start to question Eva about the house, and her family's connections to the Caribbean?'

'Which suggests what? That he was planning to dig the dirt on Eva's family?' Grant's eyes narrowed, and then she laughed. 'Well, he hit the jackpot there, alright. She has connections to the Lancefield family, and through that to Marcus Drake, newly convicted of manslaughter after a crime of passion.' Grant blew out a breath. 'But Eva McWhinney herself isn't that well known, is she? Is there another angle?'

'Outing the connection to slavery?'

'Because she's living in a house built on slave money, and raking in the rental income from the two adjacent houses, also built on slave money? That's hardly a novelty these days, is it? Every week there's an article in some paper or other, telling us all to atone for the sins of our fathers. What are they going to do? Demolish half the New Town because it was built on dirty money? Knock down half the city's statues, and rename all the streets that were named after Caribbean connections?'

Pearson frowned. 'Could he have been looking for a story about the benefits of privilege and influence? I've heard a rumour that Marcus Drake's sentence was lenient because it was handed down by a contact of Richard Lancefields.'

'I don't know, Ross, but it's a possibility.' Grant folded her arms. 'Do you think Alec's relationship with Geraldine was genuine? Or do you think that he somehow found out that she knew Eva McWhinney, and could be useful to him?'

'Did she die because she tried to stop him digging for a story?' Pearson pondered the possibility. 'He has an alibi for the time of death, doesn't he? We found the taxi driver who took him back to Leith?'

'We did. But a journalist's network can stretch far and wide, can't it? He could have paid for the alibi. He could even have paid for someone else to commit the murder.'

'Do you think he has a connection to Cornwall?'

'I don't know that either. But I do think it might be worth making our way back down to Pitt Street, to ask him.'

\*

Ennor Price hesitated in the doorway, almost reluctant to cross the threshold. He'd made many visits to Salvation Hall in the months since Lucy Lancefield's death, but this was the first time he'd returned to her suite of rooms, and the sight of it made him feel uncomfortable. 'Why on earth have they put you in here?'

'They could hardly have put Eva in here, could they? It would have been like resurrecting a ghost.' Kathryn was standing by the bed, unpacking her overnight bag. 'They've put her in the room next door.' She pulled a cashmere jumper from the bag and held it up to examine it. 'I really need to go back to The Zoological. All I have here are the casual clothes I took up to Edinburgh. I have nothing to dress for dinner.'

'I'll run you over there now if you like.' He sounded keen. 'We can be there and back in an hour.'

'I'm sure we could. But I thought you were at Salvation Hall to make sure that nothing happened to Eva. You wouldn't be much of a guard dog if you were fifteen miles away in Penzance.'

He ignored the reprimand and stepped into the room. Nothing appeared to have changed since he'd last set eyes on it. The large Liberty sofa and polished glass console tables still dominated the seating area, and the wall above the marble fireplace still bore its impressive collection of silver-framed family photographs. He crossed to the mantelpiece and lifted a large, ornate frame to his eyes, to take a closer look. The picture was familiar to him – it had been his first ever sighting of Marcus Drake – and he stared at it, remembering. 'Marcus has aged in the last few months.'

'Are you surprised, after everything he's been through?'

'No.' Ennor put the picture back on the mantelpiece. 'But I am surprised that this room hasn't been changed in any way. It's almost like a shrine.' He turned to look at the opposite wall. 'And that damned picture is still hanging there.' He crossed the room to examine a framed print, a period study of two young women dressed in silken finery. 'Lady Elizabeth Murray, and her cousin Dido Belle, attributed to the artist David Martin.' He smiled and turned to look at Kathryn. 'That was your very first history lesson for me, wasn't it? Nieces to the Earl of Mansfield, one born into a privileged British life, and the other born into slavery, and then claimed and brought to England by her father.' At the time, he had found the image both beautiful and terrifying, and the discovery that the print had been a gift to Lucy Lancefield from Richard's secretary, Nancy Woodlands, had only piqued his curiosity. 'Why would Nancy leave this picture hanging here, when it was a gift?'

'Why would she feel the need to remove it?' Her overnight bag emptied, Kathryn zipped it shut and lifted it down off the bed. 'You don't rescind a gift, just because the recipient has died.'

'No?' Perhaps he was still attributing too much

significance to it. 'Talking of Nancy, she didn't seem too pleased to see me when I arrived. Or too keen on the idea of leaving me alone with Richard. But I know he was worried that Marcus had been implicated in the hire of the blue van, and I wanted to put his mind at rest.'

'Has there been a development?'

'Yes. I took a call from Tom just before I left Penzance. The clerk at the van hire firm has confirmed that Mick Smith hired the blue van, and Robin Smith collected it.'

'Becca's brothers? They hired the van in Marcus's name?'

'It appears so. We still haven't managed to track Robin down, but Tom is planning to bring Mick Smith in for questioning this afternoon. He can bring him in for false representation when the van was hired, we have a witness now.'

'Which one of them do you think drove the van to Edinburgh?'

'We don't know yet that it was either of them. My money is on Zak, but we can't do much more until we've questioned Mick to see what they were up to. I have no grounds yet to bring Zak in for questioning. Even if we could find him.'

Kathryn sat down on the edge of the bed. 'I still can't quite believe that one of them would go so far as to murder a girl they mistook for Eva.'

'Neither can I. But the signs are there. At least we have pretty much confirmed that Marcus was being framed. The murder was nothing to do with him.'

'Isn't it also possible that the murder was nothing to do with the Smiths? After all, hiring a van and driving it to Edinburgh and back doesn't make you a killer.'

'You always have to play devil's advocate, don't you? What else would that van have been doing at the back of Hemlock Row on the night that Geraldine was murdered?'

'Staking out the house? Trying to take a look at Eva?

Possibly intending to warn her away from the Lancefields?'

'Don't waste your time making excuses for the Smiths, Kathryn. They don't deserve it. They were always bound to go too far one day.'

'So what happens now?'

'We question Mick, carry on looking for Robin and Zak, and question the whole family about their whereabouts on Wednesday evening. I have to eliminate them, if nothing else.'

'Have you established yet how they knew about Hemlock Row, or that Eva was a Lancefield?'

'No. That's a mystery for which I still don't have an answer. But that won't stop me from looking after her while she's here at Salvation Hall.'

\*

Becca Smith's new home was a tiny, two-up two-down council house on the outskirts of Penzance, a depressing concrete-covered shoebox far removed from the pretty-though-run-down tied cottage that she had enjoyed on the Salvation Hall estate.

She had been slow to answer the door when DS Parkinson rang the bell, and reluctant to invite him in. She had shown him into the small living room with a grunt and a shrug, and pointed unenthusiastically at a grubby sofa, in an indication that he might take a seat.

Parkinson, for his part, wasn't exactly overjoyed to be questioning Becca again. Like his senior officer, he was beginning to tire of the Smith family's escapades, and the sympathy he had borne for the girl over her loss of Philip McKeith was waning with each new strike against the Lancefields. But there was still her child to consider, the innocent living with the consequences of her mother's irrational behaviour. 'Where's Frankie this afternoon?'

'She's with my mum. They've gone to the park so that I can have a couple of hours to myself to do some housework.'

Parkinson cast a glance around the room and guessed that wasn't something that happened with any frequency. 'It must be handy, having your mum to help out with her.'

His attempt at small talk fell on deaf ears. Becca scowled and sat in a nearby armchair, folding her arms across her chest. 'So, what's my family supposed to have done now?'

The policeman frowned. 'What makes you think they've done something?'

'That's usually why you turn up on my doorstep, isn't it? When you want to accuse us of something?'

'Maybe. That, and when we think one of you can assist with our enquiries.' He leaned forward and rested his forearms on his knees. 'Where's Zak, Becca?'

'How should I know? He's probably at his lock-up.'

'No. We've been there, and funnily enough for a lock-up, it's all locked up.' Parkinson cleared his throat. 'And the tenant of the neighbouring unit reckons that Zak hasn't been seen there since Thursday.' He was watching Becca's face as he spoke. 'And before you suggest it, I've already spoken to Amber, and she hasn't seen him either.'

'I know.' Becca glowered and rolled her eyes. 'If you must know, I've been worried about him myself. He had a bust-up with Amber, and he's disappeared.'

'So you think he's disappeared because he had an argument with his girlfriend?'

'Do you have a better idea?'

The sergeant certainly did. 'I think his disappearance might have something to do with a blue van that was hired from a firm in Truro, and driven up to Edinburgh to murder a girl called Geraldine Morton.'

'Like the way you thought he'd murdered that girl Emma Needham last year when it was nothing to do with him?'

Parkinson ignored the jibe. 'At one o'clock this afternoon, we took your brother Mick in for questioning.

He hired a van from a firm called Trennick Rentals in Truro last week, and he gave his name as Marcus Drake.'

'You mean he decided to have a bit of fun at Marcus Drake's expense?'

'Do you call driving a van to Edinburgh to commit a murder "a bit of fun"?'

'Mick wouldn't do that. Apart from anything else, he doesn't know any girls in Edinburgh.'

'This particular girl was staying with Eva McWhinney.' He didn't have to elaborate further. Becca's eyes widened in momentary panic. 'I can see that the name is familiar to you.'

'I've heard the name, yes. She's another Lancefield, isn't she?'

Parkinson nodded. 'The murdered girl was staying with her, and the murder took place behind the house that she owns. The van Mick hired was seen driving away from the area very close to the time of death.'

'Mick wouldn't do anything like that.'

'Would Robin?'

The suggestion left her momentarily speechless. 'Robin wouldn't hurt a fly. You know that.'

'The van was hired by Mick, and driven away by Robin. We have a witness prepared to identify them both.' The policeman let her think about it. 'Where's Zak, Becca?'

'You think this was Zak?'

'If it wasn't Mick or Robin, then what's the alternative? Where were you on Wednesday evening?'

A deep crimson flush suffused her cheeks. 'You're mad.'

'Am I? There's no love lost between you and the Lancefields.' He lowered his voice. 'Wise up, Becca. If nothing else, do the right thing for Robin and Mick. Help us to find Zak, so that we can question him.'

'You're off your head. How could Zak have even known about this Eva McWhinney?'

'We're hoping he's going to tell us that... when we find

him.' Parkinson could feel his temper rising. Saturday afternoon and he should have been enjoying the day with his family, celebrating his niece's birthday. And here he was again, in the dog house with his wife for having to work, and on the receiving end of Becca Smith's bile. 'Do you think I have nothing better to do with my Saturday afternoon than sit here arguing the toss with you?' He needed to cut to the chase. 'I heard on the grapevine that Zak was supposed to be staying with you on Wednesday evening. Is that true?'

'You shouldn't believe everything that people tell you.'

'Was he here? Because if he wasn't, you're not just committing an offence by giving your brother a false alibi for the time of a murder. You're putting Robin in the frame.'

'Robin is in Devon. He's been there since Wednesday.'

'So you say. But we can't find him. We've been told that he's touring the coast with his girlfriend, but who tours the Devon coast in February? Maybe he was driving the blue van after all. Maybe he was up in Edinburgh, committing a murder.' Parkinson threw up his hands. 'Of course, if you can tell us where Zak is now…'

'I can't tell you what I don't know, can I? I've already told you that I don't know where Zak is. I haven't seen him since Thursday. But you can't pin this on Robin. Robin never hurt anybody in his life.'

# 19

'Do you think I look like Lucy Lancefield, Inspector Price?'

It wasn't an easy question for him to answer, given that the only time he had seen Lucy in the flesh she was a water-bloated corpse. 'Based on the photographs I've seen, there is certainly a very strong resemblance.' They had the library at Salvation Hall to themselves. Price pointed towards a pile of documents on the coffee table in front of the sofa. 'I take it that Richard has been regaling you with his favourite subject. Did it make you feel like a fully-fledged member of the Lancefield family?'

'Touché.' Eva laughed. 'Ask me that again tomorrow, after I've experienced a full-blown dinner party with them.'

'Oh, I think you'll enjoy that. I've witnessed the trappings of a Lancefield family dinner party before. They certainly know how to push the boat out.' Price relaxed back into his armchair. 'How do you like Salvation Hall?'

'It's breath-taking. I was expecting something larger, perhaps more imposing. But even though it's full of history, it feels like a home.'

'I've heard that you have a pretty breath-taking property of your own, up in Edinburgh.'

'Yes, but nothing quite like this.' She bowed her head. 'You know, I feel rather foolish now, thinking that I would be at risk here.'

Really? 'It's understandable. You've taken a great deal on trust.' Price was choosing his words carefully. 'But I'm hoping that you might feel a little more at ease, now that we've taken Mick Smith in for questioning.' The policeman rested his elbows on the chair's arms and steepled his fingers. 'You know, it's clear to us now that the Smith family hired the van that was seen leaving Hemlock Row on Wednesday night, and we strongly believe that a member of the family was responsible for Geraldine's death. But what we don't understand is how the Smith family came to hear about you. How might they have known to come to Hemlock Row?'

'I wish I had the answer, Inspector Price. I did tell Geraldine that Richard and David had reached out to make contact with me. We had quite a long chat about it. But she was the only person I shared that with. So they must have gained the information from someone here in Cornwall.'

'But this isn't an isolated incident, is it? DCI Grant tells me that you had a visit from Geraldine's boyfriend yesterday. And that he knew all about your connection to the Lancefield family.'

Eva drew in a sharp breath. 'Are you suggesting that there might be some link between Alec Henderson and the Smith family?'

Was that what he was suggesting? Price wasn't sure of that himself. 'If there wasn't some sort of link or connection between them, then the fact that both parties were mysteriously aware of your existence, and the fact that you lived at Hemlock Row, could only be attributed to a coincidence. And I can tell you now, in my line of work there is no such thing as coincidence. Only cause and effect.' He frowned. 'What do you know about Alec Henderson?'

'Very little, I'm afraid. I know that he's a freelance journalist, and when he came to see me yesterday evening I had the distinct impression that he was looking for a story.'

'Did you ask him how he knew of your connection to the Lancefields?'

'I didn't have to. He told me that Geraldine had talked to him about it.' Eva looked suddenly crestfallen. 'I didn't think she was that sort of person. I mean, I didn't tell her specifically to keep it to herself, probably because I didn't think I needed to. She wasn't the sort of person to gossip.'

'Had she known Alec for very long?'

'About six weeks, I think. She met him at a friend's birthday party.'

'And when did you tell her about the Lancefields?'

Eva frowned, remembering. 'I only received Richard's letter about three weeks ago, so probably a day or two after that. You surely weren't going to suggest that Alec only formed a relationship with her because he wanted a story about me?'

'I'm sorry if the idea offends you. But I had to ask.' That, and many more uncomfortable questions. 'What sort of a person is he? Alec Henderson?'

She gave an involuntary shiver. 'Truthfully? He's rather good-looking, very self-assured and he could probably charm the birds off the trees if he put his mind to it. But I found him...' She seemed to struggle for the right words. 'I found him intrusive. He wasn't invited to visit me, and I didn't particularly welcome his line of questioning. I'm afraid I had to resort to a small untruth to get rid of him. I told him that I was expecting a visit from DCI Grant.' She sounded embarrassed by the confession. 'Now, I have a question for you, Inspector Price. What sort of people are the Smith family?'

That wasn't just a question. It was *the* question. And one that she was perfectly entitled to ask. 'They're a mixed bag. There are five siblings. Becca, who used to be the housekeeper here, and four brothers. Zak and Mick are older than Becca and don't mind operating on just the wrong side of the law. They both indulge in a spot of poaching, like to work cash-in-hand when they can get away with it, and it was Zak who masterminded the harassment campaign against Richard and David last year. Robin and Adam are younger, and pretty much keep their noses clean. Adam in particular keeps himself to himself. Becca usually plays a straight enough bat, too, but her grief at losing Philip McKeith has fuelled a vindictive streak in her.'

'Could you imagine any of them having a connection with a sophisticated Edinburgh journalist?'

'No. Any more than I could have imagined one of them driving to Edinburgh to commit a murder. But then that's the trouble with being a detective. We can never afford to be constrained by the limits of our imagination.'

\*

Becca pulled her mobile phone from the rear pocket of her jeans and stared at the display. The screen was flashing with an incoming call, and she swiped at it with an impatient thumb. 'Robin? Where the hell are you? Is everything alright?'

Robin's voice sounded tired at the end of the line. 'We're back in Torquay. Everything's alright here, but Kim's aunt said the police have been looking for us. What's going on, Becs?'

'I've been trying to call you. Where the hell have you been?'

'We took off for a couple of days. It's no big deal.'

'Why didn't you answer your phone.'

'I turned it off. We just wanted some time to ourselves.' He sounded bemused. 'I don't see why it's such a big deal.'

He wouldn't. Becca swallowed down her frustration. 'Robin, did you and Mick hire a van before you went away?'

The silence at the end of the line was deafening. Eventually, he said, 'We hired a van for Zak. He said he needed it for a job. He didn't want to use his own van because it was a long drive. He didn't want to run the miles up on it.'

Becca's heart began to pound. 'A job? What job?'

'He wouldn't tell us. You know what he's like.'

'So whose idea was it to rent the van in Marcus Drake's

name?'

Robin snuffled a laugh. 'That was Zak's idea. A mate put him on to a firm in Truro that rents vans out for cash and doesn't ask any questions. Zak said it would be a laugh to put it in Drake's name. No one needed to know about it. Mick went in and paid for it on Monday, and I went back the next day and picked it up. We dropped it off for Zak at the lock-up on Tuesday afternoon.'

'And it was definitely Zak's idea? To use Marcus's name?'

'Well, it wouldn't be my idea, would it?' A hint of annoyance had crept into Robin's voice. 'Why all the questions? You used to be up for a laugh.'

A laugh? 'You idiot.' Becca spat the word into her phone. 'Did you have any idea what Zak was going to do with it?'

'No.'

'And you didn't think to ask what the job was?' Could he have been any more stupid? 'I've had Tom Parkinson round here this afternoon, asking questions. He thinks Zak drove that van to Edinburgh and murdered somebody.'

There was a moment's silence at the end of the line, and then Robin giggled. 'Come off it, Becs. Zak has never been to Edinburgh.'

'How do you know?' Becca's voice began to waver. 'Robin, I'm scared. We need to find him. We need to know where he was on Wednesday. He told Amber that he was staying with me, and I backed him up because I thought… well, it doesn't matter what I thought. But I can't keep lying about that if he's done something stupid. It's one thing to make the Lancefields' lives a misery. But murder?'

'The Lancefields? What's it got to do with them?'

'The girl who was murdered was staying with one of their cousins. The police think the wrong girl was targeted. That the killer was aiming for the cousin.' Becca bit her lip. 'Robin, do you think he would go that far? Do you think he would kill to get back at the Lancefields?'

'No.' Robin hesitated. 'At least, I hope he wouldn't. Have you asked Mick if he knows where Zak is?'

'I can't get hold of him. He's been taken into Penzance police station for questioning.'

'On what grounds?'

'Hiring the van under a false name.' She was struggling to keep the fear from her voice. 'Robin, we have to find him. That cousin of the Lancefields is here in Penwithen. She's come to stay at Salvation Hall for the weekend. I even told Zak that she was coming.' Becca swallowed hard. 'What if he did kill the wrong girl, and now the girl he was looking for is here in Cornwall? We've got to find him before he does something else stupid.'

'Becs, slow down. You're jumping to conclusions. That murder might have had nothing to do with Zak.' Robin thought for a moment. 'Does Zak still have the van?'

'No. It's been torched and left in a layby.' She was struggling to hide her distress. 'They think Zak did that too, to cover his tracks.' She put a wrist up to her face and wiped her tears on the sleeve of her jumper. 'He's used me as an alibi. He asked me to lie to Amber, and I thought I was just covering his back for a bit on the side. But murder? If they take me in for covering up for him, what will happen to Frankie?'

'They won't take you in for telling a white lie.'

'Of course they will. And it won't just be me, will it? What about you and Mick? They know Mick hired the van, that's why they're questioning him. And you drove it away from the depot. They could call you both accessories to the murder.'

'Now you're just being ridiculous. There's no evidence that Zak killed anybody.'

'Robin, we can't take the risk. You'll have to come back to Penzance now and talk to the police. If you admit that you helped to rent the van, but you didn't know what Zak was going to do with it, they'll take that into account.

Sergeant Parkinson said he would help you.'

'And you believed him?'

'Does it matter whether I believed him or not?' Becca stifled a sob. 'Right now, I can't see what other option we have.'

*

Eva reached down into the smaller of two leather bags at her feet and pulled out a small tablet device. 'I have something else to show you.' She pressed the power button to boot it up and then tapped on the screen with a deft finger as it flashed into life. 'Here.' She handed the device to Richard. 'These portraits of James and Charlotte McWhinney hang in the dining room at Hemlock Row.'

Richard took the tablet from her hands and lifted it closer to study the screen. 'James and Charlotte?' His mouth twisted a little, and his eyes widened. He glanced across at Kathryn. 'Is this really James and Charlotte? Have you seen these portraits for yourself?'

Kathryn smiled at him. 'Yes, I saw them when I visited Hemlock Row.'

His pleasure was undeniable. 'Eva, my dear, these are magnificent.'

She was sitting beside him on the library sofa, and she stretched out a hand to point to the corner of the portrait of Charlotte. 'The artist's signature is clearest on this one, and you can see that he hasn't just signed the portrait. He has noted Charlotte's name.' She placed her fingers on the tablet and stroked the screen to magnify the image.

'Well, this is indeed a treasure. We have seen the family Bible, and now a pair of splendid portraits we have never seen before.' He held the tablet back towards her. 'Are there any more pictures on this device, Eva?'

'Yes, I took pictures of all the rooms in the house before I came. And close-ups of those pieces of art and furniture that I thought might interest you the most.'

'And the conservatory?' It was Kathryn, sitting quietly

in the captain's chair, who asked the question.

'Yes, the conservatory, with my collection of plants.' Eva leaned a little closer to Richard and lowered her voice to a conspiratorial whisper. 'And my orchids.'

'Orchids? My dear, I am almost speechless. And that is not a regular occurrence, as Kathryn will attest.' The thought appeared to amuse him. 'I hope you will let me show you my own collection of orchids in the morning. I would very much appreciate the thoughts of a fellow enthusiast.'

'I would like that very much.'

'Then it's settled.' The old man looked down again at the portraits. 'James McWhinney was a medical man, wasn't he? And Kathryn has hinted to me that his medical interests were the reason for the family rift.' He cast a questioning eye at Kathryn. 'Are we to have more than a hint today?'

Kathryn frowned. 'I've shared the full story with David, and his reaction was just as I feared. But I suppose you will both have to hear it sooner or later.' She forced a smile. 'McWhinney was very keen to make a name for himself within the medical community and, to that end, he carried out medical experiments on a number of the Lancefields' slaves. And he did it without the family's permission.'

'And likely without the permission of the slaves themselves?' The stark question came from Eva. 'That's really the crime, isn't it? Not that he went against the wishes of the owners, but that he overrode the choices of the individuals. Individuals who were unable to advocate for themselves.' She turned to look at Kathryn. 'What kind of experiments were they?'

'He was trialling a new vaccine for smallpox.'

'And people died?'

'I'm afraid so.'

'Then what on earth possessed the man to do something like that?'

What, indeed? 'Ambition? Greed? Simply the desire to

make a name for himself?'

Richard growled softly under his breath. 'Might you not be doing the man a disservice here, Kathryn? You seem to forget that he lived in exceptional times, times when men were seeking to advance scientific knowledge.'

'At any cost?' It was Eva who asked the question.

'Perhaps.' Richard sucked in his cheeks. 'You might consider that men like James McWhinney also paid a price. Kathryn knows how dearly I love the island of St Felix. But I can love it with the benefit of clean water, sanitation, air conditioning, good food and the knowledge that any ailment to befall me while I'm there will be treated with first-rate medical attention. McWhinney was amongst those men, like my own ancestors, who risked a damnable climate, unsanitary conditions and tropical diseases to which they would have had no natural resistance in order to advance in their chosen fields.' Richard turned to Kathryn. 'Now, Kathryn, in your diligent examination of our family's papers you must have come across evidence that James McWhinney did some good work? He was responsible for the care of slaves on the Woodlands Plantation, so he must have treated ailments? Mended broken bones? Saved lives that might otherwise have been lost?'

'Of course. He certainly didn't shy away from treating the more difficult conditions. And some of the cases he attended would have been distressing.' Now wasn't the time to talk of the horrors of treating leprosy or dysentery, or of tending to those poor souls who suffered accidents during the dangerous practice of boiling sugar cane. 'But you must admit there is an ethical question to answer here? He conducted experiments on those who were in bondage and couldn't refuse.'

Richard responded with a wry smile. 'You know me better, Kathryn, than to pose a question like that.' He turned to look at Eva. 'Slavery was a bloody business, whichever way you looked at it. There is no question that men, and women, suffered on all sides. It took considerable courage for a man to pursue his fortune in the Caribbean. So my question to you, Eva, is this. Were our ancestors scoundrels, or were they heroes? Should we praise them for being adventurers and pioneers, for advancing medical science and industry and commerce at a time when most of their fellow men were seeking an easy life and looking only to their own interests? Or should they burn in hell for all damnation for the miseries that they inflicted on their fellow man in the name of profit?'

# 20

Stella's appearance at Salvation Hall was never going to be easy for Nancy. But she had hoped, at the very least, that David's wife would be as keen as she to keep a polite distance between them. Regrettably, the hope was a forlorn one.

'I wanted to speak to you about Marcus, Nancy. I hope that you're going to look after him when he goes to St Felix.' Stella pulled a chair away from the dining table and sat down. 'He's been through a great deal in these past few months, and the legal process has left him feeling very low.'

Nancy, busy arranging crystal wine glasses on the table, made no attempt to hide her displeasure. 'Do you have to sit there, Stella? You can see that I'm trying to set the table for dinner.' She held a glass up to the light to examine it for smudges. 'And Marcus doesn't need looking after, he's a grown man.'

'He may be a grown man, but he's still my son. And I don't think you can blame me for being concerned, after the way you let him down.'

'Let him down?'

'Last September. One minute you were telling the police that he was with you when Lucy and Philip were murdered, and then you decided that it was a lie. I still don't understand why you did that.'

'What is there to understand?' Nancy ran a soft cloth across the glass, buffing away an invisible fingerprint. 'Marcus admitted to Philip's murder. Nothing I could say, true or otherwise, could make a difference after that. Anyway,' she placed the glass gently down on the table,

'Marcus has forgiven me. Not that there was anything really to forgive. It's all water under the bridge now.'

Stella bridled. 'It will never be water under the bridge where my son is concerned.' She picked up a dessert knife from the table to examine it through critical eyes. 'And Marcus may have forgiven you, but I have not.'

Nancy scowled. 'Please put the knife down, Stella. I would appreciate you not tampering with the place settings.' She wanted to ask the woman to get up from the table and leave the room: to leave the house, the village, the county if she could. But she must think of Richard. 'I do hope you're not going to make difficulties while you're here for the weekend. Richard is very keen that Marcus should be given a loving send-off before he goes. It would be a pity if there were any unpleasantness to spoil that.'

Marcus's mother smiled and went on examining the knife. 'There won't be any unpleasantness from me, Nancy. I hope the same can be said of you.' She raised an eyebrow. 'Have you met Eva yet?'

Nancy's scowl deepened. 'Only briefly.' She stared at the knife in Stella's hand. 'Her resemblance to Lucy is astonishing, isn't it? I do hope it isn't going to upset Marcus when he sees her.'

'Upset him?' Stella placed the knife back down on the table, lining it up against the adjacent cutlery. 'What are you suggesting?'

'I'm just thinking of Marcus. How do you think he is going to feel?' Nancy skirted the table as she spoke. 'Surely you have given some thought to how he will feel, being asked to share his farewell supper with a girl who looks just like his dead fiancée?' She put a hand down to the table and gently nudged the dessert knife that Stella had moved, pushing it back into perfect alignment beside a table knife. 'Surely that's the sort of thing a mother would think of?'

'Frankly, I don't think it will give him any cause for concern. He'll be far too busy considering his new life.

And it's not as if he'll see her again after Monday.'

'You mean, after tomorrow. She's flying back to Edinburgh tomorrow evening, isn't she?'

'Good heavens, no, whatever makes you think that?' Stella lifted a dessert fork from the table. 'No, she isn't going back until Tuesday. She'll be here to see Marcus off, and then when he's gone she and David plan to spend some time talking to Richard about the future of the estates.'

'Eva is to be involved in the estates? What do the estates have to do with her?'

Stella examined the fork and then lifted it to her lips to breathe on it. 'Nothing, as yet.' She eyed the misty metal surface and then rubbed it gently on the sleeve of her cardigan as if removing a smudge. 'But that's all going to change soon, isn't it? Eva has declared herself to be willing to support David as he manages the Lancefield estates going forward. They're going to persuade Richard that there is no need to look for any more family now. David, Eva and Barbara can manage things between them, with help from Kathryn in this country and from Marcus in St Felix.' She placed the fork back down on the table. 'Didn't you know, Nancy? I'm surprised that Richard didn't mention it to you. With you being his secretary.'

It was a cruel barb, and it hit its mark with ease. Nancy flinched and snatched up the dessert fork. 'But Eva is hardly known to the family.' She examined the fork. 'And I asked you not to touch the cutlery.'

'Eva is directly descended from the Lancefield line. That, in itself, will probably be enough for Richard. And coupled with the fact that she and David get on so well… I think it's inevitable that she will be involved with things. I must admit that I had my reservations about her at first. But she has such a lovely, easy-going personality. I'm quite warming to her myself.' Stella smirked and picked up a soup spoon. 'Of course, there will have to be changes, especially as David and I plan to spend so much more time at Salvation Hall.'

'But you hate Salvation Hall.'

'I know. But I've promised David that I will make a real effort to change the way I feel about it. After all, it is his birth right. And I wouldn't be much of a wife if I refused to support him, would I?'

Nancy could feel her pulse begin to quicken. 'It would appear that you don't mind being a hypocrite.'

Stella laughed as she twirled the soup spoon around between her fingers. 'Oh, come on, Nancy. The Lancefield family has always been rife with charlatans and dissemblers. What difference would it make if one more hypocrite were to make themselves at home under this roof?'

\*

DCI Grant offered Alec Henderson the most disarming smile she could muster. 'I am sorry to disturb you again, Mr Henderson, but I was sure you'd want to be kept in the picture.' Almost as sure as she was that he had not been pleased to see her arrive on his doorstep with DS Pearson. 'Do you mind if I take a seat? Only it's been a long day.' They were standing in the lounge of his Pitt Street flat, and she sat down on the sofa without waiting for an answer. She hoped he'd got the message that she wasn't intending to leave without getting some answers to her questions.

Backed into a corner, Henderson sat down in an adjacent armchair and gestured for Pearson to join the inspector on the sofa. 'I take it there has been a development?'

'Yes. We have a definite lead now, and an individual is being questioned about a van we believe is relevant to the investigation. The van was hired in Cornwall.' She watched Henderson's face as she spoke, and detected the slightest flicker of recognition in the cool, brown eyes.

'I see. And where is it now?'

'In Cornwall.' She gave a vague nod. 'I wonder, Alec, would you mind telling us where you met Geraldine?'

'We met at a mutual friend's birthday party. She was charming, rather shy... and that appealed to me. They say that opposites attract, don't they?'

Grant ignored the question. 'That must have been before the work started on her flat in Marchmont then?'

'Yes. She was in the process of scheduling the work when I met her.'

'Did you ever visit her in Marchmont?'

'Yes, I did. It's a lovely flat.' Alec put a hand up to his ear and pulled on it. 'Forgive me, Inspector Grant, but is this relevant to your investigation?'

She wanted to say, 'Everything is relevant to my investigation until I catch Geraldine's killer'. But he could work that out for himself. 'I'm just interested. It helps me to build a picture of Geraldine, and what was going on in her life before she died.' She gave him a moment to think about it and then said, 'You didn't visit Geraldine at Hemlock Row though?'

'No. But then I wasn't invited.'

'Were you invited yesterday evening?'

Alec Henderson's jaw tensed suddenly. And then he smiled again and nodded to himself. 'You've been speaking to Eva McWhinney.' He cleared his throat. 'No, I wasn't invited. But I don't see anything wrong in taking the trouble to pay my respects.'

'Of course.' Grant stood up and looked around her. 'I see that you're a keen reader, Alec. I like a good book myself. Do you prefer fact or fiction?' She crossed the room to a tall, slim bookcase that filled an alcove beside the fireplace, and pulled a book from the middle shelf to examine the cover. '*An Essay on the More Common West Indian Diseases.* Is that regular reading for a financial journalist?'

An angry, red flush began to spread across Henderson's neck. 'I have many interests, Inspector Grant. A journalist can't afford to be a one-trick pony these days. Not if they want to eat and keep a roof over their head.'

She put the book back on the shelf with a smile. 'I suppose Geraldine told you about James McWhinney and Eva's connection to the Lancefield family?'

'Geraldine knew that I had an interest in local history. Particularly the late eighteenth century. I've always been interested in the New Town and its construction; the way Edinburgh developed into the city it is today.'

'A lot of it was built on slave money, wasn't it?'

Recognition flickered again in his eyes, but he didn't speak.

'Did Geraldine know about your other line of journalism, Alec? The line where you dig around in the lives of private individuals, with a view to selling their stories to the highest bidder?'

'Just what the hell do you mean by that?'

'Sergeant Pearson here told me about an interesting piece you wrote about Albie Andrews.' She indicated her colleague, still sitting silently on the sofa. 'I just wondered whether you were planning to do a similar piece about Eva and her connections to the Lancefield family. "The dark and unpleasant history behind some of Edinburgh's finest homes." That sort of thing.'

Alec slumped back into his chair. 'There's no law against writing about the past. And writing about slavery is fair game these days. It's trendy. People love it. It's always been trendy to diss the establishment. And right now, it's particularly trendy to diss an establishment that made its money on the backs of others.'

'The establishment has always made its money on the backs of others. Factory workers, coal miners… there's nothing new in that.'

'Factory workers and coal miners are old hat when it comes to provoking indignation.' His smile was cynical now. 'And these days, indignation sells newspapers.'

Grant held up a hand towards him. 'Let's cut to the

chase, shall we? You met Geraldine at a party, and a few weeks later she was invited to stay at Hemlock Row. And not long after she moved in, she told you that Eva had links to the Lancefield family of Penwithen in Cornwall. And the journalist in you thought that sounded worth following up, and after a bit of digging, you thought you'd hit the jackpot. You thought you'd come up with an article or two about wealthy, slave-owning families to sell to the liberal press; the dirty link between Edinburgh wealth and the misery of slavery.' Grant drew in a breath. 'Did you tell Geraldine that you were planning to write about her friend's family, Alec?'

'No, of course not.' He looked suddenly deflated.

'Because she wouldn't have liked it, would she? In fact, it would clear the way for you, wouldn't it? If Geraldine wasn't there to stop you.'

'What are you suggesting?'

'Eva was very unsettled by your visit yesterday evening.'

'I was just trying to be kind.'

'Were you?' Grant feigned surprise. 'Tell me, Alec, were you only planning to write about Eva's connections to slavery, or did Marcus Drake come into the equation in any way?'

The colour in Alec Henderson's neck headed north, spreading angrily across his cheeks and chin. 'Marcus Drake?'

'Don't play the innocent, Alec. It doesn't suit you.'

For a few seconds, he sat silently in the chair, breathing heavily, contemplating his next move. And then he put up his hands in surrender. 'Okay, originally I only planned to write about the slavery. But I had a tip-off from a friend in the business. He'd heard of the Lancefields, and he told me to look at the case against Marcus Drake. When I saw the details, I thought it would add something extra to what I was writing, that slavery didn't just bring wealth for the establishment, it brought influence. Drake should have gone down for years for killing Philip McKeith. But the wealthy can always defend their own, can't they?'

Grant had heard enough. She shoved her hands into the pockets of her coat and jerked her head towards DS Pearson. 'I think we're done here, Ross.' She turned to Alec Henderson. 'We'll leave you in peace now. But if I hear that you've written about Eva McWhinney's family and sold the story to the press, I'll make sure that you never work for a Scottish newspaper again. I'll make it my life's mission. Because you and I have something in common, Alec. I can't stand to see money made on the back of other people's misery either.'

\*

Marcus had been the first to arrive in the drawing room for pre-dinner drinks and was busy pouring himself a whisky and soda when Eva arrived. Hearing the rustle of movement behind him, he had turned, glass in hand, to greet the arrival, and found himself face-to-face with a ghost.

Now, of course, sitting next to her on the damask chaise longue, he could see that Eva McWhinney was no unearthly apparition.

And all he could do was gaze at her.

'I thought they might have told you how much I looked like Lucy.' Eva sipped on the gin and tonic he had poured for her. 'When you weren't here this afternoon, I wondered if perhaps you were avoiding me.'

'Not at all. I've been into Truro with a friend, and we lost track of time.' Truth be told, Marcus had been reluctant to return to Salvation Hall at all, but not for any reason concerning Eva. 'I only arrived back half an hour ago.' If he had known what he'd been missing, he would have returned far earlier. 'I hope you don't think I was rude, not being here to greet you.'

'Of course not. And I'm sorry if seeing me for the first time was a shock. They really should have warned you.'

'Perhaps. But it probably wouldn't have occurred to them. Nothing this family does ever surprises me, Eva. You get used to it after a while. The word "dysfunctional" just wouldn't begin to cover it.'

'And yet you're still here?'

'It's a long story. And not really one for polite company.' Marcus found the courage to smile at her. 'Assuming that you don't know already, of course.'

'About Lucy and Philip, and the court case?'

His stomach churned, but his nerve held. 'Well, at least they managed to share that with you.'

'Have they told you much about me?'

'I can't say that they have. You're a very distant cousin to the family, you're some sort of doctor, and you live and work in Edinburgh. And they are very, very keen to welcome you into the family fold.' He stared into his whisky glass. 'Have they managed to put you off yet?'

Now Eva laughed, a soft ripple of amusement. 'Does it look like it? If anything, I almost find the level of dysfunction endearing. Most people are generally so desperate to conform, aren't they? As if being different from the pack is something to be afraid of.' She sipped again on the gin. 'I've always been something of a loner, and perhaps that was because of my family. I always knew we were different, the last of a long line of medics living in our grand, inherited house. My father was a brilliant man. He was a surgeon, you know? And he wasn't just a skilled technician. He was a fearless mind. He would go where other surgeons would fear to tread.' She laughed again. 'And, of course, he was eccentric.' She fixed her eyes on Marcus's face. 'So, the dysfunction and eccentricities of the Lancefield family are no novelty to me. If anything, I feel strangely at home with them.'

'I'm sure they'll be delighted to hear it.' He was curiously delighted himself. 'So, you'll stay in touch with the family? With David and Richard?' His eyes glowed with mischief. 'And with my mother?'

'Yes, of course. If they want me to. They are charming, including your mother.' Eva was still looking at him, questioningly now. 'She's very concerned, you know, that you are going to St Felix. She thinks the family are using you.'

He could only laugh at the suggestion. 'Using people is one of the family's very special talents. But I've found that the trick is to look for the positives. Just because someone is using you, doesn't mean there can't be a benefit in the agreement.' Marcus hesitated, and then said, 'When I originally denied that I was responsible for Philip McKeith's death, Richard asked me to have the courage to confess to it, rather than run away from it. He said that if I came clean, he would give me every possible support. And I knew then that he was using me. I knew that there was nothing in the way of evidence to point to me as Philip's killer, but that if I confessed it would bring closure, and the family would be free to move forward. Philip would be blamed for Lucy's death, I would take my punishment with Richard's support, and everything would be neatly wrapped up by the legal process. Instead of everyone enduring a long, drawn-out police investigation while they tried to get at the truth.'

'And what was in that for you?'

'At first, I thought it was just the promise of the best legal support that money could buy, and a one-way ticket to St Felix to get the taste out of my mouth. But I can see now that there was another benefit. I would be free to move on too. I wouldn't have to keep looking over my shoulder. And although I can never escape the guilt, at least everything is out in the open.' Marcus tilted his head. 'I hope I haven't said too much. You didn't come here to listen to my life story.' She was just too easy to talk to. 'Eva, can I ask you... do you think the family is using you?'

Eva's eyes clouded. 'I didn't think so at first. But now that I've seen more pictures of Lucy, I have to admit...

well, I'm a little concerned that I'm being used as some sort of replacement. As if I'm wanted for my resemblance to her, not for myself. But time will tell, I suppose.'

'They didn't know that you looked like Lucy when they reached out to you.'

'No, I don't suppose they did. But they do now, and that makes a difference.' Eva leaned a little closer to him. 'Have they told you about Geraldine Morton?'

'Yes.' Marcus felt his pulse quicken. 'Have they told you that I've been framed for hiring the van that's key to the murder investigation?'

'Yes. It's insane, isn't it?'

'Oh, I don't know.' Marcus moved his head a little closer to Eva's and pointed upwards with the index finger of his free hand. 'Maybe someone up there is just trying to tell us something?'

## 21

Ennor Price relaxed back on the library sofa, a glass of alcohol-free lager in one hand and his mobile phone in the other. 'Alec Henderson was a dead end then?'

'I'm afraid so.' DCI Grant's voice crackled at the end of the phone line. 'The only lead we had up here, and he turned out to be just a grubby little journalist trying to make a bit of money at the expense of Eva and her connection to the Lancefield family.' She sniffed her disapproval. 'Hopefully, he understands now that trying to sell that story wouldn't be such a good idea after all.'

'It's a pity that there was no clear link between him and the Cornish end of things though.' Price had fantasised more than once about the possibility of turning up some unexpected link between Geraldine Morton's boyfriend and the Smith family. 'He and the Smiths might have been known to each other in some way; distant cousins, perhaps.'

'Distant cousins? You've definitely been spending too much time with the Lancefields.' Grant laughed. 'Do you have any news for us on the van?'

'Yes, things are moving a bit there.' It was a relief to have something positive to report. 'We've questioned Mick Smith, and he's admitted to hiring the van. But he denies all knowledge of the drive to Edinburgh, and he's produced a cast-iron alibi: he was in a local pub with his wife for most of Wednesday evening, and the landlord of the pub backs him up, as do half the bar staff.' More was the pity. 'I've known the landlord for years and he's as straight as a die. Mick also confirmed that it was Robin who collected the van, but he just isn't the type to commit a murder.'

'And what about the forensics?'

'Early indications say there's no question that it had been set alight deliberately. The full examination is going to take several days, but I don't hold out much hope of finding anything that would incriminate Zak Smith. The damage is extensive. We think it had only been burning for around fifteen minutes before it was spotted, but it was a dry evening and there was a strong breeze blowing.'

'Has Mick Smith admitted to torching it?'

'No. And he has an alibi for yesterday evening too.' There was a small pile of papers on the coffee table in front of him, and Price stretched out a hand to put down his ale and pick up the top sheet of paper. 'The layby itself hasn't revealed very much. There were the inevitable tyre marks and footprints from the fire crew to contaminate the scene, and the layby had multiple sets of additional tyre marks due to heavy usage.'

'So it's not possible to tell if someone picked the arsonist up after he set fire to the van, or whether he left the scene on foot?'

'That's about the size of it. We're working on the theory that he walked away, and maybe picked up a taxi in Helston.'

'By *him*, are you still referring to Zak Smith?'

'Yes. Mick has admitted that hiring the van was Zak's idea, so we're pinning it on him. He has an alibi for Wednesday evening, but we know now that it's not safe. Tom Parkinson has tried to break it, but it's the sister, and she won't budge.'

'Can't you just bring him in?'

'Oh, sure. If we could find him. But he's gone to ground, and that's the bit that's really troubling me. Because it's not like Zak Smith to miss an opportunity to boast about his crimes.'

'Is he biding his time until he can try again?'

Price stiffened, and felt a familiar prickle of the hairs on the back of his neck. 'Don't even joke about that.'

'We have to be realistic.' Grant was silent for a moment. And then she asked, 'How's Eva?'

'She's fine. We had a long talk this afternoon. I think she was nervous to begin with, but she's settling in here well, and the family are looking after her.'

'And you'll be there all evening?'

Price stared down at his almost empty glass. 'All evening, until the family turn out the lights. They're having dinner at the moment.'

'And you weren't invited to join them?'

'No. But then that was never the idea. I'm camped out in the library and I'm using the time to deal with some paperwork. I've been promised supper on a tray if I behave myself.'

'Well, let's hope it's something freshly prepared. You are a Detective Chief Inspector, after all. I'd hate to think that you'd given up your Saturday evening just for the pleasure of eating the landed gentry's leftovers.'

\*

'Are you sure you don't want to join the rest of them, out on the terrace?' Richard leaned a little closer to Kathryn, sitting beside him at the dining table. 'I will be quite content to sit here and enjoy the view.'

Kathryn turned her head to look out through the French windows. The windows were open, and the rest of the party was already seated around a large, wicker table. 'It was a lovely idea of Nancy's, to set the terrace for after-dinner drinks, but it's far too cold for me.' Even with the promise of a lamb's wool blanket to huddle under. 'I'd far rather be in here near the fire.' She turned back to smile at Richard. 'Ask me again when it's June.'

'I quite agree. These old bones need all the warmth they can get.' He stretched out a hand to a crystal decanter and lifted it to pour himself a brandy. 'At least we can say that the evening has been something of a success. Eva just seems to have fitted right into the family.' He lifted the glass to his lips and sipped. 'She and David seem to have a genuine connection, and if I didn't know better I would say that she has charmed Marcus.'

'She even seems to know how to handle Stella.'

'Ah yes, Stella.' Richard frowned. 'Is it my imagination, or has Stella mellowed in the last few months? She has actually promised me that she will make more effort to support David with the estates.'

'I think she feels better now that Marcus is free. I don't think she quite trusted you when you said you could secure his release.'

'Then I am glad to have proven her wrong.' Richard tilted his head. 'But I can't help wondering if I sense reservations with you? About Eva?'

'I wouldn't say *reservations*, Richard. But Marcus seems to be almost as besotted with her as David, and I'm worried it's because of her appearance.'

'She may look like my dear, late granddaughter, I agree. But I judge that the resemblance is only skin deep. There is a warmth and kindness about the girl that was never present in Lucy. Lucy was a force of nature, but not a force for humanity.' Richard sipped again on his brandy. 'As Nancy is busy in the kitchen, and the others are out on the terrace, can we take the opportunity to talk privately? It occurs to me that there is one amongst us who doesn't welcome Eva's presence at Salvation Hall.' He swirled the brandy around in his glass. 'Nancy has played her part well this evening, acting as hostess and attending to everyone's needs. But I might have hoped she would do it with a better grace.'

'She was a little short-tempered between courses, but I put that down to the pressure of serving the meal. Apart from that, Richard, I didn't notice anything particularly amiss.'

'I very much doubt that you would. But I know Nancy.

I know her moods. She cannot fully hide her grievances from me. Her acting skills are second to none. She can smile and make small talk, and pretend to be interested but her eyes give her away. I have seen how she looks at Eva when she thinks no one is looking. And Eva herself has already asked me if Nancy has taken a dislike to her.'

'She's sensed something?'

'It would be difficult for a sensitive soul to miss.'

Was this the time for Kathryn to point out the obvious? 'Perhaps Nancy feels that she is to be replaced in your affections.'

'No, never in my affections. And you, of all people, know why. But perhaps in my day-to-day life.' Richard nodded to himself. 'I wondered, my dear, how you would feel about taking over Nancy's secretarial duties again? As you did the last time she was in St Felix?'

'Of course I will. She's only going to be away for three or four days this time, isn't she?'

'I was thinking it might be a little longer than that. I would like the time and space to get to know Eva better, without Nancy hovering in the background like a mischievous sprite. After all, it was never the intention for Nancy to settle permanently here in England.'

'Is that how Nancy sees it? I rather formed the impression that she had made a life here. I know she loves to visit St Felix to see her family, but I've never heard her express a wish to return for good.'

'You are presuming that the decision is Nancy's to make. She was invited to Penwithen to spend some time here as my secretary. I viewed it as an important part of her overall education.'

'Please tell me that you're not planning to send her back against her will. Richard, that would be cruel. She loves being here with you. She's a part of Salvation Hall now. Part of the extended family. You have always said so yourself.' Never mind the fact that she was his unacknowledged granddaughter.

'Nancy will always be part of the extended family, my dear. Everyone who lives and works on our estates is a much-loved part of that family. But what concerns me at the moment is the immediate family. David has Barbara and Eva to support him now, and Stella has promised to spend more time in Cornwall. And he has Marcus.' Richard put out a hand to touch Kathryn's arm. 'And I very much hope that he still has you in his corner. The six of you will make a formidable team, not least because you have all declared on the side of mutual support.' His brow furrowed. 'It pains me to say that the same cannot be said of Nancy. She is still at odds with Stella and I see no evidence of warmth towards Eva.'

'Perhaps she just needs time. Time to get to know Eva, and to adjust to the way the family is developing.'

Richard gave a knowing smile. 'I have made up my mind. Nancy will take Marcus to St Felix, spend a few days with her family, and then she will return. And when she returns, I will speak to her about the future. We will take three months to wind up her responsibilities at Salvation Hall, after which she will return to St Felix. I will make sure that she has a responsible and rewarding role on the Woodlands Estate, perhaps as second-in-command to Marcus. There will be no question of her losing out.'

'I see.' Kathryn turned disappointed eyes down to study her hands. There would be little point, she was sure, in pointing out to Richard that the success of his plan would very much depend on whether Nancy's definition of 'losing out' was the same as his own.

\*

Nancy set the perfectly-prepared tray down on the small coffee table in front of the library sofa. 'I've set the tray for two, Inspector Price. I hope you don't mind if I join you?' She wrinkled her nose. 'I've brought chocolate biscuits, as an inducement.'

'Bribing the police?' Price clicked his teeth. 'I won't tell if you don't.' Truth be told, he had been enjoying the peace and quiet, but he could hardly ask her to leave. 'I thought you would be enjoying after-dinner drinks with the rest of the family?'

'Good heavens, no.' She dismissed the idea with a laugh. 'I wouldn't enjoy that at all.' She sat down in the armchair beside the sofa. 'No, I'm far more interested to discover what a detective chief inspector gets up to when he is moonlighting as an unpaid security guard.'

He tapped the lid of his laptop, resting idle on the sofa beside him. 'If you must know, I've been catching up on today's football coverage.' It was a harmless enough lie. 'Surely you didn't think that I'd be working?' He stretched out a hand to the tray and helped himself to a chocolate biscuit. ' How did the dinner party go?'

'Well, the food went off without a hitch. But it always does when we use an outside caterer. I hope your share was up to scratch?'

'It was delicious. I was only expecting a sandwich. I didn't realise that I was to be spoiled with roast beef and all the trimmings.' Not to mention a rather generous portion of apple pie and custard. 'And how did Eva fare, at her first official Lancefield engagement?'

'I can't say I noticed, inspector. I was far too busy carrying out my duties.'

Price balanced the chocolate biscuit carefully on his knee. 'Do you have an issue with Eva being here, Nancy?'

Nancy's lips curled into a condescending curve. 'Why should I have an issue? It is very much Richard and David's concern.' She almost sounded convincing. 'Although I will admit that I found her physical resemblance to Lucy a little unsettling at first. Of course, once I'd had a conversation with her I could see the difference. She lacks Lucy's spark.'

'And what do you think she makes of you?'

If the question was meant to catch Nancy off guard, it

failed in its quest. Nancy merely shrugged and reached out to the tray to pour herself a coffee. 'I have no idea. And to be honest, Inspector Price, I don't particularly care. I suspect that Eva will be a five-minute wonder.' She put down the cafetiere and lifted the cream jug. 'Of course, I am delighted for Richard and David, if it amuses them to find another cousin, just as I was delighted to meet cousin Barbara. But cousins who live hundreds of miles away from the family will make little difference overall. We will know they are there if we need to call on them, but that need may never arise.' She sucked in a breath as she lifted her cup and saucer from the tray. 'I rather think that this weekend will go without a hitch, everyone will be polite to everyone else, and then Eva will go home to Scotland, only to re-emerge whenever there is a family event to be attended.'

'Or if there is a crisis.'

'Do you foresee a crisis, inspector?'

'I always foresee a crisis, Nancy. The prediction of crises isn't just in my job description, it's in my DNA.'

'And what crisis do you foresee on this occasion?'

'The fall-out from the murder of Geraldine Morton.'

'I see.' Nancy nodded sagely. 'Which brings us back to the matter of what you are doing here at Salvation Hall.' She settled back in her chair, the cup and saucer still in her hand. 'I have been told very little about what happened in Edinburgh, only that Eva's friend has been murdered and that a police investigation is underway. But if her friend was murdered in Edinburgh, why would that mean that something might happen to Eva here?'

So she knew about the murder, but not about the van. 'We don't necessarily think that she is at risk in any way. But the investigating officer in Edinburgh wasn't too happy about Eva leaving Edinburgh before the killer had been found. She only warmed to the idea when I volunteered to keep an eye on her key witness.'

'How very public-spirited of you.' Nancy laughed. 'And

who will keep an eye on things when the party is over this evening? Are you planning to spend the night on guard here? Because Richard hasn't asked me to prepare a room for you.'

'Now you're making fun of me.' Ennor picked up the chocolate biscuit, intending to take a bite, but it didn't reach his lips. He sat bolt upright. 'What the bloody hell was that?' The noise had been deafening, a resounding crack from somewhere outside the house. 'Was that a car backfiring?'

'It can't be.' Nancy started, and stretched forward to put her cup and saucer back on the tray. 'The estate gates are locked.' She tilted her head, listening, and as she did so a second, loud crack rent the air.

'Jesus.' Price hurled the biscuit at the coffee table and launched himself off the armchair and across the room towards the window. 'Where did that come from?'

'It sounded like it came from the terrace.'

\*

Nancy was already beside the library door when Price turned to look at her. She flung it open and passed through into the hallway without a backward glance.

Price followed her at speed as she crossed the hall and headed through an open doorway. 'Nancy, be careful.' He bounced off the doorframe as he lurched into the dining room behind her. 'You don't know what's out there.' He strode across the room towards the French windows, his pulse quickening. Somewhere to his right, in his field of peripheral vision, Kathryn and Richard were huddled near the fireplace, and he turned to look at them, his eyes wide. 'Stay there.' He put up a hand. 'Just stay there.'

Nancy was already beside the window and she turned around to look at him, her eyes filling with tears. 'There's someone lying on the terrace.' She grabbed at his arm, her fingers digging into his flesh. 'I can't see who it is.'

'Lying on the terrace? You mean on the ground?' He tried to break free of her grasp. 'Nancy, you have to let go of me. I need to go out there and help.' His mouth was dry, and his head was beginning to pound. 'It sounded like a gunshot.' He took hold of her fingers with his free hand and prized them away from his arm. 'I want you to stay here, with Kathryn and Richard.' Out of her clutches, he stepped through the open window and out onto the terrace. 'What the hell has happened? Has somebody been hurt?'

It took a moment for his eyes to adjust to the semi-darkness. In the glow of a quartet of decorative lanterns, he could just make out the outline of David and Marcus on their knees. They were only a few metres in front of him, their backs to the dining room windows, heads bowed over a dark form on the ground. 'David? What's happened?' He stepped forward and knelt beside them.

'She's been shot.' David's voice wavered. 'We'd just got up from the table to come back into the house.' He turned a pitiful, tear-stained face to look up at the inspector. 'There was nothing I could do.'

Price put a hand on his shoulder. 'Where did it hit her?' 'In the chest. And in the neck.' David could hardly speak. 'She had just stood up when the first shot was fired.' He turned his attention back to the woman lying prone on the ground. He was holding her fingers tightly in his right hand, and he reached out with his left to stroke her gently across the cheek. 'She didn't stand a chance.' His face crumpled with grief. 'My poor, darling girl. She just didn't stand a chance.'

## 22

Price stepped forward towards the glass-topped table, counting the surrounding chairs as he went. 'Three still standing, and one on the floor.' It had fallen as the bullet hit its mark. 'We heard two shots from inside the house and both of them hit her. David said she was already on her feet, preparing to come into the house. She grabbed onto the chair and took it with her as she fell.' He blinked against the morning sunlight, and looked down towards the ground, wincing at the sight of blood splattered erratically on the York stone paving. 'I want these slabs lifted and removed.'

Parkinson jolted to attention. 'Sir?'

'I want a full set of photographs of this scene in daylight, taken from every angle. And then I want these paving stones lifted and removed.'

'But we won't be able to tell anything from…'

'It's not for examination. I don't give a damn what happens to them when you've removed them. But the Lancefield family have been through enough without staring at Stella's blood every time they step out here.' Price was snapping, and he knew it. He turned on his heel and moved towards the edge of the terrace to look out over the lake, lifting a hand to point across the water and into the distance. 'I want every inch of this bloody garden combing for evidence. The shot could have come from anywhere. And I want to know how the hell the killer got into the grounds of Salvation Hall when all of the gates were locked.' If there had ever been a time in his life when he had felt more wretched, Ennor Price couldn't remember it. 'What the hell was the point of my being here, Tom?'

The sergeant shrugged and rested a hip against the table. 'Don't blame yourself, boss. No one could have seen this coming.'

'The evening was coming to a close. I thought everything had gone off without a hitch.'

'Whoever it was will have just scaled the perimeter wall.' Parkinson spoke quietly. 'And we did search last night, sir. Isn't it possible that we might have destroyed evidence in the process?'

Not so much possible, as probable. Price turned to look at his colleague. 'It's ironic, isn't it? She was still alive last night and the primary focus was to get her to hospital. If she'd died here on the terrace, instead of the hospital, we'd have called the pathologist out. We'd have looked more closely at where the bullet might have come from. How it had entered the body... the trajectory...'

'I doubt we would have learned much. As you say, it could have come from anywhere. Whoever did it must have had a long-range weapon and plenty of experience of shooting in the dark.'

Like a poacher.

Price hissed under his breath. He turned again and spoke over his shoulder. 'I'm going to question every member of the household again this morning. While I'm doing that, I want you to lean on the Smith family.'

'Sir, there's no evidence yet...'

'I don't need evidence to know who was responsible for this. You know as well as I do that there's only one person who knew the boundaries of this estate well enough to know where he could scale the wall. Only one person who has trespassed on this estate enough times to know where the terrace is, where he could get a decent shot from.'

'But he wouldn't have known that the family would be out on the terrace.'

'Becca Smith knows the family's habits. She's catered

for their dinner parties often enough to know that they were likely to come out here after the meal.' Price hesitated. 'Check his firearms licence. And his guns.'

'Doesn't Mick Smith have a licence too?'

'Then check them both. And we'll have Mick Smith in for further questioning. He must know something about this.' Price drew in a breath. 'Where are we with Zak Smith's phone records?'

'I'll chase them again this morning.'

'Not just his. I want phone records for the whole family.' Price glanced back across the lake. 'I suppose there's no point in asking how the search is going?'

'We've tried everywhere we can think of. His lock-up is deserted and the occupants of the adjacent units haven't seen him for days. His mother says he hasn't been home since Tuesday evening. Amber is denying any knowledge of his whereabouts, as is Becca. She's sticking to her story that he stayed with her on Wednesday evening, but she hasn't seen him since.'

'Then try again. He must be sleeping somewhere.' Price barked out the words, and then checked himself. 'Tom, I'm sorry.' He softened his tone. 'Can you do me a favour? Before you do anything else, can you call DCI Grant and give her an update?'

'Sure.' Parkinson sighed. 'I suppose it was always going to go too far, wasn't it? This thing between the Smiths and the Lancefields.' He shifted away from the table and folded his arms. 'Do you think he was aiming for Marcus or Eva when he fired?'

'I think he was aiming for Eva.' Price felt a stabbing at the back of his eyes. 'David said that Marcus and Eva had already got up from the table and that Stella was still sitting. Eva had turned round to speak to her, and her body would have been between Stella and the lake.' It didn't bear thinking about. 'And David called to her. He was encouraging her to go back into the house because it was raining, and as he did so the first shot rang out. It must have only missed Eva by inches.'

*

The events of the previous evening had left an indelible mark on Richard Lancefield. Frail at the best of times, grief had left his rheumy eyes sunk deeply within their sockets and his thin lips twitched with an involuntary tremor. 'I don't see how we can recover from this.' He was sitting next to Kathryn on the library sofa, and he tilted his head towards her. 'What kind of creature would commit such a crime?'

One without conscience. Or scruples. But there would be little point in stating the obvious. 'Who knows?' Kathryn let out a sigh. 'Some minds just cannot be fathomed.'

'But what do they gain? Revenge? Against an innocent victim? I could understand it had the target been Marcus, or even myself or David. But Stella?'

'The police think that the bullet was meant for Eva.'

Another innocent party. Richard put a hand up to his mouth and gnawed at a knuckle. 'My son has already lost his daughter, and now he has lost his wife. And I have no explanation for him.'

'I'm sure he doesn't expect an explanation from you. Just comfort. At least he had Marcus and Eva to support him at the hospital.'

'Do you know the worst of it, Kathryn? Yesterday evening was the first time since her marriage to David that I had actually taken the trouble to sit down and talk to Stella at length. For years, I simply dismissed her as a self-interested harpy, intent only on fulfilling her own self-seeking intentions. But as we waited for dinner to be served, she thanked me for standing in defence of Marcus. And although she chided me for suggesting that he move out to St Felix, she told me that she knew it was an opportunity for him to make a fresh start. And that, as he was rising to that opportunity, she was going to do the same. She was going to make an effort for David and Marcus and spend more time here, at Salvation Hall.' The old man turned to Kathryn. 'She had planned to speak to you today, I believe, about the family's heritage. She thought, perhaps, that it was time she learned a little more about it, instead of just standing in judgement on something she didn't fully understand.' His eyes grew suddenly moist. 'Which, to my shame, is what I did. I stood in judgement of her, without ever really taking the time and trouble to understand her.' He cleared his throat. 'She had even warmed to Eva, you know. Just when it seemed that we had finally turned a corner, and were beginning to put the misery of the past behind us...' His words trailed away and he blinked to subdue a tear.

'You know, Richard, that if there is anything at all that I can do, you only have to ask.'

'You are already doing it, Kathryn. Just as you did when Lucy and Philip died, and when Emma lost her life. You are here for us. And that is enough.' Richard nodded to himself. 'We will need your strength in the coming days. Marcus will have to delay his trip to St Felix until after his mother's funeral, and both he and David will need time to grieve their loss. We must reach out to cousin Barbara today and let her know what has happened. With a fair wind, she will come down from Liverpool to bolster our numbers, and although Eva has struck up a bond with David, I know that Barbara's wisdom will be the greater blessing.'

'Of course Marcus must stay here for the funeral, but it will be a disappointment for Nancy. She was so looking forward to seeing her family.'

'There will be no disappointment for Nancy. Because Nancy will still travel to St Felix.'

'But the family will need her. The household will still need to run while the police investigation is ongoing. And there is the funeral to arrange.'

'Nancy has become an unsettling influence. And she has never seen eye to eye with Stella. I do not think that Nancy will greatly miss the opportunity to pay her respects at the funeral. In fact, I think it would be pragmatic to ensure that Nancy is not present on the day.'

Kathryn frowned. 'I'll admit that Nancy and Stella didn't have the best of relationships. But it's the living, not the dead, that we have to pay heed to at a funeral. I've never seen Nancy show anything other than affection for David. Don't you think he might appreciate her support?'

'Have you forgotten that Nancy attempted to give Marcus a false alibi for the night of Lucy's and Philip's deaths and then, having set the poor boy's expectation, reneged on the agreement?'

'No, I haven't forgotten. But I did rather hope that it was all water under the bridge. Marcus doesn't seem to think it's an issue. After all, he did confess to killing Philip. In the end, Nancy's alibi was immaterial.'

'The alibi itself was immaterial, but the nature in which it was offered, only to be so cruelly snatched away again, was not.' Richard looked down at his fingers. 'I have often asked myself why Nancy would do something so cruel.'

'Is it cruel to tell the truth?'

'It can be, if one takes into account the motivation behind it.'

So the events of yesterday evening had made no difference. 'Has it occurred to you that now might be the time to acknowledge Nancy? At the end of the day, she is your flesh and blood. And not just your granddaughter, but David's niece. Has it occurred to you, Richard, that now might be the ideal time to let David know that he has a half-sister and a niece?'

'What *has* occurred to me is the importance of genuine love and affection, without question. Things which I know David will receive from Marcus, Barbara and Eva. And, I hope, from yourself.'

'You don't think Nancy can offer him genuine love and

affection?'

'It isn't that.' Richard ran his tongue around his thin lips. 'I don't think that she can do it without question.'

\*

Becca Smith had hammered hard enough on the door of Amber's cottage to wake the dead. But Amber, for her part, had been less enthusiastic in welcoming her arrival.

'It's Sunday, Becs. I was hoping for a lie-in.' She muttered under her breath as she led the visitor down the small, dark hallway into the kitchen. 'I've got a lunchtime shift today, and they're putting on a Sunday carvery.' She crossed the tiny kitchen to the sink, stretching out a hand to switch on the kettle as she went. 'What's all the drama about?'

Becca leaned against the doorframe. 'You haven't heard, then? About Stella Lancefield?'

'Well, as I haven't left the cottage, and you're my first visitor of the day, what do you think?' Amber pulled two mugs from a rack beside the sink. 'Anyway, what have the Lancefields got to do with me?'

'Apart from paying your wages at The Lancefield Arms?' Becca pouted. 'Someone took a pot-shot at Stella last night when she was out on the terrace at the hall.'

'She's been shot?' Amber spun round on her heel. 'Oh, Becs, that's awful. Is she going to be alright?'

'She's dead. They took her to the hospital last night, but they couldn't do anything for her. She died this morning.'

For a few seconds, neither girl spoke. And then Amber laughed. 'You really do go in for some fancy wishful thinking, don't you?' She picked up a jar of coffee from the kitchen counter and twisted off the lid. 'Who's been feeding you this nonsense?'

'It isn't nonsense. It's all over the village. Emily's sister-in-law is a nurse, she works in the A&E unit. She was on duty last night when they brought Stella in. Two gunshot wounds, she said, one in the neck and one in the chest.'

'But why on earth would anyone do that?' Amber turned to look at Becca. 'Poor Mr Lancefield must be devastated.'

'Mr Lancefield?'

'David, I'm talking about, not the old man. David's alright. If he hadn't been so kind in the past, Zak would be inside for harassment by now.' Amber frowned. 'I suppose this will be egg and milk to your brother. He has no love for the Lancefields, does he?' She spooned coffee into the mugs as she spoke. 'Where is the toerag now? Still camping out at your place?'

'No.' Becca blushed and ran her tongue slowly around her teeth. 'That's the other reason I came to see you this morning. There's something I need to tell you. About Zak.'

'Really?' Amber put the coffee jar back in its place and stretched out a hand towards a small, adjacent sugar bowl. 'Still two sugars in your coffee, Becs?'

The question went unanswered. Becca stepped into the kitchen and sat down on a small, pine chair beside the wall. 'It's important, Amber. It's about Wednesday night.'

'What your brother does, and when and where he does it, is nothing to do with me.' Amber dug a teaspoon into the sugar bowl. 'I'm just. Not. Interested.' She scooped a spoonful of sugar into one of the mugs. 'One or two?'

'I'm sorry that I lied to you. About where he was on Wednesday night.'

'You let me believe that he was with you.'

'I know. And I'm sorry.'

A spark of fury flashed in Amber's eyes. 'I'm your friend, Becca. I've been your friend since we were five years old and at school. And you still covered up for the lying scumbag.'

'I'm sorry, alright?' Becca's agitation was growing. 'Amber, I've had a visit from Tom Parkinson. Mick and Robin have done something stupid. Something really stupid.' She was struggling to find the words. 'Zak persuaded them to hire a van for him. He told them he needed it for a long journey, and asked them to hire it in Marcus Drake's name. He told Mick that it was a joke. And Mick went along with it. He hired the van from some place in Truro that doesn't ask too many questions, and Robin collected it early on Wednesday morning and drove it over to Penzance for Zak.'

'So what?'

'They found the van torched on Friday evening, in a layby just outside of Helston. The thing is, the police reckon that the same van was driven up to Scotland on Wednesday. It was seen leaving the centre of Edinburgh just after that friend of Eva McWhinney's was murdered.'

'Murdered? Oh, come on, Becs. Zak is stupid, but he's not that stupid. You can't think that was anything to do with him.'

'I don't, but the police do. They've had Mick in for questioning already, and he's admitted to hiring the van in Marcus's name for a laugh. But he's not going to hold his hand up to a murder he didn't commit. He's got Debbie and the kids to think about.'

The kettle came to the boil, punctuating the air with a click, but Amber didn't move. She was still facing the kitchen counter, her eyes turned down towards the mugs, her hands resting stiffly on the worktop. 'Does Mick think that Zak is responsible for that girl's death?'

'Mick doesn't know what to think. None of us do. We can't get hold of Zak to ask him. He's still not returning any of our calls.'

'Where was he on Wednesday, Becca?'

'I don't know. I only know he wasn't with me.' Becca sniffed. 'He told me that he was with some girl that he met at the Embassy Club, but he didn't tell me who she was or where she lived.'

Colour flared in Amber's cheeks. 'Then he needs to ask that girl to come forward and give him an alibi.'

'I know. But I think he's scared to do that. He doesn't know I've told you the truth, does he? And he doesn't want to lose you.'

'There's nothing there for him to be scared of, Becs.' Amber took the kettle from its stand and set about pouring water into the mugs. 'Your brother has already lost me. As far as I'm concerned, he can bring as many other women forward as he likes. It won't make any difference to me now.' She set the kettle back and picked up a teaspoon to stir the coffees. 'I suppose he was with the same girl last night? When Stella Lancefield was shot?'

'I've no idea.'

'Well, let's hope for his sake that he was. And let's hope that she's willing to come forward and speak up for him because he's had his last dodgy alibi from me.' Amber clattered the teaspoon down onto the draining board beside the sink. 'Because I'm telling you now, if there is no "other woman", and Zak Smith has blood on his hands, he needn't think that I'm going to be the idiot standing by him.'

# 23

Marcus looked exhausted. Newly returned to Salvation Hall, he was sitting at the kitchen table, his forearms resting on the edge, his eyes cast down towards his hands.

'Would you rather get some sleep? In the big scheme of things, it won't make much difference if we put this off for a couple of hours.' Price was trying to extend some sympathy, but it appeared to be falling on deaf ears. 'Marcus?'

Marcus lifted his head and tried to smile. 'Have you ever reached that point of utter exhaustion, when you know the thing you need the most is sleep, and at the same time you know that sleep is the last thing you'd be able to do? Well, that's where I am now, so we may as well get this over with.'

'Well, if you're sure.' The policeman pulled a small notebook from his pocket and flipped it open. 'Tell me again how you all came to be out on the terrace.'

'We'd finished dinner, and Nancy suggested that we might like to have a drink out on the terrace while she cleared the table and prepared some coffee. She'd already lit the patio heaters and put some blankets out there so that we wouldn't feel the cold. So, we carried our drinks out there and sat down at the table.'

'We?'

'David and my mother, Eva and myself.'

'Can you remember the time?'

'Not the exact time. But I think we were out there for about twenty minutes, and then Eva said she thought she felt rain, and that perhaps we should go back into the house.' Marcus nodded to himself. 'I think I stood up from the table first, and then Eva and David followed me. But Stella, my mother, was still in full flow, talking about taking more of an interest in the family's history. She was still sitting at the table.'

'And then the shot was fired?'

'Not quite. I think she had pushed her chair away from the table, and was beginning to stand.'

'And where exactly were the rest of you standing when that happened?'

'David and I were between the table and the drawing room window, and I think Eva was close to her chair. She was still in conversation with Stella and she stepped forward to say something, and then David called out to them both to hurry up because the rain was getting heavier.' Marcus was struggling with the memory. 'Eva leaned away, and began to turn towards the house just as the shot rang out.' He bent his head and rested it in his hands. 'If she hadn't stepped away, the bullet would have hit her.' He fought away a tear. 'The bullet would have hit her, and my mother would still be alive. Have you any idea how that feels, Inspector Price?'

'For you?' The inspector frowned, uncertain. 'Or for Eva?'

Marcus started. 'For me, of course. I don't know whether to be distraught that my mother died, or elated that Eva survived. I mean, I've only just met Eva. But I already know that losing her would be a loss that I wouldn't want to face.'

Was that some sort of admission? 'Have you considered how it must feel for Eva? Survivor guilt is a terrible thing to bear.'

'My mother's loss is going to be a terrible thing to bear. For all of us.' Marcus snuffled a laugh. 'Considering that in life she was so easy to despise.' He looked suddenly ashamed. 'She'd changed, you know, over these last few months. Mellowed, somehow. Even Richard had noticed.

And now she's gone.'

Price glanced down at his notebook. 'I was in the library with Nancy when the shots were fired. We thought the first one was a car backfiring, and then we realised that couldn't be possible. It was the second shot that brought us out onto the terrace. When I arrived, you and David were kneeling beside Stella. She was still alive at that point.'

'Yes, but she was barely breathing.'

'And then, just after I arrived, Eva knelt beside her and tried to stem the bleeding.'

'Yes, she was very brave about it all. I think it took a moment for the situation to sink in. That's why she hesitated. But once she realised that Stella had been shot, her instincts just seemed to kick in.'

'Did you have any thought, at the time, where the shots might have come from?'

'No. I had no sense that anyone was close by. I wondered if they had come from the other side of the lake.'

'And it didn't occur to you that you might all have been in danger?'

'Danger?' Marcus raised his eyes, surprised by the suggestion. 'In what way?'

'Well, Stella had been shot and the gunman was still out there. He might have fired again.'

'I didn't think about that. All I thought about was trying to save my mother.' Marcus narrowed his eyes. 'Is this down to the Smith family, Inspector Price?'

'It would be unprofessional of me to say yes without any evidence to back up the theory.'

'And unprofessional to say they were aiming for Eva? Inspector Price, was this an attempt to finish what was started in Edinburgh? Was my mother just in the wrong place at the wrong time, in the same way that Geraldine Morton was in the wrong place at the wrong time?'

If that, indeed, had been the case. 'I don't know.'

'But you suspect, don't you? And as long as the person

who did this is still out there, Eva is going to be at risk, isn't she?' He didn't wait for an answer. 'Well, whoever did that had better hope that you get to him before I do, if only to gain some protection. Because I've lost Lucy, I've lost my mother, and I've lost my reputation, all because of that damned Smith family. And now that I've found her, there is no way in hell that I'm going to lose Eva the same way.'

\*

'I was looking for Kathryn.' Eva gently closed the library door behind her. 'I hoped she might be in here.'

Nancy, seated at the desk, swivelled gently to and fro in the captain's chair. 'Kathryn has taken Samson for a walk down to the village. She said she wanted to clear her head.'

Eva crossed the room to the sofa. 'Then perhaps I could take the opportunity to talk to you?' She was carrying a small, stiff, leather bag and she dropped it gently beside the sofa before sitting down. 'I can't begin to describe how I feel about what happened here yesterday evening. One minute everything was going so well, everyone was happy and talking about the future, and the next, Stella was lying on the ground with a bullet wound in her chest.'

'Two bullet wounds, surely?' It was a cold correction. 'It was very lucky that you were on hand to try to help her. And very unfortunate that you weren't able to save her.' The starkest of understatements.

Eva frowned. 'Have I done something to offend you, Nancy? I can't help feeling that you're unhappy with me in some way. And yet we hardly know each other.'

Nancy bowed her head. 'You have done nothing to offend me, Eva. But I have never agreed with Richard's insistence on seeking out distant cousins to bolster the family. I always said that no good would come of it. It led to the deaths of Dennis Speed and Emma Needham, and now it has led to the deaths of your friend Geraldine and…' She paused, as if the reality of the situation had only just hit her. 'For pity's sake, it has led to Stella's death.'

'Has it? I thought that the Smith family's feud with the Lancefields was based on the fact that Marcus murdered Philip McKeith. That was nothing to do with Richard's search for distant cousins.'

'Perhaps. But the police believe that you were the intended target last night, don't they? Just as they believe you were the intended target when your friend was murdered in Edinburgh. Has it occurred to you that both Geraldine and Stella might be alive if you had rejected Richard's invitation to connect with the family?'

'That's an unspeakably cruel thing to say.'

'I don't mean to be cruel. It just seems to me to be a statement of fact.' Nancy swivelled again in the chair. 'Don't you think it would be safer all round if you were just to go back to Edinburgh and forget about the family? David and Marcus will need time and space to grieve.'

'But David and Marcus want me here. And so does Richard.'

'Richard is just being kind. And I think it would be kind of you to give the family the privacy it needs to come to terms with its loss.'

'I see.' Eva puffed out a breath to steady herself. And then she said, 'It's a pity that we're not on the same page, isn't it? I had hoped that we might be friends.'

A flicker of annoyance flashed across Nancy's face. 'I am not in need of friends, Eva. I have the family. And I have Kathryn.'

An angry silence settled between them, the impasse seeming impenetrable. And then Eva said, 'I came in search of Kathryn because I wanted to show her something that I brought with me from Edinburgh. It's been in the family for generations and it belonged to James

McWhinney.' She licked her lips. 'Kathryn tells me that you've been studying your own family history on the Woodlands Estate. So, perhaps it might also be of interest to you?'

Nancy jutted out her chin and then cast a reluctant glance at the bag beside Eva's feet. 'James McWhinney was a doctor, wasn't he? The one who experimented on the plantation's slaves?'

'I believe so. And it's not something to be proud of, I'll grant you that. But I suppose he was trying to advance the cause of medical science.' She turned her own eyes towards the bag. 'My family have always believed this to be his original doctor's bag. It's been handed down from generation to generation.'

'Then we find ourselves in rather a curious dynamic. Did you know that my ancestors were slaves on the Woodlands Estate?'

'Slaves?'

'Yes. My ancestors were amongst the original slave population on St Felix. They were brought there in the early eighteenth century.'

Eva frowned, an expression of genuine concern. But before she could reply, the library door swung open and a familiar voice cut in. 'Oh, here you both are.'

It was the most innocent of comments, but Nancy bristled at the words. 'Yes, here we *both* are.' She smiled as Kathryn stepped into the room, Samson trotting breezily at her heels. 'I came in here to do a little family research, to take my mind off the circus outside.' She gestured towards the window and the parade of uniformed officers occupying the terrace. 'Eva was looking for you, but only finding me she has taken the opportunity to tell me a little something about her infamous ancestor and his medical experiments. I don't think she had realised that I was descended from the original slaves on the family's plantation. So it probably hadn't occurred to her, until now, that her ancestor might have conducted some of his experiments on mine.'

\*

Becca Smith had been reluctant to let Tom Parkinson into her cottage. But Parkinson hadn't been in any mood to pussyfoot around.

'Where is he, Becca?' The sergeant strode down the small, dark hallway and pushed on the living room door. 'Where's Zak?'

She followed sullenly in his wake. 'You know he's not here. I don't know where he is.' She hesitated, standing behind him in the doorway. 'You're frightening Frankie.'

'No, I'm not.' The child was sprawled on the floor in front of him, unconcerned, her attention held by a grubby, plastic tea set. He turned on his heel to face her mother. 'When did you last see him?'

'I haven't seen him since Friday. And that's the truth.' She sniffed loudly. 'Look, I'm sorry for what happened to Stella Lancefield, but it's nothing to do with us.'

'Nothing to do with you, maybe. But plenty to do with Zak.'

'Do you have any evidence of that?'

'Not yet. But we will.' Parkinson folded his arms. 'He keeps his guns at your mother's house, doesn't he? I've got officers on their way over there as we speak. They'll be checking the guns at the house against his firearms licence.'

'They won't find anything.'

'That's kind of what we're expecting, Becca. We expect there to be a gun missing from the cabinet – the one that was used to shoot Stella.'

Becca's face grew pale and she stepped forward and around the policeman, bending down to pick up her daughter. 'Even if there is a gun missing, it doesn't prove anything.' The child, separated so unexpectedly from her toys, began to whimper. 'Zak won't be the only one to possess the type of gun that you're looking for.'

'Which is why we're also checking Mick's firearms licence and guns. And why we're bringing him into the station for further questioning.' Parkinson softened his tone. 'You do know this has gone too far now, don't you? Harassing the Lancefields is one thing, but murdering them?' He shook his head. 'You know, I understand that he's your brother, and I understand your loyalty. In a way, I can even admire it. But even you must see that this has to stop.' He let out a sigh. 'Look, Zak is suspected of committing two murders. If he's innocent, all he has to do is come forward and tell us. If he has nothing to hide, he can come forward with an alibi. And even if he's struggling for an alibi because he's been stupid enough to do the dirty on a decent girl like Amber, he can come forward and admit that, can't he? If nothing else, he can assist us with the enquiry. He can come clean about setting Mick and Robin up to hire the van. But running away? What does that say to you? Because I know what it says to me.'

Becca whimpered and hugged Frankie to her cheek. 'He wouldn't.'

'Wouldn't what? Wouldn't murder Stella Lancefield? Well, you might be right there, because we think he was aiming for someone else. We think he was aiming for David's cousin, Eva McWhinney. We think that he drove to Edinburgh on Wednesday to murder her, hoping to pin the murder on Marcus. But he killed the wrong girl. So when Eva came down here to Penwithen, he took his chance and tried again. And again, he hit the wrong target.'

Becca's face crumpled, and tears began to roll down her cheeks. 'You have no proof of that.'

'Don't I? Becca, he isn't just hurting the Lancefields, is he? He's hurting you. Look at the state you're in. Because you know I'm right. This is going to rebound on your whole family. The charges are racking up against Mick and Robin, aren't they? False representation for hiring the van in Drake's name, and arson for torching the van? And that's just for starters. But Zak doesn't care about them, does he?'

'You don't know it was them.'

'We know that they hired it because Mick has admitted it and they've been identified.' Parkinson took a step towards her. 'How is your mum going to feel, knowing that her son is a murderer on the run? Do you think Zak cares about how this is going to rebound on her? No one is going to escape the fallout from this. Not even you.'

'Me?' The suggestion jolted the weeping girl into motion. 'What the hell does this have to do with me?'

'Apart from the false alibi you gave him for Wednesday night?'

'I was trying to do the best thing for Amber.'

'By lying to a policeman about a murder suspect?' Parkinson toughened his tone. 'You lied to a policeman, and you gave him a motive.'

'A motive? What the hell are you talking about?'

'We know that Zak's always had an issue with the Lancefields. We know that he enjoyed every minute of the harassment that he meted out to Richard and David Lancefield before we put a stop to it. That was nothing to do with you, or with Philip's death. It was because he enjoyed taking a pop at the landed gentry. But the Lancefields forgave him for that. So why would he try to murder David Lancefield's cousin, not once, but twice? Unless someone put him up to it. Someone who still had an axe to grind against the Lancefields.'

'You're not pinning that on me.'

Parkinson leaned still closer towards her. 'Someone who might have been enraged that Marcus Drake had walked free from court, without having to serve a prison sentence.'

Becca squeezed her eyes shut. 'I'm not listening to you. This is nothing to do with me.'

'Isn't it?' The policeman coughed out a laugh. 'Have you seen Eva McWhinney, Becca? She's the spitting image of Lucy Lancefield. The same Lucy Lancefield that your Philip was having an affair with. The same Lucy Lancefield that was rubbing your nose in it every time she slept with your man.'

'I wouldn't know that, I've never seen her.'

'But you might have heard.' He nodded to himself. 'You know, whoever was aiming for her last night was looking for an opportunity, and knew that she might be on the terrace after dinner. We think that that someone tipped the killer off to that fact. Now, who would have known that the family liked to go out onto the terrace for a drink after dinner? Apart from the family themselves?' He narrowed his eyes. 'Maybe, someone who used to work for the Lancefields, and knew their habits?'

## 24

The car park just outside Marazion was almost empty.

Kathryn stepped out of the car and slammed the door shut. Ahead of her, Ennor was already making for the shoreline, hands thrust deep into his pockets, head down against the brisk, salty breeze that was blowing off the sea. She watched him, waiting until he reached the low wall that separated the car park from the beach, and then slowly made her way forward to join him. 'So this is where you and Tom come when you want to talk privately about a case?'

'Is there anything more anonymous than a car park?' He was staring out across the water to St Michael's Mount, the island in the bay. 'The coffee here is good and we can't be overheard by anyone who might care what we're talking about.' He fell silent again, and the question... *the* question... hung heavily in the air between them. And then he said, 'I blame myself, Kathryn.'

She slipped her arm into his. 'Then don't. It's not your fault that a killer was loose in the grounds last night. And it's not your fault that Stella was hit with a bullet that was meant for someone else.'

'But how do we know it wasn't meant for Stella?'

'Ennor, you were the one who said that Eva could have been the target when Geraldine was murdered.'

'I know. But I keep asking myself if there was a motive for Stella's death that I've missed. Whether there is a connection that I'm not seeing.'

'Because if Stella was the target, then Eva is no longer at risk until the killer is caught?'

'It's a possibility.' He laughed softly under his breath.

'At least I'm not as crazy as DCI Grant. She thought Eva was a suspect in Geraldine's murder.'

'You're kidding?' Kathryn shook her head with a smile. 'What motive would she have?'

'Ah, that was the problem. Grant couldn't come up with a motive.' He frowned. 'Not that I have much of a motive for Zak Smith to murder Eva. The best I can come up with is revenge. That he set out to murder Eva on behalf of his sister, hoping to cause more pain for the Lancefields and pin the blame on Marcus.'

'So there are no other suspects, and no other motives?'

'No. And now David's wife is dead. I can't…' The words caught in his throat. 'It was my idea, to encourage Eva to come to Penwithen. It was my idea, for God's sake, to use her to draw the Smith family out. What the hell was I thinking of?'

'You were thinking, quite rightly, that lightning doesn't strike in the same place twice. You suspected Zak of killing Geraldine, and that bringing Eva down to Salvation Hall would send a message that you were on to him. Perhaps you thought it would make him panic and show his hand in some way.' But instead, Zak Smith had shown just how much everyone had underestimated him. He wasn't just a bully. He was a dangerous killer. 'Are you absolutely convinced that he's responsible for what happened last night?'

'Who else could have known the layout of the grounds at Salvation Hall? Tom has a theory that Becca was behind it, that she told Zak the family often took a drink on the terrace after dinner.'

'It wasn't a given, though, was it? They might have stayed in the dining room, or taken their drinks in the drawing room?'

'Smith is an opportunist. If last night's plan hadn't come to fruition he would have bided his time and waited for the next opportunity. He might even have camped out in the grounds, just waiting for Eva to leave the house, to take a walk around the grounds, or down into the village.'

'Will you catch him, do you think?'

'We have to catch him, Kathryn. He's still out there. And Eva is still alive.' He hesitated, and then said, 'At the moment.'

'Do you honestly think Becca would go that far? Ask her brother to murder a member of the family?'

'I don't know. Nothing in this case makes any sense to me. I've never known a family endure so many deaths in such a short space of time. It's like they're cursed.'

Kathryn slid her hand down Ennor's arm and pushed it into the pocket of his coat, taking hold of his fingers. 'That's just what David said to me, the day Dennis Speed died. We'd just heard that Dennis had met with his death on his way to meet with us, and we were on our way back to Penzance on the train. And David asked me if I thought the family was cursed.'

'Because of their heritage?'

She shrugged. 'Is it because of their heritage, or because of their legacy?'

'Is there a difference?'

'Probably not. But if they are cursed, I don't believe it's anything to do with the way they made their money. This isn't some sort of divine retribution because they owned slaves, and traded in misery. Eva's family made their fortune because her distant ancestor built his medical reputation on experiments he conducted on slaves in the Caribbean. What the hell does that have to do with Zak Smith? Or Becca? This is to do with a different sort of misery. This is to do with broken hearts. With jealousy, and deceit and betrayal.'

'So maybe Becca *would* go this far?' Ennor thought about it, and then said, 'How is David?'

Kathryn took a deep breath of Cornish air. 'He's still in shock. I don't think Stella's death has really registered yet.' She turned her gaze along the shoreline. 'We all had mixed feelings about Stella, didn't we? Richard was infuriated by her, Marcus was ground down by her... Nancy almost despised her. But David saw something in her that the rest of us seemed to miss. He loved her very much.' Kathryn felt a swell of emotion rising in her gut. 'He didn't deserve this, Ennor. Neither of them did. Stella had her faults, but I believe she loved David as much as he loved her. I had the opportunity to see that when I stayed with them in Edinburgh. She was very concerned, you know, that his connection to Eva was going to hurt him in some way. And she didn't want him to be hurt.'

But, Kathryn mused, even Stella couldn't have foreseen that his determination to bring Eva into the family fold would cost him the love of his life.

\*

'I can't imagine you will lose any sleep over Stella's death.' David, slumped into the corner of the sofa, spoke without looking at his father. 'You didn't approve of her. And you certainly didn't want me to marry her.'

Dear God, was that his son thought of him? 'I will never deny that I did not think she was good for you. And it gives me no pleasure at all to admit that I have realised my mistake too late to make things right.' Richard dropped a hand to the side of his chair, where Samson was quietly dozing, and ruffled his fingers into the dog's coat to soothe himself. 'I saw with my own eyes yesterday evening that she made you happy.'

'She was going to support me, you know.' David's words came slowly. 'We were going to move back to Salvation Hall and manage the estate together. I thought that we were going to be a family: you, Stella and I, Marcus, Eva, cousin Barbara... a family, with Kathryn and Nancy to support us.'

There was nothing that Richard could say to make it better. In truth, he knew that David was at the beginning of what could be a long and lonely journey. Soon, the shock he was feeling at the brutal unexpectedness of Stella's untimely death would be joined by denial, and then both would step aside to make way for grief. He would rail against the unfairness of it all, buckle under the guilt of not being able to prevent her death, and then would come the anger. Anger at the killer for taking her life, at the police for failing to stop him, at the world for being a cruel and dangerous place. There would be depression, loneliness, emptiness, relief that Eva had been spared, and then more guilt that Eva being spared also meant that Stella had been lost. Peace and acceptance would be a long time in coming, and no one could hurry their journey.

Richard shifted awkwardly in his seat. 'We are a family, David. Marcus and I, Kathryn and Nancy, Barbara and Eva, we are all here for you. Inspector Price has given me his word that he will not rest until the person responsible for Stella's death is found, and I believe him.' Not least since the inspector had been unable to hide his own anger and grief when the promise had been made. 'I wondered if you would consider moving out of the hall for a day or two, to come and stay here with me at the Dower House.'

David scowled his bemusement. 'And why, pray, would I want to do that? Would it help you to salve your conscience in some way?'

'I am not aware that my conscience is in need of soothing.' The old man spoke quietly. 'I was simply offering you the opportunity to distance yourself a little from the main house while the police continue their investigation.' He sighed. 'Have you had anything to eat? I can ask Nancy to rustle something up for you?'

'I'm not hungry. I don't want anything to eat, and I don't want to move into the Dower House.' Impatience crackled through David's words. 'I came to ask what's been going on while I've been resting in my room. I can't find Marcus or Eva, Kathryn appears to have disappeared with Inspector Price, and Nancy is talking to me as if I were a child in need of a nursemaid.'

'Inspector Price has been here for most of the morning. He has spoken again to us all about the events of yesterday evening, to double-check the facts. I believe that he and Kathryn have driven over to Marazion, to take a break from the proceedings and talk in private.'

'And Marcus and Eva?'

'They've taken a taxi into Penzance. They both wanted to get away from Salvation Hall.' Richard laughed softly. 'Everyone seems to want to get away from the place today.' With the exception of himself. And possibly Nancy. 'I know it will be small consolation to you, my boy, but Inspector Price has informed me that Stella will be returned to us very quickly so that we can begin preparations for her funeral.'

David flinched. 'I can't think about that now.'

'I'm afraid you must. Unless you would prefer me to take care of all the arrangements?'

His son ignored the question. 'Was it wise for Eva to go into Penzance? Surely she should have stayed here at Salvation Hall, where it's safe.'

It was not for Richard to remind him that being at Salvation Hall had hardly proven safe for Stella. 'She has been advised against walking in the grounds or walking into the village. But it was deemed safe for her to take a taxi directly to The Zoological Hotel. The police are making every effort to track Zak Smith down. He's unlikely to break cover in Penzance, where he could be seen and recognised.'

The explanation appeared to reassure David. Or perhaps in his grief and confusion, he didn't fully comprehend. He turned in his seat to face his father, his grey eyes heavy with the burden of grief. 'If you genuinely want to do something to help me, there is something I would ask of you.'

'Name it, my boy.'

'You can promise me that this is the end of it. That there will be no more talk of digging up long-lost cousins.

We are a blight on the world. And I cannot bear any more loss.' He leaned forward, out of the chair, his pale face drawn and anxious. 'I cannot imagine that Eva is going to want to stay with the family now, can you? Since forging a connection with us, she has narrowly avoided death on two separate occasions, at two locations hundreds of miles apart. I am frankly astonished that she hasn't just packed her bags and headed straight for the airport.'

'She has postponed her return flight indefinitely and intends to stay at Salvation Hall for as long as you need her. She has told me that she wishes to be here to support you. And Marcus will be here too. I have asked Nancy to cancel his flight to St Felix. Apart from anything else, we are all witnesses to last night's events, and Inspector Price needs us here until he has found his man and charges have been brought.'

A look of unmistakable relief crossed David Lancefield's face. 'Eva will stay here?'

'Certainly for the next few days.' Richard's sigh was deeper this time. 'But I hear your request, David. And I give you my word. I will make no further attempt to reach out to anyone who might be vaguely related to us. I do not think that my plans were misguided. But I can see that they have set in motion the most unbearable series of events. And it must stop.' He nodded to himself. 'We have Eva, Marcus and Barbara. And we must learn to be content with that.'

\*

The atmosphere in the restaurant at The Zoological Hotel was subdued for a Sunday lunchtime.

'The sea bass is always very good. And so is the pork loin.' Marcus ran his eyes down the menu as he spoke. 'Is it my imagination, or is everyone looking at us?'

'It's your imagination.' Eva stretched out a hand to touch his arm. 'No one knows who we are, or what we're doing here. They're all far too busy with their lunches to be interested in us.' She lifted her head to glance around the room. 'Is this really where you worked?'

'Yes. I worked as Ian's business development manager. It's a pity that he's gone over to Helston, I would have liked you to meet him.' Marcus accepted the subtle change of subject with good grace. 'But there will be another opportunity, I'm sure.' He put the menu down on the table. 'And of course, this is where Kathryn usually stays when she's in Cornwall. Richard has tried to persuade her to move into the hall, but she insists on staying here. She claims it's to maintain a professional boundary, but we all know it gives her more opportunity to socialise with DCI Price when he's off duty.'

'Are they that close?'

'I suspect not as close as they would like to be.' Marcus gave a wry smile. 'And I guess that's partly my fault. Kathryn is very loyal to the family, and DCI Price has spent the last few months building a case against me. Still, we seem to have navigated our way out of that. He doesn't seem to bear a grudge that I walked free. Which is just as well, now that he's going to have to track down whoever killed my mother.'

Eva frowned. 'I am so very sorry about Stella, Marcus. I didn't have chance to get to know her well, but I think that she and I could have been good friends.'

'It sounds odd to hear someone say that. I can't say that I ever had a good relationship with her. She wasn't much of a mother when I was young, and then later…' Marcus looked suddenly younger than his years. 'She was demanding, critical and controlling. And yet she was so supportive while I was awaiting trial. Like a different person.'

'Perhaps it was the thought of losing you to a prison sentence. Maybe she woke up and realised how lucky she was to have you.'

'And now she isn't here for me to ask. Any opportunity

to start again, to get to know her, has gone. I'm on my own.'

'You're not alone. You have a family and friends around you. Not just David and Richard, but Kathryn and Nancy.'

'Nancy?' Now there was a thought. 'And where would you put Nancy? Family or friend?'

Eva frowned and lifted her hand away from his arm. 'I don't know. I can't quite make up my mind.' She picked up a menu from the table and examined it. 'Where does Nancy think that she fits in?'

'If only we knew. She's always very possessive of Richard. She was the same when Lucy was alive.'

'Were she and Lucy friends?'

'On the surface, yes. They always seemed to be. But there's a very deep side to Nancy. She and my mother hated each other.' He pursed his lips. 'She'll be glad that Stella's gone.'

'And not too happy that I've arrived?'

'Why would you ask that?' Marcus leaned across the table. 'Has Nancy said something to upset you?'

'It depends what you mean by *something*. I tried to strike up a conversation with her this morning, and she made it pretty clear that she had very little interest in meeting me halfway.'

That sounded like Nancy. 'She won't be pleased that our trip to St Felix has been cancelled either. She was looking forward to seeing her family.'

'Has it been cancelled, or just postponed until after Stella's funeral?'

'I don't know, Eva. I can't really think about anything beyond the fact that she's gone. There's a funeral to arrange, and David to support.' He bowed his head. 'Poor David. He was utterly devoted to her. I don't know what he's going to do without her. Apart from the obvious grief, her passing throws all our plans for the estates into disarray.' He looked up at Eva. 'I suppose I'm going to have to take more control in this situation than I'm used to. Richard isn't getting any younger, and David needs time to grieve. I'm sure Kathryn will help out, and I haven't met Barbara yet but if what I've heard is true, she will rally to the cause.'

'And there's always me.'

Marcus felt a lump begin to form in his throat. 'I hardly dared to ask.'

'Well, I'm sure that's something we can work on.' Eva gave a coy smile. 'I'll stay here for as long as I can.' She placed her menu back down on the table and leaned towards him. 'Richard has offered me a job on the estate. Any job I like. I can create my own role if I wish. But I don't want to give up my career, and I don't want to give up my home. I need to give some thought to how I can keep Hemlock Row, keep my post at the infirmary, and still give support to the family. After all, cousin Barbara seems to manage it. So why can't I?'

'No reason that I can think of.' Eva's hand was resting on the table and Marcus took hold of it. He would hold his counsel for now, but he already knew that the time would come when he'd want to ask Eva McWhinney if there was anything that would tempt her to give up her career and the house at Hemlock Row.

Because if there was, he would move heaven and earth to deliver it.

## 25

'Well, you got a result. Although perhaps not the one any of us would have expected.'

Or wanted. Price swivelled gently on his office chair as he contemplated Alyson Grant's dry and painfully accurate observation. 'I'm sorry I wasn't able to call you earlier. Under the circumstances, I thought it better to focus my attention on the family.' He hoped that she wasn't the sort to be smug. 'Was Sergeant Parkinson able to answer your questions?'

'Not exactly, but only because I suspect that neither of you have the answers at this stage.' She didn't exactly sound sympathetic at the end of the phone line. 'Or am I wrong about that?'

'I suppose that depends on the questions.' Price steadied his chair and rested his elbows on the desk. 'We've made some progress with the van. We've had confirmation that a man matching Zak Smith's description called into a pub in Helston on Friday evening, just a quarter of a mile from where the van was discovered. He ordered a pint, stood at the bar to drink it, and then left without speaking to anyone other than the barmaid. No one saw where he went, but we're assuming he made his way into town to take a taxi back to Penzance. As soon as we've validated that assumption, I'll let you know.'

'But you're no nearer to picking him up?'

Did it sound like it? 'We have his mobile phone records now, at least up to and including Friday night. Early on Wednesday morning, he made a call to a so-far unidentified mobile number, and he called the same number again at eleven thirty that night.'

'Taking instructions in the morning, and reporting back after killing Geraldine?'

'It could be a working hypothesis. The same number made an incoming call to him late on Thursday afternoon, and then he seems to go into panic mode. There was no activity between the numbers for the rest of the day, and then on Friday, Smith made multiple calls to it, none of them answered.'

'The penny had dropped that he'd murdered the wrong girl?'

'Could be.' Price drew in a breath.

'And that's where the phone records stop?'

'So far. We're waiting for yesterday's data, and in the meantime, I have an officer working to identify the number he was calling.' He paused, and then added, 'And before you ask, it doesn't appear to be registered to any of the Smith family, or the Lancefield family, or Marcus Drake.' He couldn't help wondering if Grant was wondering what he was wondering – that the whole case could hinge on just who was behind that unidentified mobile phone. That the individual on the other side of those calls to and from Zak Smith was the mind behind the murders of Geraldine Morton and Stella Drake Lancefield. Or worse still, the individual who wanted the death of Eva McWhinney, and who wouldn't stop directing Zak Smith to kill until that end had been achieved?

'So, as things stand, your proposed suspect for the murder that took place on my patch is still on the loose. He appears to have taken another crack at Eva McWhinney, within the grounds of Salvation Hall – a location, I might add, that you assured me was one hundred per cent safe – and accidentally murdered another member of the Lancefield family.' Grant didn't sound disparaging, so much as incredulous. 'And he managed to do that right under your nose?'

Price felt his heart sink. 'You can't berate me any more than I've berated myself.'

'For pity's sake, man.' She exhaled a loud breath down the phone line. 'I'm not blaming you. You already know that I set off on this investigation thinking that Eva was a suspect, not a victim. Although I had no evidence to back that up.' She was silent for a moment, and then she asked, 'Where is Eva now?'

'I believe she's in Penzance, having lunch with Marcus Drake.'

'She's roaming around the streets, and Zak Smith is still on the loose? Didn't you advise her to stay at Salvation Hall?'

'You said it yourself. It didn't stop him taking a pot-shot at her last night.' Price leaned back in his seat. 'I advised her this morning to return to Edinburgh, but she wants to stay with the family. And I can't force her to go. She's a grown woman. She tells me she's planning to stay until after Stella's funeral. Unless you want to have a word? Maybe you could persuade her to see sense.'

Grant thought about it. And then she said, 'Maybe I should come down there instead. We've nothing in the way of leads up here, and the original investigation was mine. Would that be a problem for you?'

'No, but it might be a problem for you.' There was no easy way to explain. 'This hasn't exactly been my finest hour. I should have made a better job of assessing the risk.'

'Is that you talking, or has someone else made the suggestion?'

'Let's just say that my commanding officer has made his feelings known.' And that was putting it mildly. 'I need a result, DCI Grant. A result that will justify my actions.' As if anything could. Price tapped his fingers on the desk. 'Can you give me another twenty-four hours? The chances are, if I don't have Smith in custody by then, it will be out of my hands anyway.'

\*

Kathryn returned to Salvation Hall to find the library already occupied. 'I didn't know anyone was in here.' She dropped her bag onto the sofa. 'Were you looking for me?'

'No, I was just taking the opportunity to catch up with my family's history.' Nancy, reclining contentedly in the captain's chair, swivelled the seat gently to the left to smile at her and showed no inclination to move. 'Everyone else in the family seems to find the pursuit useful as a distraction when chaos rages all around, so I thought I would try it for myself. Anyway…' She arched a perfectly-groomed eyebrow. 'We have been making such good progress, I don't want to lose momentum.' She waved a hand towards a stiff, wooden chair beside the desk. 'Won't you join me, Kathryn? I'm trying to pursue a particular line of enquiry, and I would welcome your opinion.'

Kathryn felt her cheeks flush pink. She could lay no claim to the library; however much time she spent alone there, poring over the family's documents, she was still only a visitor to the house. But the captain's chair, presented to her by Richard as a gift, she considered to be her own. And while Richard and David and anyone else in the household, Nancy included, often used the thing when Kathryn wasn't there, good manners had always led them to relinquish it whenever she returned to the room.

So, what sort of a game was this? She narrowed her eyes to look at Nancy's face and saw an unmistakable flicker of mischief in Nancy's own cool, dark eyes. And then she smiled. 'Of course, Nancy. Anything I can do to help you.' She sat down on the wooden chair and rested an elbow on the desk. 'Which line of enquiry is this?'

'We have managed to construct my direct line of descent back to Gainsborough Woodlands, an enslaved carpenter on the estate who was born in 1805.' There was a document on the desk in front of her, a roughly-drawn sketch of her family tree, and she traced a finger across it. 'But we haven't yet established his parentage.' She tilted a sly eye in Kathryn's direction. 'And it occurred to me that his parents would have been alive when Eva's ancestor James McWhinney conducted his experiments on the slaves at Woodlands.'

Ah, so that was the game. 'Where is this leading, Nancy?'

'Where is it leading?' Nancy shrugged. 'I would like to know if Eva's ancestor conducted his experiments on my own family. But I have no evidence. I thought, perhaps, you could help me to find some?'

'And what do you think that would achieve?' Kathryn placed a hand on Nancy's arm. 'Nancy, we can't change the past. What James McWhinney did was unspeakably cruel. He put the pursuit of medical science ahead of the well-being of those people he was paid to care for. But his wasn't the only crime. What about the Lancefields' crimes?'

'I thought the rift between the two lines of the family came about because Benedict Lancefield forbade him to carry out those experiments? He tried to protect his people.'

'He didn't try to protect his people. He tried to protect his property.' Kathryn made no attempt to hide her irritation. 'It appears to me, Nancy, that it serves your purpose to ignore the fact that the family owned slaves because you consider yourself to be a part of that family. Just as it serves your purpose to find fault with Eva's line because you are trying to find fault with Eva herself.' She drew back her hand. 'And in the big scheme of things, what the hell does it all matter? If you have to go looking for a reason to throw rocks at Eva, don't you think that it should wait until after Stella's funeral?'

'To be frank, I am not sure what to think any more. But I do not have to "find fault with Eva", as you put it, when it is clear that Eva is the problem. Like everyone else, I believe that Becca's family are responsible for Stella's death. But it is Eva who is drawing them here. If only she would just go back to Scotland, we might finally have some peace.' Nancy turned her head away and spoke without looking at Kathryn. 'I just want all this nonsense to stop. Richard is an old man. And he doesn't deserve what is happening.' She lifted the document from the desk. 'We were happy here until Richard decided to pursue the wider family. It is a folly which has brought him, and the rest of us, nothing but misery.' She wafted the paper towards Kathryn. 'He shows very little interest in this, you know. Very little interest in *my* family tree.'

Wrong on both counts. At least, in Kathryn's opinion. 'You seem to forget that the unhappiness began when Lucy and Philip died, and that was before my work on the family connections began. And as for your family's history, I have spoken to Richard about it myself. He is incredibly interested in it. He shares your belief that the Woodlands Plantation has one history, belonging to all of its people. But in the last few months, he has lost his friend, his granddaughter, a distant cousin, and now his daughter-in-law.' She ventured a cynical laugh. 'Surely even you can see that "history, for the sake of history" has to take a back seat for the moment?'

'You think I am wrong?'

'I think that you're being unreasonable. And it isn't like you.'

Nancy considered the reprimand. And then she bowed her head. 'You are right, of course, Kathryn. And if I have disappointed you, then I apologise.' She dropped the paper she was holding onto the desk. 'But you are not alone in being disappointed.' She rested her hands in her lap. 'I understand that Marcus must stay here at Penwithen until after Stella is buried. But I don't understand why I am still to go to St Felix. I feel that I am being banished.'

'That's not how I understand the situation. I

understood that Richard was sending you in Marcus's place. He is trusting you to be his representative on the island until Marcus is ready.'

'But that could be weeks. Perhaps even months.' Nancy pouted. 'And then just as I get used to the role, I'll be surplus to requirements.'

'Nancy, you will never be surplus to requirements.'

'Marcus is not even a true member of the family. He is only David's stepson.' Nancy tilted her head. 'Perhaps you could speak to Richard, and ask him to let me stay until after the funeral? He would listen to you.' She nodded. 'I want to be present at Stella's funeral. As a part of the family.'

To be present at Stella's funeral? To take part in the obsequies of a woman that she almost despised? 'Were you planning to make your peace with Stella's memory?'

Nancy winced and turned a questioning eye in Kathryn's direction. 'My peace? Perhaps. Although my main intention was to support David and Marcus in their loss.' She arched her neck. 'Now it would appear that Eva will take my place.'

'Nancy, are you jealous of Eva?'

'Good heavens, no. I'm not jealous of the woman, I just don't trust her. She is using her resemblance to Lucy to beguile the family.' Nancy narrowed her eyes. 'Have you also been taken in by her?'

'It's not a question of being "taken in", as you put it. I happen to like Eva. And I think she will be good for the family.'

'So I cannot speak freely with you. I cannot trust you?'

'You can always trust me to do and say what I believe to be the right thing.'

It was the only answer that Nancy was going to get.

\*

Amber Kimbrall spread the butter slowly to the edge of

the bread. 'You ought to have something hot to eat.' She put down the knife and carefully peeled a slice of freshly-cooked ham from the paper parcel on the counter, dropping it onto the bread as she spoke. ' A sandwich isn't enough.'

'I just need to sleep, lover. I need a shower and a sleep. And then I'll be on my way.' Behind her, at the kitchen table, Zak was watching her intently. He leaned back, pushing his chair up onto its back legs. 'I knew you would come through for me when the chips were down.'

'I'm feeding you, not coming through for you.' She sliced angrily through the sandwich with a bread knife and spun on her heel to look at him. 'Becs said they want to question you about that van.'

'Stay out of it, Amber.'

'How can I stay out of it? You're in my cottage, sitting in my kitchen. You're waiting for my food. And then you'll be showering in my bathroom and sleeping in my bed.' Her mouth was dry as she spoke. 'Why the bloody hell should I stay out of it?' She clattered the plate bearing the sandwich down onto the table in front of him. 'Now, tell me about the van.'

'I was trying to set Marcus Drake up. The bastard deserves to be in prison for what he did to Becs and little Frankie.'

'So, you hired a van just to torch it, for him to take the blame?'

'Since when did you care about Marcus Drake?'

'I don't care about him. But I care about you.' Was that even true anymore? Did she care? 'You torched the van.'

'Yes, I torched the van. Alright?'

'And then you hid like a coward, and let Mick and Robin take the blame. You do realise that they're going to be charged with false representation and arson?'

'It's not that simple.'

'Well, it never is with you, is it?' She pulled a chair away from the table and sat down on it. 'Where were you on

Wednesday night?'

'I can't tell you.'

'Becs reckons you were up in Edinburgh, trying to frame Marcus Drake for something a bit bigger than torching a van.'

'Becs doesn't know what she's talking about.' He looked away, avoiding her gaze. 'I was with a girl I met at the Embassy Club, alright? I haven't come forward because I knew how it would make you feel if I said where I really was.'

'So you went on the run to save my feelings?' How dare he? How dare he make it her fault? 'Where have you been sleeping?'

'I spent Thursday night in the van, and last night on a mate's sofa.'

'Which mate?'

'What the hell does it matter? I'm here now, Amber.' He turned back to her and stretched out a hand to take hold of her arm. 'I was made up when I got your text. I know I screwed up, lover. I won't do it again, I promise.'

'And the girl?' She looked down at his hand. 'The one you spent Wednesday night with?'

'She's history.'

'She can't be, though, can she? She has to come forward and back you up. The police aren't just going to take your word for it. About Wednesday.' She twisted her arm, pulling it free of his grasp. 'Or last night.'

'Last night?'

She arched her neck and forced a smile. 'Never mind. Finish your sandwich, and then you can go for a shower and get some sleep.'

'Amber...' He began to stammer, his anxiety growing. 'If I can't find that girl I spent the night with on Wednesday...'

'Never mind her now.'

'But you're right. If I can't find her, I won't have an alibi. And I need an alibi, don't I?'

'You need to rest.' Amber pushed herself up from the chair. 'I'll put the kettle on and make a coffee, you can take it up with you.'

Back at the kitchen counter, she took the kettle from its stand and pulled off the lid. She had to keep it together, had to stay calm until he had finished the sandwich and gone upstairs to shower. And then what? She stepped sideways to the kitchen sink, holding the kettle under the tap and flicking the lever tap down with a trembling finger.

Then she would need to make a phone call.

# 26

'David and Marcus have gone into Penzance to speak to the funeral director.' Richard, wrapped up warmly against the continuing February chill, was just on his way out of the front door. 'Perhaps I can help you, Inspector Price?'

Price, just a few feet away, bowed his head slightly. 'I wanted to give David an update on our investigation.' He shuffled his feet like a nervous schoolboy. 'I haven't had the opportunity to speak to him since yesterday evening.'

The old man nodded to himself. 'I would expect nothing less of you.' He stepped forward. 'Samson and I were just about to take our afternoon walk, and this afternoon we are confining ourselves to the grounds. Perhaps you would like to join us?' He stretched a hand out behind him, snapping his fingers, and the ever-obedient Samson set off at a pace along the front of the house, before disappearing through the archway in the hedge. 'He doesn't need to be told twice. Much like myself.' Richard chuckled to himself. 'It takes us around twenty minutes to circumnavigate the lake, if you have the time.'

Ennor nodded and stuffed his hands into the pockets of his overcoat. 'I have as much time as it will take.' He followed Richard through the archway and down the short run of steps that led to the path around the lake. 'There have been a couple of developments this afternoon. As you might be aware, Zak Smith claims to live with his mother in a house out on the Newlyn Road.' Not that he spent much time there. 'That house is where he keeps his gun collection.'

'Licenced, and suitably locked up, one hopes?'

'Indeed. That's how we know there is a gun missing from the cabinet.' Ennor drew in a breath. 'The missing gun uses the same ammunition as the bullet that hit Stella yesterday evening.' He blew the breath out again. 'There is no doubt, now, in my mind who fired that shot.'

'Until now, you suspected but lacked the evidence to back up your theory?'

'Yes. Of course, it's still circumstantial until we can prove that it was Zak Smith's gun, and not a similar make and model belonging to a third party. But on the balance of probabilities...'

'I understand.' They were beside the edge of the lake now, the waterlily-laden waters gently rippling to their right and the wide, York stone terrace where Stella met her death to their left. 'You said there had been two developments?'

'Yes. We believe that we've identified a mobile phone that could be critical to the enquiry.'

'A mobile phone?' Richard stopped abruptly. 'You suspect that he had an accomplice?'

'We believe that Smith set off for Edinburgh sometime on Wednesday morning. In examining his mobile phone records, we noted a number that called him early that morning. He made an outgoing call to that same number on Wednesday night, just after the time we believe Geraldine Morton was murdered.'

'And how is that relevant to Stella's death?'

'The same number called him on Saturday morning, and he returned the call on Saturday evening, just after Stella was shot.'

'Was the call answered?'

'No.' Price turned his head to gaze out over the lake. 'He made repeated calls to that number all through Saturday night. None of them were answered.' He glanced back over his shoulder. 'We think that phone is what we call a "burner phone" – a pay-as-you-go mobile phone, not registered to any individual.' Even now, it seemed ludicrous to Price that such a device was still possible within the law, given how many unlawful uses it might have. 'The service provider for the SIM card in that phone has confirmed that it was purchased two weeks ago, and loaded up front with fifty pounds of airtime credit. But they can't yet tell us where it was purchased. That's going to take some time to trace.'

'Are we talking days?'

'Possibly weeks.'

'Ah.' Richard set off again down the lakeside path. 'And if it can't be traced?'

'That's not an outcome I'm considering.' Price pulled his eyes away from the lake, and stepped forward to follow Richard. 'We do know that the phone is pinging from a mast in the Penzance and Penwithen area. So we think it's in the possession of someone local. Becca perhaps, or another member of the Smith family.' There were other possibilities, but Price didn't want to share them just yet. 'We have tried the old-fashioned way of trying to find the phone by calling the number. Of course, no one answers.'

'Is it possible, Inspector Price, that the phone could have been purchased in Edinburgh?'

Trust the old man to be ahead of him. 'Yes, that's possible. And the calls were all made after Marcus had returned to Cornwall. But I would struggle to understand why he would go to such astonishing lengths to frame himself for a murder that he didn't commit.'

'Indeed.' They had reached the length of the lake now, the point where the path curved around towards the shrubbery. 'So, where will your investigation head next?'

'The investigation hinges on two things: finding Zak Smith and identifying the individual using that burner phone. Finding Smith will bring us the fastest result, but it's like looking for a needle in a haystack. And we don't have much time.' Price slowed his pace. 'And I have to advise you that there is a slim possibility of my being removed from the case.' More than a slim possibility, and he knew he didn't have to explain the reason why.

But Richard Lancefield merely stopped in his tracks. 'I will not hear of it.' He turned to look at the policeman. 'Inspector Price, I have the utmost confidence in your ability to bring my daughter-in-law's killer to justice. If there is anything I can do to bring my influence to bear with your superiors, you have only to say the word.'

*

'I was looking for Kathryn. ' Eva hesitated in the library's doorway. 'I hope I haven't disturbed you.'

'Of course not, Eva.' Nancy, still firmly entrenched in the captain's chair, beckoned for the incomer to join her. 'I was actually about to come and look for you. Kathryn has gone out to the Dower House to look for Richard, but she and I have spoken at length this afternoon, and I believe that I owe you an apology.'

'Not at all.' Eva closed the door behind her and crossed to the desk. 'I know these last few days must have been difficult for you.' She sat down on the hard, wooden chair beside the desk. 'And I haven't exactly helped by making an appearance.'

Nancy bowed her head. 'The fault is on my side. You are right that there has been a lot of disruption, but I've been in this household long enough to know that disruption just comes with the territory.' She swivelled gently in the captain's chair. 'I should be able to handle it better, but sometimes I'm afraid it all gets a little too much. We have had the trial against Marcus hanging over us since last September, and all the unpleasantness with Becca and her family. Not to mention the fallout from the murders that took place when I was last out in St Felix.'

'Dennis and Emma?'

'Yes. I was visiting my family when all of that happened. I didn't even get to meet them. By the time I returned, Dennis and Emma were already buried and Jason was on remand awaiting his trial.' Nancy smiled. 'Of course, there was good news. We were all so relieved when we learned that Marcus was to walk free.' She wrinkled her nose. 'And delighted to see him when he came home. But that happiness has been short-lived because now we've lost Stella. Just when it looked as though the family was about to find a little happiness again. Richard had such plans for Marcus.'

'And plans for you?' Eva rested her hands in her lap. 'You were supposed to be taking him out to St Felix, weren't you?'

Nancy's smile stiffened. 'Playing nursemaid to Marcus was only a small part of my duties. As it happens, I will still be travelling to St Felix tomorrow, but now I will be staying a little longer. At least until Marcus comes out to join me.' There was a smug tone to her words. 'I will be taking on his duties in St Felix until he is ready to pick up the reins. And then I'll return to Salvation Hall to resume my post as Richard's secretary.'

It almost sounded like a warning. 'How long have you been Richard's secretary, Nancy?'

'Almost ten years. I came just after my eighteenth birthday.'

'And your family have always lived on the Woodlands Estate?'

'Always.' Nancy spoke the word softly. 'My family's history is irrevocably interwoven with that of the Lancefields.' She laughed. 'There is no need to look shocked, Eva. If you had ever visited St Felix, you would understand.'

'But your family were enslaved by Richard's.'

'I know. But that was many centuries ago.' Nancy nudged Eva's arm. 'Does it look to you as though Richard beats me soundly every night? As if he locked me in my room to prevent me from running away?'

If Nancy's suggestions were meant to be a joke, they fell far short of the mark with Eva. 'I didn't mean to offend you, Nancy. I'm afraid I don't know a great deal about it.'

'You haven't offended me. I don't believe in taking offence. And your ignorance on the subject is only to be expected. Most people are ignorant on the subject unless they have first-hand experience of it. It's not something that you can grasp by reading a book. Books are written by people with opinions. But I believe that you will only learn about this family by spending time with us. Just as you will only learn about the Woodlands Estate by visiting it.' She softened her tone. 'Do you think Richard will ever invite you to visit St Felix?'

'I don't know. But I hope so. I would like to learn more about it.'

'There is a great deal to learn.' Nancy's smile had become immovable. 'Perhaps I can help you with some basic facts.' She pulled up the right-hand sleeve of her cardigan to reveal a thick, gold chain, lifting her wrist for Eva to see. 'My grandmother gave me this chain for my eighteenth birthday. Do you see the charm that hangs from it? The seahorse is one of the island's national emblems.' She slipped the cardigan off her shoulder. 'Along with the orchid.' She leaned the shoulder towards Eva. See, I have it tattooed. A seahorse, interwoven with an orchid.' She waited for Eva to examine it, and then added, 'The family used this emblem on their branding irons, to show which slaves belonged to them.'

Eva shuddered and shrank back. And then she prodded the tattoo with a gentle finger. 'Nancy, I think you're playing with me. You're trying to shock me. And it isn't going to work.'

Nancy took hold of Eva's finger. 'And now you're getting the measure of me.' She laughed. 'I wonder, would you come with me for a walk down to the village? We could call in at The Lancefield Arms and have a drink to cement our new understanding. Wipe the slate clean, and begin again as friends.'

'I'd love to, but Inspector Price said that I shouldn't leave the house again until he gave me the all-clear.'

'Oh, nonsense. You can't stay cooped up here in the house forever. It's like being under house arrest.' Nancy pushed the captain's chair away from the desk and rose to her feet. 'I think we should ask Kathryn what she thinks. I always think that Kathryn is the voice of reason.' She frowned down at Eva. 'Will you come with me if Kathryn thinks it is safe?'

\*

Tom Parkinson's call had come through to Ennor Price's mobile just as he and Richard Lancefield were completing their circuit of the lake.

It had taken him scarcely five minutes to reach Amber Kimbrall's cottage, speeding his car down the lane to Penwithen village, his heart pounding with every turn of the wheels. And as he flung the car round the corner into Quintard Street, he couldn't help wondering just what he was going to find when he got there. Zak Smith was armed and Parkinson wasn't, and it would take the backup they'd requested at least twenty minutes to get there.

As he slammed on the coupe's brakes, bringing the car to a screeching halt just inches from the rear of Parkinson's Audi, the first thing that struck him was the silence. The silence, and the open door of the cottage, swinging gently on its hinges in the breeze.

He pulled the key from the ignition and launched himself out of the car and down the short, York stone path that led to the cottage. 'Tom?' He rushed through the doorway without a moment's thought. 'Tom, are you in here?' He halted in the hallway and listened.

'We're in here, sir.' Parkinson's voice echoed from the door at the end of the hall. 'It's okay. Nobody's hurt.'

Adrenaline was coursing through the inspector's veins.

'Jesus.' He pushed on the kitchen door. 'Where is he? Have you got him?'

'He's gone, Inspector Price.' Amber was sitting at the kitchen table, her face wet with tears, her lips trembling uncontrollably behind a sodden, crumpled tissue that hung loosely between her fingers. 'I did my best to catch him. But he's gone.'

Parkinson, sitting beside her, put an arm around her shoulders. 'We know you did your best, Amber. It was very brave of you to call us when he was still here.' He cast frustrated eyes up at Price. 'Amber did more than call us, sir. She lured Smith over here, and then she hid his gun.'

Price walked up to the table and bent over it, bracing his hands on the edge. 'You hid his gun?'

She lifted her eyes. 'Sergeant Parkinson has locked it in his car for safekeeping.' She sniffed into the tissue. 'I sent Zak a text, asking if he was alright. I knew he'd take it as a green light to come round here. He wanted food and a place to sleep. So, I made him a sandwich and then waited until he'd gone upstairs for a shower. And while he was in the shower, I took his gun and I hid it in my car. And then when I knew it was safe, I called Sergeant Parkinson and I gave him the gun.'

'And I called you, and the rest is history.' He nodded towards the weeping girl. 'Apart from Amber's second bout of heroics.'

For the first time, Price noticed the burgeoning bruise that was beginning to spread across her cheek. 'Did he do that?'

Amber nodded. 'He came downstairs and told me he couldn't relax enough to sleep, and he noticed that his gun had gone. I wouldn't tell him where it was, so he hit me.' She stifled a sob. 'I wanted to keep him here, Inspector Price, but I was so scared I didn't know what to do. I told him that I wouldn't give him the gun and that the best he could expect from me was the chance to make a run for it.' She twisted the tissue between her fingers. 'So he did.'

Price leaned farther over the table. 'Amber, this is important. Do you have any idea, any idea at all, where he might have gone?'

'No. All I know is that he went out of the back door and over the garden fence.'

'And where would that take him?'

'We're right on the edge of the village here. The garden backs onto open countryside.' She folded her arms across her body, hugging herself for comfort. 'But at least he isn't armed, Inspector Price. That's the main thing, isn't it? He isn't armed, so he can't really do any more harm, can he?'

## 27

The footpath from Salvation Hall to the centre of Penwithen village was lit by a procession of tall, cast-iron lampstands. To one side of the path, a run of wooden railings was all that stood between the path and the arc of open countryside that curled around the perimeter of the estate. To the other, high timber fences kept prying eyes from the cultivated splendours of a row of private cottage gardens.

'These cottages belong to the family and are rented out to retired estate workers.' Nancy waved a hand in the direction of the fence. 'Richard has always had a very strong sense of "noblesse oblige". He looks after everyone who works for or has ever worked for the Lancefield estates.'

'Like the old-fashioned lord of the manor?' Eva stretched her neck upwards as she walked, but couldn't see over the fence. 'Do you think David will continue in the same vein?'

'I hope so.' Nancy slipped her hands into the pockets of her coat. 'There was a time, you know, when David refused to have anything to do with the estates. He has always struggled with the way the family made its money, and we all thought it more likely that Lucy would step in and take over.' Nancy laughed softly to herself. 'She had a fancy idea to turn Salvation Hall into a health spa, and the Woodlands Estate into a holiday resort. That's one reason she was so keen on the idea of marrying Marcus; he had experience in the hospitality trade and an understanding of business development.'

'Were they very much in love?'

'In love?' Nancy scoffed at the thought. 'Good heavens, no. I think that for Lucy it was a marriage of convenience. And poor Marcus just did whatever his mother told him to. Although afterwards, I think we all realised that he had truly loved Lucy, we just hadn't known how much.'

'I can't imagine what he went through, discovering Philip in the act of murdering her, and then accidentally taking Philip's life.'

'Accidentally?' Nancy tilted her head as she walked. 'Philip's death wasn't accidental, Eva. Marcus knew what he was doing. You know, I once overheard Richard say that he had underestimated Marcus. And I don't think he was alone in that. Marcus may look calm and cool on the outside, but what about the inside?' She lowered her voice. 'I hope you don't mind me making the observation, but you have only just met him.'

Eva smiled, a knowing curve of the lips. 'I don't mind at all. But as you said yourself, yesterday, there is no substitute for first-hand experience of a thing. And I prefer to get to know a person and judge for myself.' She pushed playfully at Nancy's arm. 'You were the one who said we needed to get the measure of each other, Nancy. I may look like Lucy, but I'm not Lucy.'

Her companion muttered under her breath. 'I suppose I asked for that.' She took a hand out of her pocket and pointed along the lane. 'Can you see the church now? That's St Felicity's.' Ahead of them, the first impressions of an illuminated clock tower were beginning to glimmer through the trees which lined the churchyard. 'The church dates back to the eleventh century and contains many points of interest which relate to the family. There are memorials to many of Richard's ancestors and a marvellous stained-glass window at the eastern end which depicts sugar workers cutting cane in the fields. Richard's father had it installed on the death of his own father, as a tribute to a man who loved the Caribbean.'

'Now that sounds like something I would like to see.'

'Then we must come back tomorrow when it's light.' Nancy appeared to warm to the idea. 'Many of the family are buried there, of course, both within the church and in the churchyard.'

'There's no mausoleum at Salvation Hall?'

'Yes, but its use was discontinued in the nineteenth century. One of Richard's ancestors took exception to the idea of private interments, and wanted the family to lie side by side with the villagers.' Nancy turned to look at Eva as she walked. 'You can see the bend in the lane up ahead? We follow the path around to the right, and then we are almost at the village centre. From there, I can take you into the churchyard and show you where Lucy is buried. And Philip. And then we can cross to The Lancefield Arms, and enjoy a drink.'

'Has the village pub always been named after the family?'

'Yes, as far as I'm aware.'

'Are you absolutely sure about that, Nancy?' The unexpected voice rang out from somewhere in the lane behind them. 'I thought it used to be called The Black Swan until the Lancefields decided to grab it for themselves?'

Nancy started and turned on her heel. 'Who's that?' She put out a protective arm towards Eva. 'Stay back, Eva, until we know who it is.'

'Until you know who it is?' The voice was still disembodied. 'That's not a very nice way to talk about an old mate, is it?' The words were coming nearer. 'And who's this walking out with you? Eva McWhinney?'

They saw his hand first, pointing at Eva through the darkness as he stepped into the glow of a street light. 'Of course it is. I can see now why they say you look so much like Lucy Lancefield.' He leaned against the cast-iron post. 'Just like I can see how easy it was for me to mistake

Geraldine Morton for you.'

\*

'Just what the hell was Nancy thinking of?' Marcus pulled his mobile phone from his pocket as he spoke, and swiped at its screen with his thumb. 'And why isn't she answering her phone?' He was striding out across the drive at Salvation Hall, heading towards the lane, Kathryn following silently in his wake. He pressed the phone to his ear, cursing as the call was answered and a familiar mechanical voice began to speak. 'I just keep getting the answering service.'

'She must have the phone switched off because the signal is usually okay in the village.' Kathryn, her own heart full of fear, was trying to sound calm and not quite sure that she was succeeding. 'Marcus, we thought that Zak Smith had been found. It was the last thing that Ennor said to Richard before he left. Amber Kimbrall had called to warn Tom Parkinson that Zak had turned up at her cottage. Do you honestly think I would have considered it safe for them to walk into Penwithen if I had known that Zak was still on the loose?'

He didn't answer the question. 'I swear to God, if anything has happened to Eva... if Nancy...'

'Why are you blaming Nancy? If anyone is to blame here, then it's me. I was the one who said it was safe for them to leave Salvation Hall.' Just as she had been the one to take the call from Ennor not five minutes since, telling them that Zak had got away. 'I know it's only a small consolation, but at least he isn't armed now. Amber took his gun away and hid it.'

'He didn't need a gun to murder Geraldine Morton, did he? All he needed for that was his bare hands, and the scarf around her neck.' Marcus growled under his breath. 'Do they really hate me that much? Becca Smith's family. Do they really hate me so much that they would go around murdering young women just to make me suffer?'

That, and much more besides. But now wasn't the time for Kathryn to point it out. Instead, she grabbed onto his arm, hooking her own around it in an attempt to slow his pace. 'Zak doesn't know that Nancy and Eva have gone for a walk, does he? And even if he did, do you honestly think he's going to hang around in the village when he knows the police are on his trail? Ennor and Tom have called for backup, but even before those officers arrive... well, they could find him in a heartbeat, couldn't they? Penwithen is tiny, only a couple of streets, a pub and a churchyard. There aren't that many places for him to hide out. No,' she shook her head, 'he'll be well out of the village by now, and trying to make his way across country.'

'I wish I shared your confidence.' Marcus's voice crackled with anxiety. 'I can't lose her, Kathryn. Not after everything else. Losing Lucy, losing my freedom, losing Stella...'

'Marcus, you hardly know Eva.'

'What the hell does that have to do with it? Don't you think I deserve to find some happiness in light of everything else that's happened?'

'Of course I do. But you only met Eva for the first time yesterday.'

'How long do you have to know someone, to just know?' He shook his head. 'Okay, I've only known her for twenty-four hours. And yes, she looks like Lucy. I'm not a fool. I know how easy it would be to make that mistake. But she isn't like Lucy. Even you must be aware of that? Lucy was almost the embodiment of her own vivid imagination, but Eva? Eva is real.'

\*

'I haven't come here to hurt you.' Zak was still leaning against the cast-iron lamp post, hands in his trouser pockets, his tired, unshaven face illuminated by the lamp's eerie, orange glow. 'I'm going on the run again. But I wanted you to know that someone agreed to pay me to get rid of you.'

'I don't believe you.' Eva was calm, composed beyond reason, considering that she had found herself face-to-face with the man who had been trying to kill her. 'Why on earth would anyone pay you to murder me?'

'Who cares? The only bit I care about is the fact that they were willing to pay me twenty thousand quid.'

'Twenty thousand?' Eva turned to look at Nancy, standing dumbstruck in the lane beside her.' Have you ever heard anything so ridiculous?'

'No, I don't believe I have.' Nancy's reply was barely audible. 'Zak, did you murder Stella?' Her voice was trembling.

'Of course I did.'

'And you were aiming for Eva?'

'Yes. And I'm sorry for my mistake. I can't say I had much time for Stella Lancefield, but killing her was an accident.' Zak chewed on his lip, and then said, 'Killing that other girl in Edinburgh, that was a mistake too.' He bent his neck and stared down at his boots through long, dark lashes. 'I watched her walk along Hemlock Row that night and I thought, she looks about the right age, the right build, the same blonde hair. And when I saw her grab onto the handrail outside number three and start to walk up the steps, I thought that has to be her.' He drew in a breath. 'I stepped out behind her and took hold of the scarf around her neck. I never thought to stop and ask her name. I just assumed that she was you.' He lifted his gaze to Eva. 'And then I pulled the scarf tight, so tight that she couldn't scream. It was so easy to drag her down the steps and round into the alleyway behind the house.' Tears had begun to well up in his eyes. 'I was too strong for her.'

'And all the time, you had the wrong girl.' Eva took a cautious step towards him. 'And you tried to pin the blame on Marcus.'

Zak held her gaze for a moment, and then he laughed. 'If you like.'

If she liked? Eva studied his face, trying to make sense of something that seemed to have no sense behind it at all. 'How did you know that I was coming to Cornwall, Zak?' She used his name as if using it was the most natural thing in the world. 'And how did you know I'd be on the terrace last night?'

'The same way that I knew what you looked like. I was told. By the person who wanted you dead.' He grinned, a sardonic twist of the lips. 'I was told that you were a doctor in Edinburgh, so I searched for you on the internet, and I found your picture on the infirmary's website under the list of resident consultants.'

'And that same person told you that I was coming to Cornwall? And that I would be on the terrace last night? So that all you had to do was break into the grounds of Salvation Hall and wait for the dinner to end.'

'They did.' He leaned forward from the lamp post and winked at her. 'At least, they told me that you were at the hall and that you might come out onto the terrace. I knew there was a chance that you would stay indoors if the weather turned, but it was worth a punt to see if I could get a shot at you. All I had to do was scale the wall and hide out in the garden.'

'So where did you scale the wall?' It was Nancy who asked the question. 'Most of the perimeter wall has security wire around it.'

'Ah, well, saying I scaled the wall was a bit of poetic licence. It might be more accurate to say that I scaled the double gate that opens onto the Helston road. That's the gate you use for deliveries, isn't it? I wouldn't want it to be said that I didn't know my place.' He put a hand up to his head and tugged on a forelock. 'The tradesman's entrance is always round the back.'

'This is all very well...' Eva's voice was growing stronger. '...but what happens now? We were told not more than twenty minutes ago that the police were on the verge of arresting you. They must be combing the village.' She turned her head towards the church. 'It won't be long before they reach us here.' She took another step towards him. 'Have you come to finish the job, so that you can collect your twenty thousand?'

Zak Smith flinched. 'No. As far as I'm concerned, the job is finished. I just wanted to let you know that I was being paid. It was nothing personal.'

'Who told you that I was related to the Lancefields?'

'I'm going to be on my way now.' He stepped away from the lamp post, lifting his hands into the air as he edged along the fence, back in the direction of Salvation Hall. 'I just wanted you to know…'

The sound of a police siren rent the air and Zak jerked his head towards the village. 'They're here.' He began to walk backwards down the path. 'Don't forget that I let you go, Eva.'

'You haven't answered my question. How did you know that I was related to the Lancefield family? How did you even know my name?'

Zak Smith's laugh echoed as he backed into the darkness. 'Did you hear that, Nancy? Eva wants to know how I knew her name?'

# 28

Eva McWhinney shivered against the cold and huddled into her soft, cashmere coat. 'All of this commotion because of me.' She was sitting on the low stone wall that ran around the churchyard of St Felicity's, watching the unfolding circus of police activity with a weary, if curious, eye. 'Seven police cars for one, insignificant individual.' Across the road, blue lights were flashing from a line of parked police cars, illuminating the front of The Lancefield Arms with an eerie, cerulean glow.

DCI Price, standing beside her, tilted his head with a wry smile. 'Two individuals. You and Zak Smith. And I don't consider either of you insignificant.' Just both incredibly lucky. 'In a little while, I'll have to take a formal statement from you. For now, I just need the basic facts.'

Eva turned her head to the left, where farther down the pavement Nancy and Kathryn were deep in conversation with DS Parkinson. 'Nancy was very brave. I don't know what I would have done if she hadn't been there.'

'If it hadn't been for Nancy, you would have been safe inside Salvation Hall.'

'If I had been safe inside Salvation Hall, I would never have heard that Marcus offered Zak twenty thousand pounds to kill me.'

Price stared at her, and then laughed. 'He actually said that to you?'

'Yes. I asked him how he knew I was related to the Lancefields and he thought it was funny. He seemed to be... I don't know, sort of taunting Nancy about it as he backed away. And then he said, "Marcus Drake offered me twenty thousand to drive to Edinburgh and get rid of you." He had started to back away from me before he said it, and then he suddenly stopped and began to walk towards me again. Nancy screamed at him to leave me alone, but he didn't take any notice of her. And then the police sirens started to get louder and we heard footsteps running down the lane from the village. That was when he just turned and ran off, towards Salvation Hall.'

'I tend to have that effect on the Smith family.' More was the pity. 'Do you have any sense of where he came from?'

'He was behind us. But I don't understand how he could have been. Nancy told me that he'd been found at his girlfriend's house, at the other end of the village.'

'It depends where he was heading. He could have been making for the road that runs to the north of the Salvation Hall estate. It's narrow and secluded, and it eventually leads to the main road that runs from Penzance to Helston. The path you were walking with Nancy is the fastest way to reach it.' The inspector pointed along the road. 'There's a cut-through from the village down the side of the newsagents. He could have joined the path just north of where you were walking, and heard the two of you talking.'

'And decided to double back to suggest to me that Marcus wanted me dead?' Eva whistled through her teeth. 'If that's the case, then he was taking a hell of a risk, wasn't he? We might have just screamed to raise the alarm. He must have known that you were searching for him?'

'He never was the sharpest knife in the drawer. He couldn't have known that Amber had called Tom Parkinson, but equally, he didn't know what she had done with the gun. And she'd made it pretty clear that she wasn't going to cover for him anymore.' Somewhere in the distance, a dog let out a bark, the eager, playful yapping of a hunter after its quarry. 'He won't get far. If we don't find him, then the dogs will. There aren't that many places he can make for.'

'Are you sure of that, Inspector Price?'

If only he could say yes. 'We'll do everything that we can to catch him, Eva.' It was beginning to sound like an empty promise. 'Kathryn tells me that you're planning to stay with the family for Stella's funeral.'

'Yes. It's the least I can do. To be here for Marcus and David.' She looked up and smiled. 'And talk of the devil.' She nodded towards the road, and a familiar figure making its way towards them. 'I was just telling Inspector Price that I'm staying until after the funeral.'

'And does the inspector think it will be safe?' Marcus reached the pavement and eyed Price with a hint of reproval. 'We don't want a repeat of this evening, do we?'

'Of course we don't.' Price met the challenge with a curl of the lip. 'But then I'm not the one who supposedly offered Zak Smith twenty thousand pounds to murder a girl I didn't know.' He turned back to Eva. 'Smith told you that he had no intention of killing you, didn't he? That the game was over now he'd met you?'

'Yes. He said it was enough for him that I knew it was Marcus who had tried to have me murdered.' A faint blush had made its way into her cheeks, and she seemed reluctant to look at Marcus now. 'Of course, I don't believe him for one minute.'

'He hired a van in my name, and tried to pin Geraldine Morton's murder on me.' Marcus sat down on the wall beside Eva and put an arm around her shoulders. 'Wasn't the whole point of that to punish me in some way? A clumsy attempt on his part to put me back through the legal system.'

'And isn't that what he's doing now?' Price offered the young man a wry smile. 'Trying to blame you for the attempts on Eva's life?' He let Marcus think about it, and then to Eva he said, 'Did Zak and Nancy say anything else to each other?'

'Not that I can remember.' Eva shook her head. 'Nancy was brilliant. She defended me from him.'

Marcus frowned. 'Earlier today, you told me that the two of you weren't hitting it off.'

'I know. But she apologised to me for that. It was all a misunderstanding. That's why we came out for a walk. She wanted to go to The Lancefield Arms to talk and clear the air.'

'And that was Nancy's idea?' Marcus turned his head to look up at DCI Price.

The two men exchanged a knowing glance, and as they did so the policeman felt an all-too-familiar prickling of the hairs on the back of his neck.

\*

'I cannot remember when I ever faced a worse day in my life.' David Lancefield slumped onto the sofa with an air of defeat. 'Darling Stella gone, Eva threatened by a delinquent, Marcus falsely accused of the most dreadful of crimes...' He turned sorrowful eyes to his father. 'Can you tell me now that this family isn't cursed?'

Richard reclined in his armchair with a shrug. 'Out of every adversity must come an opportunity.' It would take a harder heart than his not to feel the pain of his son's sorrow. But now was not the time to wallow in self-pity. 'I think some fresh air might do us good. I thought we might pull ourselves together and walk down to The Lancefield Arms for a drink.'

'A drink?'

'Sitting here in the Dower House, brooding over the week's events, sends completely the wrong message. It's time that we made ourselves visible.'

David blew out an incredulous sigh. 'Are you party to some piece of information that has escaped me? When Kathryn called from the village, she said that they were all safe, but that Zak Smith was still on the run. I would hardly call that an opportunity to make ourselves visible.' He pursed his lips. 'And when have you ever visited The

Lancefield Arms for a drink?'

'I think the last occasion was when Lucy was baptised. Didn't we hold a celebration in the bar for the villagers?'

'That was twenty-seven years ago.'

'Well, then it's high time we did it again.' Richard gave a wry smile. 'Perhaps I am just beginning to realise that there is little point in having a public house named after the family if we never make the effort to frequent it.' He nodded to himself. 'Now, where are Marcus and Eva? And Nancy and Kathryn? Are they still in the village?'

'Yes, I believe Harry has opened up the back room at the inn for them to speak in private. Inspector Price is with them.'

'Then we will join them. We will take Samson with us, and we will insist that Harry also opens up the kitchen to prepare us some supper.' He took a decisive breath. 'Now that the Smith family have taken it upon themselves to breach our walls, and invade the safety of our home, there is nowhere else for us to retreat. And when the enemy cuts off all lines of retreat, the only option left is to advance.' He tilted his head. 'I think it's time that we took steps to remind the Smiths that we are not afraid of them. We have allowed that family, and their hangers-on, to use The Lancefield Arms as their own preserve for far too long. I have always done my best to be a compassionate and paternalistic employer. But perhaps my leniency has been my downfall.'

'I hope you're not proposing to embark on a campaign of revenge?'

'Indeed not.' Richard softened his voice. 'I cannot bring Stella back for you, David. And I don't think I can ever express the sorrow that I feel, knowing that her involvement with our family is the thing that led to her death. But I do not want that death to be in vain. I know that when Smith is brought to justice for her murder, and for that of Geraldine Morton, the law will do its utmost to make sure that he never commits such unspeakable crimes again. But the responsibility lies with us, to make sure that his family understand that there is no justification for the pain that he has inflicted on our family.' Richard's voice suddenly filled with emotion. 'That there is no justification for the pain that he has inflicted on my son.'

\*

'I don't think Harry was too pleased when you asked him to evict the regulars.' Kathryn glanced across at the bar, where the landlord of The Lancefield Arms was busy venting his frustrations. 'If he polishes that bar top for much longer he'll take the veneer off the wood.'

Ennor's lip curled. 'I don't give a damn what Harry Blackstone thinks. If he gives me any more grief, I'll take his licence away.'

'I don't believe you. You wouldn't be that mean.' Raising Ennor's spirits was going to be an uphill struggle, then. 'There's still a lot of activity out there.' They were sitting at a table by the window, a ringside seat for the ongoing search of the churchyard across the road. 'I don't understand why there are so many officers combing the graveyard. Zak must be miles away by now.'

'They're looking for anything that might suggest where he's been hiding out. He can't just go randomly on the run. He must be heading for somewhere.' There was a glass of Cornish ale on the table and Ennor lifted it to his lips. 'What?' He sipped on the ale. 'No, you're right, I shouldn't be drinking on duty. And yes, it is ridiculous that all that manpower is being spent on a thorough search of the churchyard when Smith has already gone. It's called procedure.'

His free hand was resting on the table and Kathryn took hold of it, wrapping her fingers tightly around his knuckles. 'Ennor, you can't take all the responsibility for this.'

'No?' He didn't look convinced. 'Even when we catch

Smith, we're going to struggle to find enough evidence to charge him. We still haven't worked out how he knew who Eva was.'

'So you don't believe it was Marcus who told him?'

'I… no, of course I don't.'

'You hesitated then.'

'Only because I can't close off any line of enquiry.' Price blew out a sigh of frustration. 'I can't see any way at all that Zak Smith and Marcus Drake would come to an agreement over anything. The most obvious answer is that Becca found out somehow and told him. We know he didn't hire the van, he was clever there. And even if we can find CCTV footage of him, either in Edinburgh or any of the service stations he might have used on the way home to Cornwall, that doesn't directly tie him to Geraldine's murder. The best hope we have is that DCI Grant's team can come up with something forensic from the victim or the crime scene to nail him with.'

'But you'll be able to charge him with Stella's murder?'

'Will we?' Ennor sipped again on his ale. 'We have the gun that was missing from the cabinet at his mother's house. We're pretty certain that we'll be able to prove it was the gun used when Stella was shot. But we don't have cast-iron evidence that he was in the grounds of Salvation Hall on the evening she was killed, any more than we have evidence to prove that he was the one who fired it. It's all circumstantial at the moment.'

'But he confessed everything to Eva and Nancy. He admitted to both murders.'

'And that's just hearsay until he makes a formal confession to us. Which isn't going to happen.' Ennor looked up at the ceiling. 'I had twenty-four hours to catch him, Kathryn. Twenty-four hours. And he's slipped through my fingers.' The inspector growled. 'What a bloody mess. And it's all of my own making.'

Kathryn squeezed his hand. 'None of this is of your making.'

'Try telling that to my superior officers.'

'Ennor, no one in the family holds you responsible. Richard told me that he has absolute confidence in your ability to catch Zak and hold him accountable for Stella's death.' She hesitated, and then said, 'When you catch him, do you think he'll hold on to that story about Marcus offering to pay him?'

'It wouldn't surprise me. After all, it will be Marcus's word against his.' Ennor turned his head to look out of the window. 'I suppose that you'll be going back to Cambridge, now that Richard has finally decided to stop digging up more victims for the Smith family to target.'

Kathryn bridled. 'I'm going to give you the benefit of the doubt, after everything that's happened, and let that little spurt of bitterness go.' She drew back her hand. 'Just because Richard has decided to draw the line at Eva doesn't mean that my work is complete. Even if her trip has to be delayed, Nancy is still going out to St Felix, so I'm going to cover for her again until she returns. In addition, I still have two other branches of the family to document, and the artefacts from the storeroom to deal with. Richard and David are still debating whether to preserve them here or donate them to a museum.'

'They could just do the decent thing and destroy them.' Ennor put down his glass and leaned his elbows on the table. 'I can't imagine why anyone would want to look at, let alone own a set of manacles or a collection of inhumane branding irons.'

'Destroying those artefacts won't eradicate their history.' There was a half-finished glass of wine on the table in front of her, and Kathryn ran a finger absently around its rim. 'To be honest, Ennor, I have no idea how the next few months are going to pan out for the family. Stella's death has hit David very hard. He's putting a brave face on it, but he's going to need time to grieve. And Marcus may not have always seen eye to eye with his mother, but he isn't unaffected by her death. The plan to send him out to St Felix will have to be postponed. What we need now is a period of calm and stability.' Kathryn picked up the glass and sipped from it. 'I had hoped, in the meantime, to use the extra downtime to give my favourite sceptical pupil a few more lessons in the history of the Lancefield family. But I think he might be losing interest in the subject matter.'

At the other side of the table, Ennor met her gaze with a rueful smile. 'The subject matter, maybe. But I hope it's understood that I'll never lose interest in the teacher.'

# ABOUT THE AUTHOR

Mariah Kingdom was born in Hull and grew up in the East Riding of Yorkshire. After taking a degree in History at Edinburgh University she wandered into a career in information technology and business change, and worked for almost thirty years as a consultant in the British retail and banking sectors.

She began writing crime fiction during the banking crisis of 2008, drawing on past experience to create Rose Bennett, a private investigator engaged by a fictional British bank.

Hemlock Row is the third Lancefield Mystery.

www.mariahkingdom.co.uk

Printed in Great Britain
by Amazon